Sincerely,
Mayla

A Novel

Virginia Smith

Kregel
Publications

Sincerely, Mayla

© 2008 by Virginia Smith

Published by Kregel Publications, a division of Kregel, Inc., P.O. Box 2607, Grand Rapids, MI 49501.

Scripture taken from the *Holy Bible, New International Version®*. Copyright © 1973, 1978, 1984 by International Bible Society. Used by permission of Zondervan. All rights reserved.

Scripture also taken from the New King James Version. Copyright © 1982 by Thomas Nelson, Inc. Used by permission. All rights reserved.

ISBN 978-0-8254-3692-5

Printed in the United States of America

08 09 10 11 12 / 5 4 3 2 1

For my daughter, Christy Delliskave.
God blesses me every day through you.

Acknowledgments

I have a confession. Writing a follow-up story to *Just As I Am* was a daunting task. People fell in love with Mayla Strong as they read that first book. What if the second didn't turn out as well? What if I let someone down? But I shouldn't have worried. The minute my fingers touched the keyboard, Mayla herself showed up and practically dictated the story to me. She's such a control freak!

Sincerely, Mayla would not exist without the encouragement and support of my family: Amy Barkman; Christy Delliskave; Beth Marlowe; Susie Smith; and of course, the love of my life, my husband, Ted. They have no idea how much I value each of them.

Thanks to my awesome critique partners on this project: Jill Elizabeth Nelson, Lee King, Tracy Ruckman, Lisa Ludwig, and Tambra Rasmussen.

I deeply appreciate the members of the American Christian Fiction Writers group who opened their hearts to me about their abortion and adoption experiences. My prayer is that God will continue His work of healing in each of your lives, and that He will heal others through your generous sharing with me.

Special thanks to Jacquie Markowski of the Pregnancy Resource Center in Salt Lake City for giving me a personal tour and so much great information. May the Lord continue to save lives through the vital work done there.

I'm so grateful to my agent, career partner, and respected friend, Wendy Lawton.

And where would Mayla be without the dedicated and talented people at Kregel Publications? Thanks to Dennis, Steve, Becky, Esther, Amy, Leslie, and Nick. And thanks to the rest of the Kregel team who do their jobs behind the scenes with excellence. I don't know all their names, but I know how grateful I am for their work.

But primarily and above all, I owe everything to Jesus. Without Your wisdom, Lord, my stories are just dead words on the page. Thank You for giving them life.

Chapter 1

I've always said if the Lord had intended His people to live in snow He would have put the garden of Eden in the middle of the North Pole. And we know He didn't because Adam and Eve were wearing only fig leaves. If the first couple had lived in the frozen north, the Bible would have described them shivering around a bonfire for warmth, and surely one of the temptations offered by that snake would have been ankle-length wool coats. No, snow and the cold weather that goes along with it are a part of the curse.

In Kentucky, we live with that curse for four months every year, sometimes more. We hole up in our homes, paying outrageous prices for gas to run our heaters, and we bundle ourselves up like Arctic explorers just to run from the front door to the car. Don't even get me started about scraping ice off the windshield.

The cold makes us cranky. I have a theory that it's because of all the recycled air we breathe since we spend so much time inside during the winter, but when I voiced the idea to my roommate, Sylvia, she said that's just my excuse for being bad tempered. "Mayla Strong, you need to just *get over it!*" she hollered as she stomped out the door with the tail of her scarf flying.

She's probably right, but I still hate the cold.

I knew I was in for a bad day that February morning before I opened my eyes. The first sound I heard was the distinctive scrape of the snowplow on the street outside my apartment window. *Terrific. More snow.*

"Lord," I grumbled into my pillow, "why do You keep sending all this snow? Is there a kid praying for a snow day because he didn't study for a test? I know You answer every prayer, but maybe You could answer this one with a big ol' no. I say let the kid flunk, Lord. I am sick of snow."

I don't claim to have second sight, but that morning, I felt like a cloud had gathered above my head while I slept. I lay in bed, my face buried in my pillow, and wished I could stay there all day. Something bad was going to happen. I just knew it.

My pastor is fond of saying, "Don't expect life to be perfect just because you're a Christian. Becoming a child of God didn't give you a magic shield. But it did give you the right to cry on the shoulder that the weight of the world rests on."

I know for sure that's true. Bad things do happen to Christians, me included. It's like supper when I was a kid. Mama made me eat all my peas before I could have ice cream. Don't ask me why she felt the need to force those nasty, slimy things down my throat; I sure won't do it to my kids. But I suffered through it, grumbling and crying and gagging the whole time, so I could get the good stuff at the end.

I hate to admit it, but I'm pretty much the same at twenty-three as I was at six. I still grumble and complain while I'm going through the hard part, but I suffer through it because I know the blessing is coming.

And I still gag at peas.

Business at Clark and Hasna Building Company was not going well. The bosses lost an important bid, one they had worked hard on for months, and then we had a run of bad luck that made another job come in a couple of months late. The penalties ate into the company's profits, and I knew from Mr. Clark's voice carrying through the cardboard walls of his office that he blamed Mr. Hasna. The construction business slows to a crawl during Kentucky winters anyway, so we were lucky to have a couple of indoor remodels to keep at least some of the guys working. But most of our payroll was drawing unemployment, and we didn't figure that would change for another month to six weeks, when spring finally moved into central Kentucky and the ground thawed.

So it made no sense at all for Mr. Clark to hire his niece to work in the office. Alison Harper, the company secretary, agreed with me. Between the two of us, we had things running as smooth as Mama's roast beef gravy, and we didn't take kindly to Miss Smarty Pants waltzing in with the ink still wet on her associate's degree from Lexington Community College. Because I don't have an associate's degree, I don't know what goes into getting one, but it seemed like she had learned enough to have an opinion on every subject that could come up in normal office conversation and several more that nobody had ever heard of or cared about. Especially Alison and me.

Her name was Elizabeth Clark Payson, but she went by Clarkie. I mean, really! Clarkie? I had struggled with *Mayla* all my life because no one had ever heard it, but at least it sounded like a first name. Her nickname was almost enough to make me feel sorry for her . . . almost.

We heard her life story on her first day. Her *entire* life story, with nothing left out from the moment of her birth to her family Christmas in Hawaii two months before. And then she told us how Uncle Eric—that would be Mr. Clark—had been so interested in all these new ideas she'd learned at LCC that he hired her to modernize his office and how she expected to have things running shipshape in no time.

By the time we left work that first day, Alison and I had decided if anyone deserved a name like Clarkie, it was her. Actually, it was nicer than some we would have given her if we weren't Christian women.

So that morning in late February when I sledded to work in my little Honda, praying the whole way as I slipped over the icy Lexington roads like a moose on ice skates, I was not happy to walk in and find Clarkie sitting at my desk. I was twenty minutes late because of the weather, and Alison had not arrived yet.

"What's up?" I asked, allowing a hint of irritation to seep into my voice when I saw her fingers poised over my keyboard.

"Oh hi, Mayla! Awful morning, isn't it? The radio said we got three inches and black ice everywhere. I got a ride this morning with Uncle Eric."

"Yeah, so now you're doing what?"

"Oh." She had the decency to look embarrassed. "Uncle Eric asked me to pull up some payroll figures for him, but I'm having trouble getting into the database."

"That's because the database is password protected." I gave her a tight smile. "Payroll is pretty sensitive stuff, you know. Can't leave it sitting there for just anybody to hack into."

She ran a finger down the edge of her straight, honey-colored hair, giving it a flip at the end to toss it over her shoulder in a perfect Jennifer Aniston imitation. "Of course not. But I'm not just anybody, you know, and Uncle Eric did ask me."

I stood staring at her for a moment, trying to decide if I should give her the password or grab the back of the chair and dump her on the floor. I used to be a lot more menacing when I had purple hair and a stud beneath my lower lip. Though I still wore a tiny diamond in my left nostril, my slim, five-five frame and milk chocolate brown hair didn't intimidate anyone, especially Miss Associate's-Degree-Whose-Uncle-Owns-the-Company. She sat there in my chair, smiling sweetly at me with a glint of something in her brown eyes that I didn't like one bit. A secret lurked around in there, and I didn't even want to think what kind of secrets the boss's niece might know.

At that moment, Mr. Clark stuck his head out from his office behind Alison's empty desk. "Mayla, would you give her the password, please?"

He posed it like a question, but he was not asking. My back to Clarkie, I didn't bother hiding my discomfort from him. "If you need some payroll numbers, I can pull them for you."

His smile moved his lips but nothing else. "I'm sure you can, but then Clarkie will never learn how, will she?"

I wanted to say she seemed to think she knew everything that needed knowing anyway, but I clamped my jaw shut and wrote the password on a sticky note—JOY4LIFE. Clarkie read it, gave a tight smile, and typed it in. The payroll system opened.

I pointed to the top of the screen. "So now you click on Week Ending, and then—"

"Thanks, I can figure it out from here."

She grabbed the mouse and clicked with authority while Mr. Clark disappeared back into his office. She did know her way around a computer; I had to give her that. I didn't have to like it, though.

Alison arrived at that moment, bringing an icy blast of wind through the door with her.

"It's snowing again," she announced, collapsing a purple umbrella and shaking the flakes onto the dirty welcome mat. "Can you believe all the snow we're getting this winter? The roads are awful. I almost wrecked my car three times between home and here."

As usual, Alison managed to look elegant even dressed for snowy weather. A pink wool scarf knotted loosely under her chin protected her hair from the wind and painted a splash of color on her full-length black coat. Her gloves matched the scarf, her boots matched the coat, and she looked like she had stepped off the cover of a winter fashion catalog.

Seeing Clarkie seated at my desk, her eyelids narrowed for a moment, and then she arched her brows in my direction. I shrugged and nodded toward Mr. Clark's office. Rolling her eyes, she hung her coat on a peg on the wall and took her seat.

I didn't want to hover, and given that my seat was occupied, I sat in Clarkie's. She had shared a corner of my L-shaped desk since she'd arrived in our happy little family three weeks before, and Mr. Clark had promised to get her a desk of her own soon. It would mean rearranging the office and giving me a smaller desk, but that was okay. The sooner Clarkie moved into her own space and out of mine, the better.

From where I sat, I couldn't see the computer monitor, but since she was writing neat figures in a spiral notebook, I assumed she had figured out how to get what she wanted. I couldn't see what she wrote, though I did strain my neck in the attempt. After a few minutes, she tore the page out of the notebook and got up from my desk.

"There you go." She vacated my chair and flashed a bright, fake smile.

She ignored Alison on the way into her uncle's office. When Clarkie closed the door behind her, Alison and I looked at each other.

"What was that all about?" Alison whispered.

I shrugged, uneasy. "Whatever it was, I don't like it."

Alison glared at the door. "If it involves Clarkie and closed doors, it can't be good."

I felt exactly the same. I was trying not to feel paranoid, but I had sensed bad feelings from the little brat all week. She had been secretive and not nearly as chirpy as before.

"It's probably nothing," I said trying to convince myself as much as Alison.

"Hmmm." She gave the door one final glare, then turned away to boot up her computer.

We both spent the rest of the morning trying to avoid Clarkie. Not an easy task, because she not only shared a desk with me, but Mr. Clark had asked me early in the week to show her the company's books. Supposedly, she learned some great new things about bookkeeping at LCC and had ideas about ways we could be more efficient in ours. I couldn't imagine what new advancements could have come about in bookkeeping in the past few years, but I kept my opinions to myself. I learned by working with the woman who hired me to take her place, so what did I know? But if Clarkie had new ideas, she wasn't sharing them. She spent her time listening to me and making notes in her spiral notebook.

The day dragged. During the summer, the office was as active as a playground at recess, but that winter day was long and boring. Finally, just before three thirty, Mr. Clark came out of his office and said, "Mayla, could you come in here for a minute?"

Clarkie had suddenly become absorbed with whatever she was writing in that notebook and didn't look at me as I passed her chair. Alison's eyes asked a silent question, and I shrugged. As I stepped past Mr. Clark, Mr. Hasna came out of his office and followed me. Mr. Clark closed his door and sat behind his desk.

"Have a seat, Mayla. Jack and I want to talk to you about something."

I sat in one of the two chairs in front of the desk. Mr. Hasna took the other. He didn't look at me, keeping his gaze fixed on Mr. Clark. His jaw was clenched shut, his lips tight, and I got the impression he wasn't too happy about whatever Mr. Clark was getting ready to tell me. I knew right then that I wasn't going to be happy about it, either.

"As you know," Mr. Clark continued, "business has been slow lately. We've got some things in the works, but we don't see any improvement in the financial situation for at least another few months." He paused, waiting for me to say something, but I just nodded. "When times are tight, as they are now, we're required to make difficult decisions. Sometimes those decisions impact people, and I'm afraid this time our decision has impacted you."

"Wait a minute," I interrupted. "Are you firing me?"

"Laying you off," Mr. Hasna responded quickly. "Not firing you. There's a difference."

"I understand the difference." I struggled to keep my voice level. "We lay off the crew when a construction job ends, but they know when we land another one we'll bring them back on the payroll. So are you saying you intend to bring me back on the payroll when business picks up again?"

Mr. Hasna looked away, and Mr. Clark answered. "We would certainly hire you in the future if we have another opening for which you are qualified."

"For which I'm qualified," I repeated. "What does that mean?"

He gave a small, embarrassed cough. "We've decided to upgrade your position. It will include several new responsibilities and will now require a minimum of an associate's degree."

White, hot anger rose up inside me as the light dawned. This was Clarkie's doing, the little brat.

"I see," I said levelly, pinning Mr. Clark with a direct stare to let him know I really did see.

He looked down at the paper in the center of his desk. I saw it had been torn from a spiral notebook, and the sight of the figures written in Clarkie's neat handwriting set my teeth together.

"Of course, we've prepared a generous severance package for you in appreciation of the excellent job you've done for us. One full month's pay—one week for every year you've worked for us—and after that, you will be eligible to draw unemployment. I wanted to have your checks here for you to take, but the weather prevented the payroll service from delivering them. They will be mailed to your home instead, and you should have them within a few days. Your health insurance deductions will be taken so your coverage continues through the end of next month."

One part of my mind realized that the deal wasn't bad. Construction workers never got severance pay at the end of a job. But the other part of my mind was fuming, so the offer didn't make me feel better.

Lord, I need Your help right now, or I'm going to say something I'll regret.

Mr. Clark went on. "And of course if you need a reference, we will give you an excellent one. We are very happy with your work here at Clark and Hasna, Mayla." He paused, obviously waiting for me to say something. When I didn't, he asked, "Do you have any questions?"

I looked him directly in the eye. "No, I think I understand everything."

He had the grace to look away. Then he stood, and Mr. Hasna and I stood, too. He handed me the paper.

"Here are the figures for your final check, so you'll know what to expect."

I took the paper without a word and turned toward the door. As I reached for the handle, Mr. Hasna's hand stopped mine. Glancing up at him, I realized he looked more miserable than I felt.

"I'm really sorry, Mayla." From the look in his eyes, I believed him. He probably didn't like Clarkie any better than I did. "When you need a reference, give them my name. And if I hear of any jobs you might be interested in, I'll let you know."

For the first time, I felt something other than anger. Mr. Hasna was a nice man, and I liked working for him. I would miss him, and it made me sad. A lump formed in my throat.

"Thanks," I told him. "I appreciate it."

He opened the door for me, and I stepped through to see Alison waiting with teary eyes. She caught me in a hug while Mr. Hasna stood watching, wringing his hands.

"She told me," Alison said, meaning Clarkie. "I got a box and started packing for you."

Clarkie had made herself scarce, which was probably a good thing. A box sat on my desk, and most of my personal things had been piled inside. I opened the desk drawers and got one or two things Alison had missed, like my favorite gel pen I had bought myself and my letter opener shaped like King Arthur's sword Excalibur that Mama had put in my Christmas stocking one year. Then we both put on our coats, and Alison opened the door for me and walked with me out to my car.

The snow had stopped falling, thank goodness, but the air was still bitterly cold. I was actually kind of grateful, because the chill would make our good-byes short. Alison grabbed me in a hug, and when she clung to me, I felt tears start to build up in my eyes.

"I'm going to quit," she told me, sniffling. "I can't work with that little snot one more day if you're not here."

"Don't you dare. That's just what she wants—to get rid of both of us. Besides, they gave me enough severance pay to last until I find another job. You wouldn't have that, and then I'd feel responsible when you got kicked out of your apartment because you couldn't make the rent."

She sniffed. "I'm glad they did that, anyway. But I'm still going to look around for another job. I don't like the way things are shaping up here."

I thought that was probably a good idea, but I didn't say so. "Listen, you've got my number, so keep in touch. Say a prayer for me, but don't worry. God will take care of me."

"I will, Mayla," she promised. "And you call me, too, okay?"

"Sure, Alison. Good luck."

"Bye, Mayla."

She stood shivering in the cold and waving as I backed out of the parking place. I thought sadly that today would probably be the last time I saw Alison. She had renewed her relationship with Jesus nine months ago, shortly after I began mine, and it had been good to work with someone who was as excited about her new life in Christ as I was. We weren't really close friends, just friendly coworkers. Still, I would miss her.

Wiping a tear from the corner of my eye, I fixed my gaze straight ahead. The roads had been scraped, but snow and patches of ice still covered them. I focused on driving, my hands clutching the steering wheel in the ten-and-two position. A feeling started growing inside me, an empty sort of feeling. That was the only job I'd ever had, outside of waiting tables. I had joined Clark and Hasna as a temporary summer clerk when I was nineteen. I never left.

Until now.

Where would I work? My stomach tightened into a knot of anxiety. My night job as a waitress would help, but I couldn't make the rent on tips alone. I didn't know anything except bookkeeping at Clark and Hasna. I wasn't qualified to do anything else. And I didn't have a college degree. Would any company want to hire me?

"Lord," I said, swallowing past the tightness in my throat, "I know the Bible says You'll take care of me. I guess now's Your chance to prove it. And I sure would appreciate it if You don't wait too long, okay?"

❀ ❀ ❀

My roommate, Sylvia, had already left for her job as a bartender at The Max, the restaurant where I worked part-time. So instead of bending her ear with my problems, I called Mama.

My mama is just about the best person in the world when it comes to taking up for me. You could put her up against a mother tiger, and that cat would end up cowering in the nearest hole like a kid in a thunderstorm. She has been known to take the protection bit too far, though. Once in high school, I came home heartbroken because I saw James Mills, the guy I had been going out with for two months, making out with Ashley Grimes under the bleachers at a football game. Mama patted my back while I cried on her shoulder, and then she called James Mills and told him off. I was so embarrassed I wouldn't go to school for three days.

Part of me almost wished she would call Mr. Clark and tell him off, too.

"Oh, baby, that's terrible," she told me on the phone. "Do you need some money?"

"No, Mama, I'm okay."

"How 'bout groceries? You got enough groceries to last you?"

"Mama, they gave me enough money to cover my salary for a month, and I can still wait tables at The Max. I'm going to ask Jolene if I can pick up the lunch shift a few days a week until I find another job. I won't starve."

She started in then. "The idea of that man hiring his niece and firing you! Ain't that against the law? It's called nesemistics or somethin'."

"It's nepotism, and I don't think it counts for small family businesses."

She snorted. "Well, it oughta, that's all. But don't you worry 'bout a thing, baby. I'll get my Tuesday night ladies praying, and you'll find you a job before you know it."

The last thing I wanted was Mama's Tuesday night ladies' group knowing I had lost my job. I believe in prayer, for sure, and I had no doubt that actual praying did happen in that group. I knew my mama prayed, for one, and I'm sure some of the other ladies did, too. But before a single one of them discussed the matter with the Lord, they'd all have a good jaw about it with each other first.

"Mama, don't go telling the Tuesday night ladies." I heaved a little sigh because I knew she would tell them even if I asked her not to. "It'll be all over the church by Sunday."

There was a pause, and I could almost hear her spine cracking as she sat straight up in her chair. I know my mama well, and I know when she's getting ready to go off on me.

"And what's wrong with the church knowin'? It ain't like you did anything wrong. You're havin' a time of trouble. It's the job of the church to hold each other up in times of trouble. That's your problem, Mayla, you ain't learned to lean on the Everlasting Arms yet."

I sighed louder this time. "Okay, Mama, if you say so. I've got to go now, or I'll get fired from the only job I have left. Love you."

"Love you, too, baby. And don't you worry 'bout a thing. It's gonna come out all right; you'll see."

I hung up and pulled a clean black shirt out of my dresser. Not that I really minded the church ladies gossiping about me. I had been the subject of their gossip lots of times. There wasn't one other person in Salliesburg Independent Christian Church with four earrings in each ear plus one in her nose. I didn't mind that, though. I knew most of them liked me even with the jewelry, and in the nine months since I had been baptized, they had even come to accept me. I figured if they were talking about me, they were giving someone else a rest—someone they might not be as nice about.

No, what I minded was that sooner or later one of those ladies would call the preacher. And when he found out I had lost my day job, Pastor Paul would call me. I minded that a lot.

We had not talked in more than a week. Except for last Sunday when I shook his hand by the door after church, but that didn't count. I was waiting for him to call me. Childish, yes, but I wanted to see how long he would go before he called or sent an e-mail.

Pastor Paul Rawlings is one of my favorite people in the whole world; he really is. When I was first baptized, he spent a lot of time explaining things to me, answering my Bible questions, and helping me find a place to fit in the church. He and I worked together every month to produce the church's newsletter, a magazine-type booklet called *The Torch*, with all sorts of interesting items about life at Salliesburg Independent Christian Church.

We still talked a lot, but he never called me. In the past few months, I had begun to realize that I called him all the time. My cell phone bill was proof of that. Then I paid careful attention to our e-mail conversations—same thing. He answered my e-mails quickly, but his were always a reply to mine.

It hadn't taken me long to realize I wasn't comfortable with that arrangement. I mentioned it to Sylvia, who listened with her eyebrows edging slowly up toward her hairline. When I finished, she shook her head.

"Mayla, you've got a thing for the preacher."

"I do not!" Heat rose up my neck, but by sheer force of will, I stopped it before it came into view above my turtleneck.

"It's okay if you do," she went on with an indulgent grin that made me want to smack her face. "He's a good-looking guy and smart, too."

"He's a preacher!"

She shrugged. "Preachers have girlfriends. It's usually a prerequisite for getting married."

I walked away, not prepared to discuss my feelings about Pastor Paul with anyone until I worked them out myself. What I worked out was that I did have some feelings for the guy. Or could have if I let myself. But obviously if he had any feelings for me, he hadn't realized it yet. And I certainly wasn't going to ask him to consider it. So I had decided to cool it for a while, just to see how long he would wait before calling.

If he heard that I lost my job, of course he would call. He's a pastor, so he would call anyone in his church who was in trouble. That was a kink in my plan. I wanted him to have no excuse for calling. I wanted him to call because he missed me.

I grabbed a can of Diet Coke and a couple of pieces of bologna from the refrigerator, making extra sure I sealed the plastic bag the bologna was in. Sylvia had a ballistic meltdown if the meat got hard around the edges because the bag wasn't sealed. Rolling the bologna into a thick tube, I gulped it down in three bites and snatched a handful of Doritos as I headed out the door.

As I was leaving, I ran into Stuart in the breezeway of our apartment building. Stuart and his roommate, Michael, lived upstairs, and we'd been friends since they'd moved in a little over a year before. When I became a Christian last year, Stuart and Michael were the first of my friends to accept the "new Mayla," which is pretty amazing since they were not Christians. But Sylvia and I had started praying for them early on, so I held out hope for both of them.

As I trudged down the wooden stairs in my snow boots, clinging to the handrail so I wouldn't slip on the ice, Stuart stomped up. He was hard to miss, looking like he had just came down off the slopes in his fluorescent pink and black ski jacket and matching pants. A few stray flakes of snow rested in the nest of his spiky blond hair and on the shoulders of his jacket. Both hands held the handles of white plastic sacks bulging with groceries.

"Hey, what's up?" I said, stopping.

He thrust his nose high into the air and breezed by me as though I was the invisible woman. Surprised, I turned and watched him stomp across the landing. He had placed a foot on the stairs to go up to his floor when I stopped him.

"Stuart, is something wrong?"

He stood with his back toward me for a few seconds before swinging around dramatically. "If you must know, there is. And it's all your fault."

I slapped my hand to my chest. "My fault? What did I do?"

"You snatched Lou from the jaws of hell, that's what you did."

Tattoo Lou was a mutual friend who had become a Christian a few months after I did, when Sylvia led him in the prayer that changed his life. He had altered rather dramatically since then. Now he spoke to high school youth all over the state about his former life of rebellion and how finding Jesus had given him the peace he had been looking for all those years. Because he was a big muscular guy with tattoos covering his arms, torso, and neck, his testimony was pretty effective.

"First of all, I didn't do it. Sylvia did. And second, what did Lou do to you?"

"You're responsible for Sylvia, so Lou is your fault, too." His glare slapped at me all the way across the breezeway. "He's trying to convert Michael, that's what he did. He quoted the Bible at him and told him we're all going to hell because we're gay. I *knew* this would happen. I just knew it!"

He turned away from me so violently one of his bags smacked into the wall with a loud thud, and then he stomped up the stairs. My mouth hung open while I searched frantically for something to shout after him, to make him come back and talk to me. For once, I couldn't think of a single word to say.

Chapter 2

The Max, the restaurant where both Sylvia and I worked, wasn't far from our apartment. She worked nearly every day as a bartender, and I worked as a server on weekends and a couple of nights a week. The tips were pretty good.

I got there a bit early and went to the bar, where Sylvia stood idly staring at the television screen hanging above her head. She is one of the cutest women I've ever seen. Not drop-dead gorgeous, but just plain cute. She's petite, for one thing, a shade over five-feet tall with her shoes on, and she doesn't weigh ninety pounds soaking wet. But after you've been around her for a few minutes you forget how tiny she is because she's so full of energy she makes me tired.

Very few customers had braved the cold to come to the restaurant that evening, and no one sat in the bar. It was still a few minutes before five o'clock on a Thursday night, and with the icy roads, the night would probably be dead for both of us.

"Hey," I said, sliding onto a barstool, "I ran into Stuart a few minutes ago. Man, was he steamed!"

She nodded. "Yeah, Lou came by here last night after he left their apartment. He apparently leaned on Michael pretty hard. Quoted Leviticus and everything."

"Whew." I shook my head. "I wish he hadn't done that."

Her eyebrows arched. "It's not like he made anything up."

"Yeah." I toyed with a stack of thick cardboard coasters. "But if someone had started spouting Bible verses at me last year and telling me I was going to hell, I would have been spitting mad. I'm pretty sure I wouldn't have wanted to join their club, you know?"

She nodded. "Yeah, I know. I talked to Lou about it, and I don't think he'll come on so strong the next time."

"Stuart was really mad. There may not be a next time for him."

A server walked up to the serving alley, and Sylvia left to fill her order. When she had set a couple of full glasses on the rubber drip mat, she came back to where I sat hunched over the bar. I realized I hadn't told her my bad news.

"Guess what happened to me today."

Sylvia shrugged. "You won a million dollars?"

"I wish. I got laid off."

"Huh?" Her eyes bugged. "How could they fire you? You've been there, what? Five years?"

"Four. And they didn't fire me, they laid me off. As for why, take a guess."

Sylvia leaned her elbow on the bar in front of me, resting her chin in the palm of her hand. "You finally decked the boss's niece."

"I didn't deck her, but I wanted to. They laid me off and gave her my job. Said business hasn't been good and they didn't need me anymore. But they did give me four weeks' pay."

"Well, that's better than a handshake and a pat on the back. What are you going to do?"

I sighed. "I don't know. I haven't had time to think about it. But I am going to ask Jolene if I can pick up some extra hours here until I find something else."

"Hey, I know what you should do!" Sylvia stood up straight, her eyes wide. "You've just been handed a paid vacation. Go somewhere warm, away from the cold. Take a cruise or go to the beach or something. You won't have any trouble finding a job when you get back, and maybe this is just what you need to get your head on straight and figure out what you want to do next—about several things."

She gave me a look, and I knew she meant Pastor Paul. I refused to rise to her bait. "Yeah, that's what I need to do right after I lose my job, spend a bunch of money on a cruise."

She shrugged. "That's what I'd do. It's just a thought."

Just a thought. A moment later, I decided it wasn't necessarily a bad one.

"You know," I told Sylvia, "my grandmother has asked me several times to visit her in Orlando. I could take a week before I start looking for another job. I wouldn't have to worry about food or a hotel, just getting there. I wonder how much a plane ticket costs."

"Only one way to find out." She took her cell phone from beneath the bar and slid it toward me.

"I have a phone."

She shook her head. "Use mine. You're unemployed, remember?"

A couple of phone calls during an exceptionally slow night told me I could fly to Orlando for around three hundred fifty dollars, but I had to buy the tickets seven days in advance or the price was twice as much. After jotting a couple of possible flight numbers on the back of a napkin, I worked until close and fell into bed around eleven thirty, exhausted.

I was awakened out of a deep sleep by the sound of the theme song from *The Flintstones* blaring from my cell phone. I kept the volume set loud enough to wake me and half the apartment complex. Fumbling around in the dark, I knocked the phone off the bedside table, then pulled it up on the bed by the tail of the charger line.

"'Lo?"

"Mayla, hey. It's Lindsey."

Lindsey Markham, the fifteen-year-old sister of my friend Alex, who had died of AIDS last summer. I hadn't talked to her since the day after Alex's death, so of course I was glad to hear from her. But I would have been happier if the digital face of my clock didn't say 12:24.

"Lindsey, what's going on?"

"Is it too late to call? Are you in bed?"

I lay back on the pillow, which fluffed invitingly around my ears, trying to lull me back to sleep. "Well, it is late. Is everything okay?"

There was a pause. "I guess." Another pause and a sniff. "No, not really. I was wondering if I could come up tomorrow and stay with you for a couple of days."

"Huh?" I sat up and shook my head, trying to wake up enough to talk to her. "What for?"

"I need to get away from here for a while." Her voice wavered.

"Lindsey, are you crying?"

"No. Yes. A little." Sniff, sniff.

My brain started to wake up. "Did you have a fight with your father?"

Alexander Markham Sr. was not a nice man, in my books. He may be a fine human being in many ways, but my only exposure to him had been when he refused to see his dying son because Alex was gay. He had also refused to let his wife and daughter have any contact with Alex because it might tarnish his reputation at work. But Lindsey had ditched school and, with my help, gone to visit her brother before he died.

"Something like that."

I sighed, not surprised. Mr. Markham liked to control every aspect of his family, and Lindsey was a headstrong teenage girl. Their relationship was destined to be volatile.

I liked Lindsey. She reminded me of myself at her age. But that didn't change the fact that she was fifteen years old. A minor. Something in her voice told me there was more to her request than a weekend vacation away from the little Appalachian town of Pikeville, where she lived.

"Are your mom and dad cool with you staying here?"

She remained silent. As I suspected, she wanted a place to disappear for a few days and had not planned to inform her parents where she would be.

"Listen, Lindsey, you know you're welcome here, but only if your parents say it's all right. I can't let a fifteen-year-old—"

"Sixteen," she corrected. "My birthday was in November."

"Okay, a sixteen-year-old come up here and hide out if her parents don't know where she is. I could get into a lot of trouble. If you ask, will your dad let you come for the weekend?"

"I don't know. Maybe."

"Ask him or your mom, and if they don't care, it's fine with me."

"All right."

She sounded depressed. I felt sorry for her. Mama and I had butted heads when I was a teenager, but Mama was a dream compared to Mr. Markham.

"Hey, cheer up," I told her. "Look at it like this. In two years, you'll be out on your own, going off to college and coming home for long weekends and holidays. You'll be surprised how much better you'll get along with your parents then."

"Yeah. Right. I'll keep that in mind."

She hung up without saying good-bye, and I lay in the dark, worrying about her. I wanted to be Lindsey's friend, but I had enough troubles of my own without taking on a rebellious teenager.

My thoughts turned to those troubles, and instead of drifting back to sleep, my mind ran marathons, leaving the rest of me to twist the blanket into knots. Should I go to Orlando, or shouldn't I? I could afford it, but I worried about spending that much money without knowing when I would have another steady job. On the other hand, when I did find a new job, I certainly wouldn't be able to take a week off to visit my grandmother, so this would be the last chance I had for a while.

Mama would not be happy about the trip, and I dreaded telling her.

"Lord," I prayed, "what do You want me to do? I could use some advice here."

I waited, staring toward the dark ceiling, but the Almighty remained silent.

Finally at two in the morning, I got out of bed and fired up my computer. My hopes swelled briefly as my e-mail software opened but deflated after a quick scan of the new mail in my inbox. Nothing from the preacher. There were a couple from other people in the church telling me about things they'd like to see in the next church magazine, as well as a couple of forwarded jokes from Mama. There were several e-mails advertising things I didn't want to think about, and I deleted those unopened.

Sighing, I closed my e-mail and went to the Internet browser, where I spent the next thirty minutes searching for instructions on preparing a résumé. Then I shut down the computer and got back into bed. Opening my Bible at random, my eyes fell on a list of "do nots" in Deuteronomy 22. If anything could put me to sleep, I figured that would. I read until I felt a delicious drowsiness creep over me, and when I fell asleep, I dreamed of finding mother birds on the side of the road and taking their eggs.

I awoke at six o'clock Friday morning, looked at the snow falling heavily outside my bedroom window, and pulled a pillow over my head.

"Thank You, Lord, that I can sleep in," I mumbled into the spongy foam and fell immediately back asleep.

The phone woke me four hours later.

"Mayla, it's Jolene. Feel like pulling a double today?"

"Huh?"

I sat up, groggy, glancing at the clock and then outside. The snow had stopped, and amazingly, the sun had decided to put in an appearance after a three-day absence.

"Kathy's kid is sick again. I know you're on tonight, but you said you needed the extra hours."

"Yeah, sure." I stretched, yawning. "I'll be there in an hour."

I made coffee quietly so I wouldn't wake Sylvia, then jumped into the shower. When I opened the bathroom door, the odor of strong, black coffee invaded the room, overpowering the steamy clean smell of Dial soap. Wrapped in a towel, I filled an oversized mug and took it into my bedroom.

The phone rang again just as I turned off the hairdryer. Diving across the bed, I managed to grab it on the first ring. "Hello?"

"I wanted to make sure you're up," said Mama's voice. "You sound up."

"I *am* up," I told her. "I'm getting ready to go to work at The Max."

"I just wanted to make sure you weren't planning to stay in bed all day and mope about getting fired."

I sighed. "First of all, I did not get fired. I was laid off. And what difference would it make if I did stay in bed all day? Maybe I deserve a day of rest."

"I'll tell you what difference it makes." She spoke in her about-to-deliver-a-lecture voice. "Essie Caldwell's son got fired from his job a couple years back, and he sunk into the depths of depression. His wife had a chore taking care of them babies and working at the Dairy Dip, and all he did was go from layin' in bed to layin' on the couch. Essie stayed out of it as long as she could, but she finally had to step in for his own good, and she went over there with the baseball bat she keeps behind the bedroom door for burglars and threatened to knock him off that couch if he didn't—"

"Okay, Mama," I interrupted, giving her a chance to gulp some oxygen. "I get the point. Keep your baseball bat behind the door. I am not about to sink into the depths of depression. But I am about to leave for work at the restaurant, so I need to hang up."

"Okay, baby. Love you."

"Love you, too, Mama. Have a nice day."

Twenty minutes later as I parked my car in the snow-covered back parking lot at The Max, I realized what Mama had told me without saying so. Essie Caldwell was in her Tuesday night ladies' group. That meant all the grapes on that vine would be vibrating with the news by lunchtime. And that vine had a big fat tendril wound around the telephone in the office of the pastor of Salliesburg Independent Christian Church.

The call came on my cell phone at two thirty. I leave my phone turned on at work but on the desk back in the manager's office where we lock our purses. I heard *The Flintstones* song playing all the way from the server's alley and charged through the kitchen, dodging around a startled kid at the salad station to get to my phone. When I picked it up, I saw the church's number on the display. Watching in an agony of indecision, I resisted punching the Talk button until finally the music stopped after the second chorus. Relieved, I heaved a sigh and waited for the chime announcing a new voice message.

The tone came quickly. He must have left a short one. I punched the number to check my messages, my stomach giving a little flutter when I heard his voice.

"Hi Mayla, it's Pastor Paul. Elizabeth Pritchard just called with the news that you've been fired." I groaned. "I want you to know you're in my prayers. Give me a call if there's anything the church can do."

That was it? The flutter in my stomach instantly transformed itself into anger. I pressed a button and listened again, the anger building into a hot rage. Anything *the church* can do? The *church*? What about him? Didn't he want to do something for me on his own, outside of the church? I could think of about a million things he could do, including inviting me out to dinner to commiserate on my bad luck.

I deleted the message, my rage evaporating as quickly as it had come. Of course he wouldn't offer to take me to dinner. He obviously didn't think of me that way. To him, I was nothing more than a member of his congregation. If he had been looking for an excuse to ask me out, he would have seen this as the perfect opportunity.

Depressed, I went back to the server's alley and gulped down two glasses of Pepsi.

During my evening break, I called Florida. My aunt Louise answered the phone.

"Guess who this is?"

"Is it Mayla?" She turned her head away from the telephone and shouted, "Mother, Mayla's on the phone!" After a pause, she said to me, "Mother can't come to the phone right now; she's in the bath."

"You need a portable phone."

"I know, but she says this one works just fine and there's no sense spending the money. How are you, Mayla?" She lowered her voice to a whisper. "And how's your mother?"

"We're both fine. I was wondering if you could stand having a houseguest for a week or so."

"Really?" She sounded surprised and so happy I found myself smiling. "We would love to have you. When can you come?"

"I was thinking about flying down next Friday if that works for you and Grandmother."

"Friday's perfect," she said. "Do you know what time you'll get in?"

"Not yet. I wanted to make sure it was all right with you and Grandmother before I booked the flight."

"Book it! Call me back with the flight number, and I'll pick you up at the airport."

"Great. I can't wait to see you both."

"I can't wait, either, Mayla. And Mother will be so excited. I know she's going to start planning things for you to do as soon as I tell her you're coming."

I laughed. "Well, tell her not to plan too much. I just want to spend time with you both, that's all. Bye, Aunt Louise."

"Good-bye, Mayla."

I hung up with a feeling of smug satisfaction. Who needed to wait around for some guy to call? I'd just go off to Florida by myself. That would show him.

Chapter 3

Since I had not heard back from Lindsey, I assumed her parents had put the kibosh on her visit. No surprise there. I'm not sure I'd let my sixteen-year-old daughter go off to the big city of Lexington, Kentucky, to stay with someone I barely knew. Hopefully, Lindsey and her dad had gotten over whatever crisis caused the midnight call. Putting thoughts of Lindsey Markham out of my mind, I pulled another double shift at The Max on Saturday, which was a good thing because it kept me from obsessing about my troubles.

I almost prayed for snow Sunday morning so I would have an excuse to stay in Lexington and go to church with Sylvia. She had found a big Baptist church not far from our apartment, and I tagged along with her every now and then. Thousands of people attended. Going to church with a crowd that big made me uncomfortable, but I had to admit the music was a lot better than Ted Davis's old-fashioned choir music at our church. The big church had an orchestra with drums and guitars and trumpets and violins, and singing was led by people with really good voices using microphones and lifting their hands to worship. If anyone ever had the nerve to lift their hands at Salliesburg Independent Christian Church, half the congregation would drop to the floor with heart palpitations.

The preacher at Sylvia's big church was good, too, but he couldn't hold a candle to Pastor Paul. 'Course, Pastor Paul was exactly the reason I had almost prayed for snow. But I woke to a bright sunny morning and grumbled through my shower and my morning prayers. By now, the whole church knew I didn't have a job. The announcement was probably in the morning bulletin, in the Prayer Request section. If I skipped church, they would think I was too embarrassed to show up. My absence would look like I had done something wrong.

"Lord," I grumped as I gelled the ends of my hair into their normal flippy arrangement, "I'm going to need Your help today. Please don't let me say anything I shouldn't to Pastor Paul. Because I really want to tell him a few things, only I don't want to embarrass myself. I mean, I know You love him and all, but You have to admit he can be really irritating sometimes. But church isn't the place to tell him about it, so please help me keep my big mouth shut."

A couple of days of sunshine and no new snow had done wonders for the roads. The thirty-five-mile drive to Salliesburg brightened my mood considerably, with K-LOVE blaring positive, encouraging music through the radio speakers, and the sun sparkling on the clean, white snow that covered those softly rolling Kentucky hills. I sang at the top of my lungs, and by the time I pulled into the parking lot of Salliesburg Independent Christian Church, I had a smile plastered on my face and one in my heart, too.

It was pure bad luck that the first person I saw inside the door was Mrs. Elswick. She stood right in the middle of the doorway, wearing a white nametag that warned people she was going to pounce on them and there was nothing they could do to escape her. The tag said GREETER.

Now Mrs. Elswick is a child of God just like I am, and I'm supposed to love her with the love of the Lord. The Bible says so. But some of God's children are easier to love than others, and Mrs. Elswick was one of the others. She did not approve of my nostril stud or my earrings, and she never let an opportunity to tell me about it pass her by.

"Ah, Mayla," she said, standing by with a hanger while I peeled off my coat, "I was sorry to hear you were fired from your job."

I ground my teeth. "I wasn't fired; I was laid off. Happens all the time in the construction business, you know."

She smiled and patted my arm. "Of course it does. But a word of advice, dear." She leaned forward and whispered, "When interviewing for a new position, try to look a little more normal."

Handing me the hanger, she brushed past me to get at the people coming in behind me. My high spirits dropped a notch, but I shrugged off the tickle of irritation and went down the stairs to my Sunday school room. Mama always insisted that Mrs. Elswick didn't mean to be rude; it was just her personality. In general I didn't think rudeness was a genetic trait, but after meeting Mrs. Elswick's daughter over the Christmas holidays, I was prepared to revise my opinion.

At the bottom of the stairs loomed the tall, stooped figure of Mr. Holmes. A seventy-something widower, Mr. Holmes worked at the church as a part-time janitor and full-time grouch. We'd gotten off to a rocky start when we first met but had reached an unspoken truce after I made him a local celebrity by printing his picture in the church newsletter. He still glared at me, as he did at every other person below the age of forty-five, but I refused to take it personally. Underneath the gruff, he had a couple of soft spots, and every so often I got a glimpse of them. He wore his habitual jeans with dingy red suspenders and stood scowling as I approached.

"Hi, Mr. Holmes," I greeted him, grinning into his frown.

His expression cleared for the flash of a second before the grimace of disapproval returned. "Heard ye got fired."

I suppressed a sigh. As I suspected, the entire church knew. If I looked, I might even see a sign posted on the bulletin board in the Fellowship Hall. "Not fired. Laid off."

Glancing up the stairs as though to ensure no one lurked there listening to our conversation, he growled, "If yer needin' work, I got a guy owes me one. Runs th' dump."

I couldn't begin to imagine what sort of job might be waiting for me in a dump. Picturing myself sorting through building-high mounds of smelly, disgusting garbage, I forced a smile. "Thanks. I'll keep that in mind."

He gave a nod and turned to glare at a ten-year-old who ran by us at that moment, taking the stairs three at a time. I continued to my Sunday school room.

Mama was already seated at the table, talking with the teacher, Sam Mullins. I've always thought my mama was a pretty woman, though she has an extra fifteen pounds she's been fighting with as long as I can remember. She tends to like dresses in wild flower patterns that look like they were meant for upholstery instead of clothing, and she only wears flat shoes on account of her extra-high arches that hurt if they don't get enough support. But her hair is one of Clairol's nicer shades called Cinnamon Stick, and her eyebrows are dark and full and move constantly when she talks. Those eyebrows stopped moving abruptly when I came in.

"Ah, here she is," said Sam. "Mayla, Angela and I were just talking about you."

"No kidding?" I said, not bothering to keep the sarcasm out of my voice as I pierced Mama with a look. "Imagine that."

Mama gave me a sharp look in return, and the crease between her eyebrows deepened into a warning. "Sam here was sayin' he might know of a job for you."

I looked at him with interest. Sam Mullins was some sort of manager for Midstate Insurance and Investments, a big company in Lexington. I liked him. Besides being a good Sunday school teacher, he had gone out of his way to make me feel welcome when I joined the church last year at a time when people like Mrs. Elswick were making me feel like a freak. He and Mrs. Elswick were about as opposite as two people could be.

"What I was saying," he told me, "is that I get an e-mail with all the open jobs every week, and I've noticed that the accounting department almost always has something listed. You do accounting, don't you?"

"Officially I'm a receptionist, but I've handled the company's payroll and accounts payable for years. I don't have any formal training or anything, just what I learned on the job."

Sam gave a shrug with one shoulder. "In my opinion, that's just as good and sometimes better. I'll forward the next one to your e-mail address, and you can see if there's anything that interests you. If so, I'm happy to be a personal reference for you."

I sat down next to Mama, my good mood fully restored. Sam Mullins would give me a reference!

Mama leaned over and whispered, "See, I told you. That's what havin' a church family is all about."

I managed to avoid Pastor Paul all morning. I sat in my usual place beside Mama on the second pew, and he looked at me a couple of times during the sermon, but after church, I slipped through the crowd waiting to shake his hand at the door.

I got in my Honda and headed to Mama's house for dinner. It was a Sunday routine and one thing Sylvia said she missed when she found her Baptist church in Lexington. My mama was the best cook in the entire state of Kentucky, in my opinion, and most everyone in Salliesburg agreed with me. Every few weeks, she invited other people to join us, and no one ever turned down an invitation to Sunday dinner at Angela Strong's house.

I beat Mama home and let myself in the back door. When I stepped inside the kitchen, I was wrapped in a heavenly cloud of aroma, and I stopped right where I was to breathe in the delicious smell of Mama's Crock-Pot turkey breast. I could smell the diced onions and the tang of chopped celery with a hint of Italian seasoning. There's nothing like walking into the house when my mama has something cooking in her Crock-Pot. When I was a kid, I would go outside and come back in a dozen times so I could catch that delicious first smell all over again.

I saw that Mama had set four places at the dining-room table, and on the buffet alongside the wall, I caught sight of a glorious, deep-dish pie. The gently swirling peaks of meringue were lightly browned at the tips, and I hovered for one long moment, resisting the urge to pinch one of them off and pop it in my mouth. I hoped for my favorite, coconut cream.

Just then, Mama came in the back door, followed by her friend Mrs. Caldwell. A widow like Mama, Essie Caldwell lived in a run-down house a couple of miles outside of town and worked at the Bundle-O-Savings grocery store where Mama was a checker. I liked Mrs. Caldwell all right, except that she put on airs sometimes. She pronounced her name Ca-WELL instead of CALD-well, and that got on my nerves.

Mama kissed my cheek and bustled over to get a can of buttermilk biscuits out of the refrigerator.

Mrs. Caldwell nodded a greeting and said, "Wasn't that a good message the preacher gave today?"

Mama answered, "It sure was. Mayla could you reach me that cookie sheet from the drawer under the oven? I just love it when he takes somethin' from the Old Testament like that and makes it fit today." I tried to give her the cookie sheet, but she shoved the biscuits into my hand instead. "Could you open those and set them out, baby? Thanks. And Essie, if you'll just get that jar of pickles outta the refrigerator and put 'em in that little dish, it would be a big help."

As Mrs. Caldwell went for the pickles, I turned the oven on to preheat, then washed my hands and peeled the paper wrapping off the can. "Who else is coming for dinner?"

Lifting the lid of the Crock-Pot to peek inside, Mama said over her shoulder, "The preacher. He'll be along in a minute."

I stopped peeling and stared at her. "The preacher?"

"Mmm-hmm." She scooped up a few vegetables with a spoon and nibbled at them experimentally. Apparently satisfied, she put the lid back on and unplugged the Crock-Pot.

Pastor Paul coming to dinner. Well, wasn't that just dandy? *Lord, is this Your idea of a joke? Are You doing this to me on purpose?*

I whacked the can on the edge of the counter so hard the cardboard exploded with a loud *pop*, and both Mama and Mrs. Caldwell jumped.

"Sorry," I muttered, freeing the biscuits with a vicious twist. I had managed to avoid him all morning, and now he was coming to my house. As I put the biscuits on the cookie sheet, I realized that only part of me was upset. The other part was trying to twitch the edges of my mouth up into a smile, and that made me downright mad. What business did I have, being happy to see a man who didn't even bother to call me until I lost my job? And then he never called back. I could have committed suicide from grief and despair, and the soonest he'd find out about it was when he read my obituary in the morning paper!

If I could have thought of an excuse to leave, I would have. But about the time I put the cookie sheet into the hot oven, we heard the crunch of tires rolling across the icy snow on the driveway.

"The preacher's here," announced Mrs. Caldwell unnecessarily while closing the lid on the jar of pickle juice.

Standing on tiptoe to reach one of her good china bowls from the top shelf above the counter, Mama said, "Mayla, you get the door and take his coat. Find out if he wants Diet Coke or sweet tea with his dinner."

Obediently, if a little sullen, I left the kitchen. I waited by the closed door, listening to the sound of his feet as he came up the wooden porch stairs and then stomped on the mat to knock the snow off his shoes. The doorbell rang, and I let him stand out there a moment before I opened it. I didn't want him to think I was waiting by the door for him.

"Mayla! It's good to see you. I looked for you after church."

Pastor Paul Rawlings was a handsome man; I had to admit that, even if I was mad at him. His dark brown hair had started to show a few strands of silver around his temples in the past few months. He had eyes so dark they sometimes looked black, especially when seen from the second pew while he preached with a passion only a man truly called by God could have. He loved the Bible, loved the church, and loved the Lord, and he could talk nonstop about any topic related to any of the three. He was thirty-two years old—nine years older than me—and he worked out four times a week at the YMCA.

Oh, and he liked the Garbage Burger at The Max but didn't like the shoestring fries.

I knew all this because I had spent a lot of time talking to the guy over the past nine months since he baptized me. But I realized I didn't know much else. What were his goals? Who was his favorite teacher in high school? What was his favorite color? Oh, I knew the basics because he used examples from his childhood and family in his sermons, but when he talked to me, he never talked about himself. He was a great listener, though. He knew everything there was to know about me.

That made me angry all over again. I took his coat without a word, jerking it away from him a little more roughly than I should have, and he gave me a startled look.

"Are you okay? Did you get my message the other day? I heard about you getting fired."

I hung his heavy black coat in the hall closet and said through gritted teeth, "I did not get fired. I got laid off."

"Oh." He sounded surprised. "That's still upsetting, but it happens to lots of people these days. Did you get a severance package?"

It was my turn to be surprised. "Yeah, I did."

His smile warmed the chill right out of the room. "You're so talented you won't have any problem finding another job. God will open a door somewhere for you. And you know that most people who get laid off end up finding a better job than the one they left and making more money."

"They do?"

"Sure, it was a study in the *Wall Street Journal* a few years ago." He raised his nose and breathed deeply through it. "Mmmm, something smells good."

"You're in for a treat," I told him, leading him through the living room toward the kitchen. "Mama is fixing one of her specialties. And I'm supposed to find out what you want to drink."

As we walked, I suppressed a sigh. It would be easier to stay mad at him if he weren't so darned nice.

❀ ❀ ❀

Dinner was delicious, as usual. The pie was banana cream, my second favorite after coconut, and Pastor Paul liked it so much he had two big pieces. Then he impressed Mama and Mrs. Caldwell by insisting that he help with the washing up. He took off his suit coat, rolled up his white shirtsleeves, and strapped on Mama's apron. Silently, I leaned against the wall in the corner of the kitchen and watched as he stood at the sink with his arms up to the elbows in hot, soapy water. As he worked, he talked easily about everything from the conflict in the Middle East to the trees on church property that had been damaged by the last ice storm.

When the dishes were all clean, he unrolled his sleeves and reached for his suit coat.

"I need to be going," he told us. "Mr. Colvin down at the nursing home expects me to come by every Sunday afternoon and give him a personal review of the morning message. Angela, this was the finest dinner I've had in longer than I can remember. Thank you for having me."

Mama took his hand and patted it. "Any time you can join us, Pastor Paul, you'll be welcome."

Mama and Mrs. Caldwell sat at the kitchen table to sip the last of the coffee, and I walked him to the front door. As he buttoned his coat, he spoke in a low voice that couldn't be heard from the kitchen. "Are you okay, Mayla?"

I shrugged. "I'm fine. Like you said, I'll find another job."

"Yes, but that's not what I mean. I haven't heard much from you lately, even before you lost your job."

I watched his fingers shoving the big black buttons through

their holes. "No, I guess you haven't. And I haven't heard from you, either."

My voice sounded funny. Suppressing a wince at the tightness in my tone, I wished I sounded less waspish. I didn't raise my eyes to his, but I could feel him staring at me even as I kept my gaze fixed on his top button.

"Are you upset about something?"

"No, of course not. What makes you think that?"

The button jerked upward as he shrugged. "I don't know, maybe because you haven't called in a while. Or maybe because you haven't been acting like yourself the past few weeks."

"Telephones work both ways, you know." A buzzing started in my head, like all the blood had rushed there and made my brain go haywire.

He shoved his hands in his pockets. "You *are* upset. Do you want to tell me what it's about?"

All that blood rushing around in my head roared through my ears on its way toward my face, drowning out any sensible thoughts that might be trying to make themselves heard. Thoughts like maybe I should shut up while there was still time to end this conversation before I embarrassed myself beyond repair. But my mouth was already moving, so I shifted it into high gear.

"I've just been thinking about us lately and wondering where this relationship is going."

"Us?"

Ah, that got him. I did look at his face then and saw his eyes round and his mouth hanging open in shock. My cheeks were burning, and I felt damp under the collar. As I stared at him staring at me, I realized I had totally blindsided him. The heat continued to build in my face, fueled by anger as much as embarrassment. Or nearly as much.

"You don't think there's an us?" I snapped.

"Well . . . I never . . ." He stammered like a woodpecker on a telephone pole.

I stepped by him to reach the door handle and jerked it open. "I guess that answers my question. It's been nice, Pastor. Please come for dinner again."

I stood in the doorway as the frigid air rushed past me into the house, staring outside with my lips pressed tightly together.

"Mayla, listen," he began, "this is all really sudden. I never . . . I mean, I like you a lot. You're a wonderful Christian soul and a good friend. I just—"

"I'm a friend?" I didn't want to snap; I really didn't. But the words came out of my mouth like they'd been fired from a ten-year-old's BB gun. "Friendship is supposed to work two ways. I don't think ours does."

"Now what is that supposed to mean?" He spoke louder then.

I had never heard him raise his voice. Looking up at him in surprise, I saw two spots of color in the middle of his cheeks. I narrowed my eyelids to mere slits.

"It means I'm the one making all the calls and sending all the e-mails."

Taking a deep breath, he spoke in a reasonable tone that made me want to stomp my foot like a three-year-old. "I'm a single pastor, Mayla. I'm not supposed to call the pretty young women in my church. It wouldn't look right."

"Oh, and above all else we must make sure everything looks right! But I do have one question, Paul. If single pastors never call single women, where do married pastors come from?"

At my mention of marriage, a fresh wave of heat assaulted my cheeks. I was being childish, and I knew it. Why couldn't I stop myself?

His voice didn't rise above a normal speaking volume again, though I could see he was struggling to keep it down. "You have obviously read something into our relationship that I never intended. If I've misled you, I'm sorry. I suggest we both pray about this and discuss it when you've had a chance to calm down. Good-bye, Mayla."

He brushed past me and strode quickly across the porch without a backward glance. I stepped inside and closed the door. Not a slam, exactly, but definitely with force. I leaned against it for a minute, my chest heaving and my heart pounding.

"Well, God," I said, "that did not go well."

As I stood there trying to calm myself down before Mama and Mrs. Caldwell saw me, two things occurred to me. First, I had never called him Paul before, always Pastor Paul. Using his name felt natural, and I liked it.

The second thought lay gloriously at the top of my mind like a cherry perched on a banana split. He had called me a pretty young woman.

Since I was on a roll, I decided I would take care of one more unpleasant little chore before heading back to Lexington. Too bad Mrs. Caldwell hadn't gone home yet, but since she hadn't made a move to leave, I decided she planned to stay the rest of the day with Mama and go home after prayer meeting that evening. I would have to talk to Mama in front of her.

I went back into the kitchen, where the two of them sat sipping coffee.

"He is the nicest man," Mrs. Caldwell said.

"Yes, he is," Mama agreed. "And helps in the kitchen, too. Not many men his age think of doing that."

"Listen," I said, not wanting to hear any more of the preacher's virtues right then, "there's something I need to talk to you about, Mama."

She picked up her fancy china coffee cup and held it daintily with her fingertips, her elbows planted on the table. "Okay, baby." She tilted the cup to her lips for a sip.

"Well, it's like this. Since I have some time between jobs, I think I might just fly down to Florida for a little vacation."

Mama's cup came crashing down onto the saucer so hard I jumped.

Mrs. Caldwell looked surprised but wisely held her tongue when she saw the expression on Mama's face.

"Oh you think so, do you?" The crease between Mama's eyebrows was as deep as the Grand Canyon. "And just where in Florida would you go, I wonder?"

I would say I'm a fairly brave person, but even I almost backed down when Mama caught me in a glare with those brown eyes of hers. My voice wavered.

"I thought now might be a good time to go to Orlando. I might not have the chance again for a long time."

The chair legs scraped against the linoleum as Mama stood up from the table. She took her cup and saucer to the counter and slung the last of her coffee into the sink. Keeping her back to me, she looked out the window as she spoke. "What do you want to visit that poisonous old bat for?"

Mrs. Caldwell's eyeballs looked ready to pop out of her skull. I took a breath and plunged bravely forward. "Because she's my grandmother, and I haven't seen her in thirteen years."

Mama's back was rigid, her hands clutching the edge of the sink so hard her knuckles turned white. "She'll bring all that old stuff up again, and she'll fill your head with her lies." Mrs. Caldwell caught my eye and pointed silently toward the living room. When I nodded, she stood as quietly as she could and left the room.

"I won't listen to her, Mama. I know what happened. I was there, same as you."

Her shoulders slumped as the rage left her. When she spoke, her voice sounded small. "You were just a little girl when your daddy died. You don't remember like I do."

A scene flashed up from my memory of Mama and Grandmother standing in the hospital waiting room. Mama was crying, and Grandmother was shouting, and I was huddled in a chair, miserable, the terrible antiseptic hospital smell filling my nostrils. I remembered Mama's expression of absolute agony as clearly as if it was yesterday.

As she stood there in the kitchen with her back to me, her head drooping and her shoulders hunched forward, I knew her face was wearing that same expression. I pushed my chair away from the table and went to stand at her side.

"I know what you went through to make the decision to turn off that respirator, Mama. You did what Daddy wanted."

She stared out the window, not moving except to lean toward me the tiniest bit, as though drawing comfort from contact with my arm.

"I know it hurt her," she whispered. "He was her son; a'course it hurt her. But she had no cause to talk to me like she did. I hurt, too, and even more to be called the names she called me."

I put my arm around her shoulders and squeezed. "You can be sure of one thing. Nobody is going to call my mama names in front of me. Nobody. I'll set her straight in a hurry if she does."

Mama's head turned toward me. I had expected tears, but instead I saw eyes so full of pain there was no room for anything else. She gave a very slight nod.

"It's probably time you saw her again. I handed her over to the good Lord years ago, but I guess maybe I held on to part of that whole mess—the part that has to do with you."

Turning, I put my other arm around her, too, and hugged her tight. She laid her head on my shoulder, and when she took a shuddering breath, I realized she was crying softly. Guilt knifed me in the stomach. I can't count the number of times I've cried on my mama's shoulder, but that was the first time she ever cried on mine. I swallowed, hard, and wondered if I should cancel my trip. The last thing I wanted to do was make Mama cry.

But the second-to-last thing I wanted to do was cancel my Florida trip. If I didn't get out of this snow soon, I would lose my mind. And besides, my grandmother wasn't getting any younger. Aunt Louise had told me her health wasn't good. This might be my last chance to see her.

Mama really didn't have any reason to be upset about this trip. I wouldn't have a good time if I thought I had gone to Florida against her wishes. I needed for her to be okay with me going. But how could I arrange that?

I heaved a big sigh. "I'm sorry, Mama. I should have asked how you felt about it before I made plans. I won't go. I'll cancel my trip."

She pulled away, her eyes widening. "You mean that?"

I bit my lip. Would she really want me to do that? Sucking in a brave breath, I nodded. "Sure. Of course, I have nonrefundable tickets so I'll probably have to pay a penalty to cancel them, but if you're not comfortable with me going . . ."

She looked toward the backyard again, then shook her head. "No, this is a good thing. It's something you need to do." She forced a smile and managed to look almost herself again. "Now where's Essie wandered off to? I'm not much of a hostess, leaving my guest to fend for herself."

She left the kitchen to find Mrs. Caldwell, and I breathed a sigh of relief that my trip was still on. I stood at the sink, looking out at the snow-covered backyard. It wasn't yet three o'clock in the afternoon, and already I had managed to make one person I cared about angry enough to shout and another one unhappy enough to cry.

I've had better days.

Chapter 4

I read somewhere in the Bible about blessings and curses and choosing between them. Cell phones are both all rolled into one. The blessing is the convenience for me. The curse is the convenience for other people—they can find me wherever I go.

I suppose I could turn it off . . .

Nah. Most of the time it's a blessing, as it was on Wednesday morning when I awoke at nine o'clock to *The Flintstones* song.

"'Lo?"

"Mayla, Sam Mullins here. Did I wake you?"

I sat up in bed, trying to untangle my legs from the twisted blankets. "No, of course not. Been up for hours."

He laughed. "Sure you have. Listen, I got an e-mail yesterday with the job postings, and there's one I think you'd be perfect for. I just came from a meeting with the hiring manager, and she would like to talk to you. Do you think you could come in today and fill out an application?"

"Today?" I was scheduled to work at The Max from three to close, and I needed to run by the bank to deposit the severance check that had come in yesterday's mail. "Sure, I can come this morning. But I haven't had a chance to put my résumé together yet."

"You won't need one. Just go to human resources and fill out an application. I'll let them know you're coming. Do you know where the Richmond Road office is located?"

I did. I thanked him and pushed the End button, then lay back on the pillows. I hadn't asked Sam anything about the job. Was it in accounting, or payroll, or maybe a receptionist? A nervous tickle started in my stomach. What would I write on an employment application about the kind of job I was looking for? I wasn't qualified to do anything. I didn't have any special training other than what I had gotten on-the-job at Clark and Hasna. People like Clarkie went to school and learned about accounting; I couldn't compete with them for accounting jobs. And as for payroll, we had a payroll service. All I did was report the guys' time to the service and distribute the checks.

What I really wanted out of a job was a big paycheck, but I didn't think that would look good on an application.

I realized that I had not prayed about finding another job and decided to take care of that right then.

"Dear Lord," I said in a quiet voice, "I know You've got the perfect job all picked out for me. I don't know what it is, but would You help me find it? Maybe it's this one at the insurance company, or maybe it's another one. But wherever it is, Pastor Paul says You'll open a door for me to walk through. Could you do me a favor, Lord? Could You open it real wide? Just so I don't walk past it by mistake. Amen."

Mentioning Pastor Paul to the Lord brought him sharply to mind, and I stewed and fretted while I showered. I had not heard a word from him in the three days since he had stomped off Mama's porch. The apology e-mail I had composed on Sunday night had been deleted unsent. He knew I was waiting for him to either call or e-mail, and he was purposely holding out. Either he was being mule-headed, or he really didn't care about me at all and this was his way of putting some distance between us. Whichever it was, I wouldn't give him the satisfaction of caving in first.

Sylvia woke up at ten thirty and stumbled sleepily out of her bedroom as I was pulling on my coat.

"Where are you off to?" she asked, yawning.

"I'm applying for a job Sam Mullins told me about at Midstate Insurance. Do I look okay?"

I opened my coat flasher-style so she could see my clothes. They were the nicest ones I owned, black slacks, a striped knit sweater I had gotten as a Christmas present, and black leather boots. I figured the jeans I wore to the construction office wouldn't go over well in a big company like Midstate.

She nodded. "Very professional. Do you have a pen?"

"Yeah, I think so. Why?"

"They say you should always bring your own pen for filling out job applications. It shows you're prepared."

She wandered in the direction of the kitchen as I let myself out of the apartment, wincing as the frigid wind bit at my unprotected face and hands. I had lost my gloves again, the third pair in as many months. I lose sunglasses in the summer and gloves in the winter. Trotting to my car as quickly as I could on the ice-covered sidewalk, I smiled to think that in just three days I would be in Florida, away from this bitterly cold Kentucky winter.

Midstate Insurance and Investments was on the other side of town. Just as I pulled onto New Circle Road, the big loop that circles downtown Lexington, a heavy snow started falling. The wind kicked up a notch, blowing snowflakes directly at my windshield and making it nearly impossible to see. Thank goodness the traffic was light at that time of day, because I slowed down to twenty-five, my windshield wipers banging at high speed while I squinted to see through the blizzard blowing outside my car.

Something moved on the road ahead of me. Instinct kicked in, and my foot slammed the brake pedal, remembering too late that slamming on the brakes on an icy road is about the stupidest thing you can do. My car skidded. The rear tires slipped sideways and threw me into a spin.

"Lord, help me!" I shouted instinctively, turning the steering wheel this way and that in a frantic attempt to get control of the whirling vehicle. After an eternity that lasted a couple of heartbeats, my car skidded to a stop off the side of the road, facing the wrong way.

My head collapsed against the steering wheel while I waited for my pulse to return to normal. The snow was falling too hard to see what had moved in front of my car, but I had definitely seen a flash of black down low, close to the road. Was it a child? Completely unaware that I'd just experienced a near-death incident, the Newsboys kept on blaring through my radio speakers.

Cautiously, I put the car into neutral and pulled on the emergency brake. I opened the door and instantly regretted that action when icy wind blasted into the warm car, bringing with it an avalanche of snow to slap me in the face. Easing myself out into the blizzard, I shut the door behind me to trap the warmth inside. The hairspray was instantly blown out of my hair as the wind whipped it with snow, freezing the strands into clumpy icicles that hung heavily from my scalp.

Shielding my stinging eyes with frozen fingers, I walked gingerly down the side of the road. What had jumped in front of my car?

I saw it then. The thing moved toward me, low to the ground, an unusual black spot in the blowing white snow. Not a child at all. It was an animal. A dog, or a cat maybe. Or a . . .

The creature hopped toward the place where I stood shivering and gathering wind-blown mounds of snow along the front of my coat and unprotected head. I stared in disbelief. It was a rabbit. A big white bunny, the biggest I had ever seen, with little black ears pinned back against its head and a black nose and a big black spot on its back like someone had poured a can of paint over it. The rabbit came hopping toward me right there in the middle of New Circle Road in a snowstorm. It hopped right up to my feet, stopped, and then rose up on its hind legs, cute little front paws dangling near its chest covered in clumps of frozen snow. Big, black eyes looked up at me.

"Where in the world did you come from?" I asked, bending down to get a closer look.

Shivering, the bunny slowly lowered itself to all fours, then edged closer to me. It rested its front paws on my boots in a clear plea for help.

I straightened and looked around. There were no cars in sight and no houses near the road on this stretch of New Circle. I couldn't see anyplace nearby where this bunny, obviously someone's pet, could have come from.

I looked down at it again, huddled against the toes of my boots, shivering. I couldn't leave it there. The poor thing was already half frozen and would surely become a rabbitsicle within an hour in this snowstorm. I reached down and picked it up. It was heavier than I expected, probably close to ten pounds, though some of that might have been the snow frozen in clumps all along its underside. The creature trembled in my hands.

"Poor bunny. I'll have you warmed up in no time."

Both of us were covered in snow. I shook my head to dislodge as much as I could before slipping back into the car. Setting the bunny gently on the passenger seat, I aimed the heater vent at him and kicked the fan up on high. He closed his eyes against the sudden blast of warm air but didn't move away.

As I turned my car cautiously around to face the right way and pulled out onto the road, I found myself smiling. I had rescued one of God's creatures from a frozen death. I'd figure out what to do with him later, after I had filled out the job application.

I got to Midstate without further incident, parked in a visitor parking space near the front door, and sat for a moment in the car with hot air blasting through the vents, gathering my nerve. The ice on the rabbit had begun to melt, and I reached over and raked as much off as I could. He opened one eye and looked up at me.

"I'll be gone for a few minutes," I told him. "Sorry I can't leave the heater on for you, but you'll be much better off in here than outside in the wind. We'll figure out what to do with you later." I looked toward the glass front doors and took a fortifying breath. "Wish me luck."

The snowfall had slowed, but big windblown flakes still slapped at my face hard enough to sting. I hurried up the snow-covered walk as quickly as I could and heaved the heavy glass doors open.

The lobby set my stomach fluttering again. It could pass for a fancy hotel lobby, with lots of shiny glass and polished, black marble floors that echoed my footsteps. Elegant wingback visitor chairs sat beside spindly little mahogany tables covered with business magazines. Huge trees in giant planters grew beneath an enormous, dome-shaped skylight, and the reception desk looked like something out of a museum, with intricate patterns etched in gold all around the edges. The receptionist, an attractive woman with red lacquered fingernails and matching lips, looked up from a magazine as I approached on tiptoe. The warm smile melted from her face when she caught sight of me.

"May I help you?" Her tone made the question sound like she was offering life support to an accident victim.

"I'm here to apply for a job," I said, irritated at myself for whispering.

Her gaze swept up to my head and then down to my snow-covered coat. She smiled again, this time nervously.

"I'll call human resources and tell them you're here." She paused, then cleared her throat. "If you'd like to freshen up, there's a ladies' room over there."

She pointed to the far wall, and I went toward it, noticing that I left a trail of wet footprints on the shiny black marble floor. The soles of my boots tapped loudly in the cavernous lobby, and I rose on my tiptoes, walking as quietly as I could.

When I looked into the bathroom mirror over the sink, I saw why the woman had stared. I looked like a flash-flood survivor. My hair, which had looked so good when I left the apartment thirty minutes before, now looked as though I had stuck my head inside an electric ice-cream churn and then tried to dry it with a vacuum cleaner. The mousse and hairspray had matted in globs to form big, gunky chunks of hair that hung like dripping dreadlocks around my head. I didn't wear much makeup as a rule, but today I had put on more than usual. I shouldn't have. Black streaks of mascara stained my cheeks and eyelids, and even speckled the bridge of my nose. My face looked like a four-year-old's finger-painting project.

"What a disaster!" I moaned, grabbing a wad of paper towels and wetting them. "Nobody in their right mind would hire me looking like this."

I'm not a primping sort of woman, so I don't carry toiletries in my purse the way some women do. I had a comb, and I tugged and jerked it through the sopping mess. After blotting the excess water with paper towels, I tried to flip the ends like I normally do. Then I went to work on my face. I had no spare makeup, so the best I could do was to wash my face clean. I scrubbed around my eyes, leaving them red and puffy as though I had been crying for a week. The result was better, but still pretty grim. Maybe I'd get some sympathy points with human resources.

When I came out of the bathroom, the receptionist gave me a sympathetic smile and pointed toward one of the high-backed chairs. I tiptoed over to it and sat. She made a call, speaking quietly, and within a few minutes, a man dressed casually in Dockers and a sweater came through a door behind her. He walked toward me, and I stood up as he held out his hand.

"Hi, I'm Justin Taylor. You're here to fill out an application?"

"Yes, I'm Mayla Strong. Sam Mullins told me to come."

His smile widened, and he shook my hand with a firm grip. "Oh yes, Sam called this morning and said you'd be stopping by. Come with me, and we'll get the paperwork out of the way."

He turned to lead me through the door he had come from and asked over his shoulder, "Is it snowing again out there?"

"Yeah, and the wind is awful. I had a problem with my car on the way over and got caught out in it."

Hopefully that would explain why I came to a job interview looking like a soup-kitchen customer.

I followed him through the door and stepped into a carpeted hallway. At the end was a wide room with four desks, three of which had people sitting at them. Someone had a radio turned on low, and one woman spoke into a telephone while the other two tapped on computer keyboards. Justin took my coat, which I had dried with paper towels as best I could in the bathroom, and hung it on a rack in the corner. He took me into a small, windowless room furnished with nothing but a round table and two chairs. Picking up a stapled package of papers from a stack in the center of the table, he motioned for me to sit and placed it in front of me.

"This is our job application. I'll be at my desk right out there if you have any questions. Do you need a pen?"

"No." I fished mine out of my purse and held it up for his inspection.

He grinned. "Let me know when you finish."

He left, and I started filling out the application. I had gotten about halfway through when Sam Mullins came into the room.

"Mayla, I'm glad you made it. This weather is something, isn't it?"

I stood, and he shook my hand. It felt weird, shaking Sam's hand in an office instead of seeing him sitting at the head of the Sunday school table at church. But he sat down in the other chair and motioned for me to sit, too. He spoke in a low voice, so as not to be overheard by those outside the little room.

"You look like you've been out in the weather."

He nodded toward my still-wet hair, and I touched it with nervous fingers. "I had some trouble on the way over."

His kind face was instantly full of concern. "Is everything okay?"

My explanation of finding a rabbit in a snowstorm seemed too improbable to explain in this office. Instead, I nodded. "Everything's fine, thanks. I'm a little wet, but I'll dry."

He settled back in the chair. "I realized after we hung up this morning that I didn't tell you about the job."

"I realized that, too."

"It's in the communications department, doing layout and design on the computer."

I sat up straight. "Really?"

"Yes, and when I saw the job description, I thought it sounded a lot like what you do with *The Torch* at church. So I brought in a couple of copies this morning and showed them to the communications manager. I told her what a wonderful job you do and how you created the look and layout yourself, and she said she wanted to talk to you."

"You talked to her about me?"

I must have looked surprised, because he smiled. "Of course. That little magazine is really good, better than some professional magazines I read. You do a great job with it. Beth would be lucky to get you, and that's what I told her."

Flattered, I couldn't think of anything to say except, "Thanks, Sam."

He stood. "Listen, I've got to get back to work, but I wanted to remind you to put my name down as a reference." He paused, then leaned toward me and whispered. "You look really nervous, Mayla. Relax. There's nothing to be anxious about."

I managed a smile as he left, then went back to the application. Justin must have been watching me, because when I closed the packet, he came into the room before I could take it to him.

"All finished?"

I nodded and gave him the application. He leafed through it.

"Everything looks good. I'll get this to the manager of the open position, and she'll give you a call to set up an interview some time next week."

"Oh." I bit my lip. "I'm going out of town Friday. I'll be gone all next week. I will have my cell phone with me, but I won't be able to come in for an interview until I get back."

"Hmmm." He glanced at his watch. "Sit tight for a sec."

He left the room and went to his desk. A few minutes later he returned.

"We're in luck," he said. "The hiring manager has a few minutes free. Come with me, and I'll take you to her office."

I gulped. "Right now?" I touched my hair self-consciously. Still damp, though the ends felt as though they were starting to look flippy, the way I like them.

"If you have time, now's good for her."

I followed him through the outer office and into the front lobby. My steps echoed on the floor again as we crossed to another door, my nerves stretching tighter with every step. That lobby was just too fancy for me. With sudden longing, I missed the dirty little construction office that was the only place I had ever worked. I fit there. How could I ever fit in a place like this?

The hallway through the other door was long, with dozens of cubicles along both sides. People stood chatting over the cubicle walls, and several spoke to Justin as he led me through the maze, finally ending at a tiny, glass-walled office. The nameplate on the open door said BETH BARLOW, CORPORATE COMMUNICATIONS MANAGER. A dark-haired woman inside sat behind a cluttered desk, piles of paper in disarray covering the surface. She stood as we approached and came around the side of the desk with a warm smile that went a long way toward putting me at ease. I relaxed the death grip I had on the shoulder strap of my purse.

Justin handed her my application, saying, "Beth Barlow, this is Mayla Strong. Give me a call when you're finished, and I'll come get her."

He left, and Beth closed the door behind him, gesturing toward an empty chair in front of her desk. The office was so tiny there was barely enough room to squeeze into it. She sat in her chair, glanced at my application, and then tossed it on top of one of the piles.

"I don't need to see that," she said, giving me another of those warm smiles. "Sam Mullins came in this morning and showed me the magazine you do for your church." Shoving some papers out of the way, she uncovered several past issues of *The Torch*. She picked one up and leafed through the pages. "It's impressive."

"Thank you," I said, genuinely pleased. "I have a lot of fun with it, and I'm kind of proud of the way it looks."

"You should be. What software do you use?"

We talked for a few minutes about my computer experience, and then she asked some questions about my work at Clark and Hasna. She had a way of looking at me with her wide, brown eyes that made me feel like I couldn't tear my gaze away.

After a while, she told me about her job.

"It's a new department for this company. They just hired me last year, and so far, I've been doing it alone. I'm in charge of all the corporate communications, starting with a company newsletter." She gave me a sheepish grin. "I'm ashamed to show it to you, because yours looks so much more professional. But I also do speechwriting for the executives, and press releases—things like that."

I cleared my throat, nervous again. "I don't actually write most of the articles; I just lay them out. I wouldn't know how to begin writing a speech."

She smiled. "That's okay. That's my job. But I've sold the executives on the need for a consistent corporate look. An internal brand, so to speak."

Her hands moved when she talked and especially when she was excited about what she was saying. Her enthusiasm was contagious as she outlined her plans for her new department.

"I want to start with the newsletter, and I've gotten human resources to agree to let me restructure all their employee materials. Things like this," she picked up my application packet, "and the employee handbook and benefits booklet, anything that is distributed to employees or prospective employees. All the content is written by the experts. We'll just do the layout."

"That sounds like fun," I told her, meaning it.

She grinned. "I think so, too. But I'm a computer klutz, so I need to hire someone who is computer savvy."

I sat straight up in my chair. "I'm computer savvy. I don't have any formal training, but if it's on a computer, I can learn it."

"That's the attitude I'm looking for." She sobered and gave me another of those direct gazes. "I want to be honest with you, though. My boss will approve the final candidate, and he places a lot of value in education. I haven't even begun to interview candidates yet—you're the first—so I don't know the background of the applicants I'll talk to. But if the choice came down to someone with a degree and someone without one, it does count for a lot with him."

My enthusiasm melted away. I swallowed. "I understand."

Then she brightened. "Don't look so down. You've got an ace in your pocket—Sam Mullins speaks highly of you." She stood and came around her desk to open the office door. "I'll walk you back to human resources. I'm planning to interview candidates next week and hope to make a decision by Wednesday of the following week. Someone will give you a call."

Encouraged by the reminder of Sam's recommendation, I followed her out the door and through the maze-like hallways. "Thanks for seeing me today," I told her. "I normally look better than this, but I got caught out in the snow on the way over."

"Oh, that's awful." She shuddered. "Justin said you're going on vacation next week. Somewhere warm, I hope."

Grinning, I said, "Oh yeah. Florida."

Her eyes closed with a dreamy expression. "Ah, sandy beaches and hot sunshine. I'm envious."

We went through the lobby doorway, and I noticed that Beth did not tiptoe. She strode confidently, her shoes clack-clacking on the marble like a tap dancer, as though she was proud of the volume. At the other door, she extended her hand. It was warm in mine.

"Have a great time in Florida," she said. "Thanks for coming in."

Then she left, clack-clacking her way back across the lobby as I went to retrieve my coat.

As I walked out the front entrance, a packet of information about the company from Justin in my hands, I remembered the bunny. Glancing at my watch, I realized he had been alone in my car for an hour. I hurried down the sidewalk and unlocked the car door, opening it cautiously. There he sat, peering contentedly up at me from the passenger seat. He seemed to have groomed himself, because there was no sign of snow or ice on his fur, and though it was still damp, he was starting to look fluffy in places. His ears twitched forward as I sat down in my seat, but he didn't move away from me.

"Hello, Mr. Rabbit," I said as I put the key into the ignition and started the engine. "I'm glad to see you behaved yourself while I was gone."

But when I looked closer, I realized he hadn't behaved himself quite as well as I could have hoped. Beside him on the seat was a scattering of black rabbit pellets.

"Eeewww," I screeched, disgusted. "We're going right now to get a box for you to ride in."

He watched me, unperturbed, as I shifted the car into reverse and backed out of the parking space, heading for the nearest grocery store.

Chapter 5

Thankfully, Sylvia wasn't home when I blundered through the door, loaded with bags of rabbit bedding, food, a pet water bottle, and a big box that deceived casual passersby—or nosy neighbors who might squeal to the apartment office—into thinking I had purchased a case of Clorox. Inside the box, the now-dry bunny was quiet, no doubt wondering what in the world was happening to him.

With my bedroom door closed in case Sylvia came home, I spent the next hour getting the bunny's new home set up. I spread a few inches of bedding in the bottom of the box and found an old, hard plastic bowl with low sides for his food. The water bottle was a challenge. I spent more than a few minutes trying to figure out how to attach the contraption—which was designed to hang on a wire cage—to a cardboard box. But I was not about to be mastered by a drinking utensil for rodents. A wire coat hanger did the trick, and when everything was all set, I put the rabbit and a carrot into his new place. As I watched, he moved slowly around the box, checking everything out. He even got himself a drink of water.

Satisfied, I washed my hands and dressed for work. Then I fired up my computer, surfed over to the *Lexington Herald-Leader* classified section, and placed an ad under Lost and Found. The Web site told me the ad would start on Thursday. Perfect. Hopefully his owners would see it and call before Friday afternoon when I left for Florida.

Before I went to work, I peeked into the box. He was munching the carrot.

"Now behave yourself, Mr. Rabbit, and we'll figure out what to do with you tomorrow."

I closed my door when I left. I needed some time to come up with a good explanation for the bunny's presence, however temporary.

Thinking of temporary houseguests brought Lindsey to mind. A week had passed since her call. I wondered if I should try to contact her and decided against it. The last and only time I had called her house had been to talk to her father when Alex was dying of AIDS. Mr. Markham had not been friendly, and I was left with the definite impression that future calls would not be welcome.

I never had pets as a child because Mama is allergic. I like cats okay. They're quiet, and I like the feel of a cat rubbing up against my leg for attention. I like to pet cats because they arch their backs up into my caress and they vibrate when they purr. The sensation gives me a warm feeling inside unless they're shedding. Then my hand comes away with a wad of fur sticking to my palm, and stray hairs go whisping off into the air to get sucked down into my lungs, and that is revolting.

Dogs and I never got along, and it's all because of Chopper. He was the bulldog who lived next door when I was a kid, and he was in serious need of orthodontic care. I never understood how Chopper could eat with that incredible underbite; his mouth didn't even close all the way. And his nose was so smooshed into his face that he snorted when he breathed. He slobbered, too. Though his owners kept him fenced in the backyard, he managed to escape an average of twice a week. He always made a beeline toward me, snorting like a bull with a sinus infection and with long slimy strings of slobber dangling from the edges of his mouth. Why did he always run after me like that? I think he just liked to hear me scream.

I had turtles when I was eight. But I set their plastic bowl—with its hill made out of blue and white gravel and its little green plastic palm tree—on the windowsill and forgot about them. The summer sun evaporated all the water so they dried out and died, and their smell acted as a homing beacon for Mama when she was putting my clean clothes in the dresser.

After the turtles, I was not allowed to get a hamster.

With my pet history—or lack thereof—in mind, I left work at eleven o'clock that Wednesday night with renewed purpose. I would take extra special care of the rabbit while he was with me. I felt sure there was a loving family somewhere mourning for him, and I prayed they would contact me soon. Preferably before Sylvia realized he was in the apartment.

Sylvia had gotten a ride to work. She worked the same shift as me on Wednesdays, so I hung around while she closed out the bar register, and then we rode home together. When we walked through the apartment door, she stopped dead in her tracks. She raised her nose and took a deep sniff.

"What is that smell?" She studied me through narrowed eyelids.

Make no mistake—my sense of smell is every bit as good as Sylvia's. I raised my nose like hers and sniffed, and I detected the odor of stale cigarette smoke from two days ago when Tattoo Lou had spent the evening here. I smelled bacon from yesterday's breakfast. And I smelled the refreshing scent of a California forest—fresh cedar from the rabbit bedding. But overpowering all those was an unpleasant odor that I had never smelled before. It had a distinct animal fragrance.

I widened my eyes as round as they would go. "What smell? I don't smell anything."

She ignored me, taking one slow step after another into the apartment, turning her head from side to side and sniffing deeply the whole time. Sylvia may be petite, but when she's upset about something, she seems to grow taller every second. By the time she got halfway down the hall, I would have sworn she was Goliath's sister. Her nose led her unerringly to my bedroom door, where she stopped and whirled on me.

"What have you got in there, Mayla?"

"What do you mean?" I asked as innocently as I could manage.

"Don't give me that," she snapped, her hand on the door handle.

I took a quick step forward, reaching to stop her. "Sylvia, wait!"

Too late. She opened the door and looked inside. From where I stood in the living room, I couldn't see what she saw, but the unpleasant odor increased dramatically when the door opened. Her eyes grew wide as she stared into my room. Then she carefully shut the door before rounding on me. I almost ducked to get away from the fire in her eyes.

"You have exactly ten minutes to get that . . . that *rodent* out of this apartment!"

I have never responded well to ultimatums. Mama learned that when I was a teenager, and every guy I had ever dated since then learned it, too. I drew myself up to my full five feet five inches, inhaling a deep breath that threw my meager chest out as far as it would go, and planted both feet firmly on the carpet.

"It's my apartment, too."

Not, perhaps, the wittiest of comebacks, but the best I could do in the face of Sylvia's fiery rage.

Her eyelids narrowed. "I told you when you moved in here that pets are not allowed. You said you didn't have any and didn't plan to get any."

"I didn't plan for this one," I shot back. "I found him in a snowstorm, frozen nearly solid. What was I supposed to do, leave him there to die?"

"Better that than bringing him home with you." She tossed her dark hair over her shoulder with a jerk of her head. "You know full well we can't have pets. We could be evicted."

"Oh, come on, they're not going to evict us over a rabbit. And besides, it's only temporary. I'm running an ad to find his owner."

We stood facing one another, glaring into each others' eyes. Finally, she heaved a sigh and shook her head. "Okay, but you're leaving here in two days. You'd better find the owner before then, or I'll take him to the pound right after I take you to the airport."

I took a step back, horrified. "You can't do that! They'll put Harvey to sleep if no one claims him!"

She ducked her head and stared at me, incredulous. "Harvey?"

Shrugging, I said, "He looks like a Harvey to me."

"Oh, puh-leeese! You don't know what a Harvey looks like any more than I do."

"I do, too." I put my nose in the air, trying to ignore the terrible whiffs I was getting from the direction of my bedroom. "A Harvey looks like the little black-and-white bunny behind that door."

She crossed her arms and gave me a disgusted glare. "Oh yeah? Well, you need to check out what Harvey looks like just now, after he has chewed holes in your bedspread and peed on your carpet."

I stood rooted to the spot as she turned away with a flounce of her hair and stomped toward her bedroom door. When she was safely behind it, I raced down the hallway and flung my door open.

The box had been turned over on its side, with cedar shavings and rabbit food spread in a five-foot radius around it. I spied dozens of disgusting black rabbit pellets littered here and there around the room, and in the center of the floor was a soggy, foul-smelling, brownish stain. Harvey sat at the foot of my bed, happily munching the flowers off the quilted bedspread Mama had given me a couple of years ago when I moved into this apartment.

It took all the self-control I could muster not to scream at the top of my lungs. But I knew Sylvia was waiting for that with her ear pressed to her bedroom door, and I wasn't about to give her the satisfaction. Gritting my teeth, I set about cleaning up after the rabbit.

❀ ❀ ❀

Rabbit pellets are pretty easy to get rid of, especially if they've been allowed to dry before you scoop them up. But rabbit pee is disgustingly thick and pungent, and rabbits produce a lot of it. At least Harvey did. I dumped the foul-smelling cedar chips into a black plastic garbage bag the next morning and was inspecting the bottom of the Clorox box when my phone rang.

"Hello, Mama."

"Hi, baby. Sam Mullins told me at Bible study last night that you went out to his company for a job interview. How'd you do?"

Tentatively, I put my hand on the outside bottom of the box, checking for dampness. I didn't feel any. Thank goodness there was a double layer of cardboard in there.

"I did all right," I told her, propping the phone against my shoulder so I had both hands free to dump fresh bedding in. "The job sounded great, but I don't think I'll get it."

"Why not?"

I sighed. "Because the lady said if someone with a college degree applies, they'll get the job instead of me."

Mama, for once, held her tongue. The topic of college was a sore subject, one we both tried to avoid. But I was still a little depressed from the interview yesterday, and because the subject was already out in the open, I found myself picking at the sore.

"I could have gone to college." My voice defied her to disagree.

"A'course you could," she responded instantly.

"You didn't want me to, though."

She heaved a sigh so heavy I swear the hair around my telephone ear moved in the breeze. "You know why I didn't think you oughta go back then."

Tossing the half-empty bag of cedar bedding into the corner, I plopped down on the edge of my bed. "Because I wasn't smart enough."

"That ain't true, and you know it. You were plenty smart then, and you're plenty smart now. You woulda got good grades in high school if you had showed up for class every now and then."

That was true, so I couldn't argue. If I was honest with myself—and I had made a pledge years ago to always be honest with myself even if I wasn't honest with anyone else—I had to admit there hadn't been much sense in paying money for me to go to college when all I really wanted to do was cut class and party with my friends. Mama said she'd make a deal with me. She would pay half, but I had to get a part-time job and pay the other half. That was her way of making me take responsibility instead of hitching a free ride on a party train. That deal sounded like too much work to me, so my friends all went off to college without me. A couple flunked out, but a couple more stuck with it and finished last year. I got invitations to their graduations, but I didn't go. It stung then, and it still stung.

"Whatever." I didn't want to talk about that anymore. "Hey Mama, are you still allergic to animal hair?"

"Worse than ever. I can't step a foot inside Olivia Elswick's house because of her dog, and sometimes I even get hives from Essie's coat because of the cat hair. Why?"

I told her about Harvey. "Think you could watch him while I'm in Florida, at least until his family calls to claim him?"

"I ain't watchin' no rabbit," she told me in a voice that left no room for arguing. "It ain't their hair; it's their urine that gets to people with allergies. Nasty stuff, I hear."

Eyeing the garbage bag full of the repulsive stuff, I did not doubt her.

"Oh, I meant to tell you," she said. "Pastor Paul asked after you last night, how you were doing on looking for a job."

I took great pains to keep my voice level. "Did he?"

"Uh huh. Told me to tell you he's prayin' for you and to remind you to be doing the same."

His parting words on Mama's porch still rang in my ears, and I felt the steam starting to build behind my eyeballs. Thankfully, Mama had to go just then because her call waiting beeped and she can't stand to let it go unanswered.

He wants to remind me that I should be praying, does he? It sure wasn't prayer for my job he was talking about. I snatched up the black garbage bag and startled Harvey, who had been nosing around beside it. I didn't need anyone—certainly not *him*—telling me to pray! And giving me a message through my mama did *not* count as contacting me, so if that's what he was thinking, he could just forget it.

I cornered Harvey beside my bed and plopped him into his newly cleaned box, then wedged it in place with my desk chair so he couldn't knock it over again. That preacher was the most infuriating man in all of God's creation!

I got to The Max at ten o'clock to work the opening shift. The front doors were still locked when my cell phone rang. I dashed through the kitchen and into the manager's office to grab it.

"Hello?"

"Yeah, I'm calling about the rabbit. Can you tell me how big it is?"

A call already! With luck Harvey would be safely back home by suppertime. "He's pretty big, more than five pounds for sure."

"Looks like it's been well fed, does it?"

At the rate Harvey was devouring carrots, I knew something about his appetite. "Oh yeah. He eats all the time."

"That's good. Where can I see him?"

Something didn't sound right. The man's voice was a little too businesslike, not at all like a person who has lost their pet. "Uh, what color is the rabbit you lost?"

There was a snort of laughter, and then, "I didn't lose a rabbit."

I held my phone out at arm's length and wished he could see the annoyed expression I was giving him. I put it back to my ear. "Then why are you answering an ad in the Lost and Found section?"

"'Cause there's good eatin' on a rabbit, lady."

I gasped, horrified. "That's terrible! This is a pet!"

"Hey, a rabbit's a rabbit. Pet rabbits get fed better, so the meat's sweeter."

I didn't even try to stop the shriek that, hopefully, split his eardrum before I hung up on him. I turned around to find the entire kitchen staff had stopped working to watch me with wary stares.

"Sorry." I ducked my head as I walked past them.

What a sicko! I would have to be extra careful, or Harvey could end up as someone's Sunday dinner. I could see the menu now—Crock-Pot rabbit, with a side of carrots.

My phone was silent the rest of the day. When Sylvia arrived for work an hour before my shift ended, she came into the server's alley looking for me.

"Did the rabbit's owner call?"

Avoiding her eyes, I shook my head.

"Listen, I called the Lexington Humane Society. They don't put them to sleep. They keep them for a while to see if anyone comes looking for them, and if not, they go up for adoption. The lady said they almost always get adopted, and the ones that don't go to a rabbit farm."

"What's a rabbit farm?" I asked suspiciously. "Do they raise them for food?"

Sylvia crossed her arms and leveled me with a disgusted look. "Of course not. They sell pet rabbits or breed them and sell the babies." Greenish-brown eyes glared into mine. "You've got to take him tonight."

"No!" I pictured him as he had looked in his box this morning before I left, his little black nose quivering as he sniffed at the fresh food in his bowl, his black-and-white ears standing at attention. I couldn't stand the thought of taking him to the pound. "I don't leave until tomorrow. There's still time for his family to call."

She stood glaring at me, and I tried to look as pitiful as I could. Sylvia's really a softie under all that tough talk. Way under.

Finally she sighed. "Okay, but if they don't call—"

"I know, I know!"

Hurrying away from her, I shot up a quick prayer that Harvey's family would call soon.

I stopped at Wal-Mart on the way home to pick up a few things for my trip. I filled my basket with travel-size shampoo and conditioner, a plastic toothbrush cover, a couple of Kit Kat candy bars, and a package of peanuts. I might get hungry on the plane, and someone at The Max had told me the airlines didn't give you food for free anymore. Heading over to the pharmacy area, I searched for sunscreen. My poor, sun-starved winter skin would roast like a chicken on a hot grill if I didn't do something to protect it. I did find sunless tanning lotion but no sunscreen.

"Excuse me," I asked a stout woman wearing a blue vest, "where can I find sunscreen?"

She straightened up from the shelf where she was stocking big brown bottles of vitamin C. Putting her hands on her hips, she threw her head back to look at me out of the bottom half of her bifocals, giving me a most unwelcome view of her nasal passages. Then she pointed.

"On that there shelf, in about three months."

Ignoring her lame attempt at humor, I said, "I need it today."

She cocked her head to one side. "Been outside lately?"

Trying to keep the smugness out of my tone, I told her, "I'm going to Florida tomorrow."

"Huh." Flipping a hand at me in dismissal, she turned back to her task. "You'll have to get your sunscreen there. It's seasonal. We don't keep it on the shelf all year long."

With a pointed look in her direction, I picked up a bottle of aloe lotion with a label promising to soothe sunburned skin and tossed it into my basket. In the checkout aisle, I added a pack of gum, and I was all set.

Well, nearly. There was still the matter of Harvey. My phone had been depressingly quiet all day, and I was beginning to worry that his family might not see the ad in time. I couldn't bear the thought of taking him to the pound. I had saved his life; I couldn't desert him until I was sure he would be happy and safe and undigested by the public.

Back at home, I let myself into the apartment a little apprehensively. Sniffing as I stomped the snow off my boots, my mood sank when I smelled Harvey again. But I had changed the bedding just a few hours ago! How much pee could one rabbit produce?

When I opened my bedroom door, what I found inside left me momentarily stunned, staring in shock. Harvey, whose grandfather must have been the rabbit Houdini pulled out of his hat, had left another disgustingly horrible puddle directly on top of the place where I had scrubbed the old one. Cedar shavings and little black pellets again littered the carpet, and there was a new and bigger hole in my bedspread. At that very moment, the little escape artist was chewing on the leg of my desk chair.

Startled by my screech, Harvey darted toward his box and disappeared through the side. I saw then that he had chewed a rabbit-sized hole right in the corner. Closer inspection revealed that those little teeth of his were sharp enough to destroy wood—several of my chair legs and the side panel of my cheap computer desk were gnawed to the point of ruin.

"What are you, part termite?" I shouted into the box where he huddled, shivering, in a corner. "Don't I feed you enough? Why do you have to eat my bedspread and my furniture? And why do you have to pee all over the floor?"

He buried his face in the tiny bit of bedding remaining in the box. A thought occurred to me. Perhaps Harvey hadn't run away from home after all. Perhaps his family had thrown him out into the cold to get rid of him. Or perhaps he had eaten the house right out from under them. Perhaps they weren't interested in getting him back.

I grabbed a bottle of Fantastik and let the puddle soak in it while I cleaned up the rest of the mess. Then I scrubbed the carpet as hard as

I could, grumbling the whole time. I'd had to clean my room twice in as many days, and trust me, that never happened. I hate housework and only do it when I absolutely can't get out of it. But when I pictured the look on Sylvia's face if she saw the mess, I scrubbed with renewed vigor. I did get the stain out, but I was pretty sure I hadn't gotten rid of the odor completely. I needed a new box anyway, so back to Wal-Mart I went.

An hour later, Harvey was all tucked away in his new home, a Charmin toilet-paper carton. It was bigger than the Clorox box, and I figured maybe one reason he kept escaping was because he needed more space. I also bought some pet-stain remover—*Guaranteed to eliminate odors so your pet won't return to the same place*—and soaked my carpet with the stuff. The entire carpet.

Then I packed my suitcase. As I filled it with sandals and summer clothes, more or less folded, I kept an eye on the bunny. He seemed content enough. But my flight left in sixteen hours. What was I going to do with him?

Sylvia worked until closing that night, thank goodness. She wouldn't get home until close to midnight. By then, I would be asleep and wouldn't have to tell her that I still hadn't gotten a call from Harvey's family. But her absence did make the evening long and boring. There are only so many times a suitcase can be packed and repacked. I let Harvey out of the box and stroked his soft fur, but I wanted him to know he was still in disgrace so I put him back after a few minutes. I would have run upstairs to hang out with Stuart, but he still was not speaking to me.

Propped against the pillows on my bed, I jotted a quick note to Bradley, a friend of Stuart's I'd been corresponding with in prison for several months, telling him that I'd be gone for a while and promising to send him a postcard from Florida. Then I turned on my computer and dealt with my e-mail before surfing the Web for a while. Finally,

I decided to try the book Mama had loaned me for the plane trip. It was a Christian romance novel, and though I had turned my nose up when she had handed it to me, I was soon involved in the story. I sat on the couch with a bag of Doritos and a Diet Coke, smudging the corners of the pages with nacho-cheese-colored fingerprints.

A few minutes after ten, the familiar chime from my computer, announcing the arrival of a new e-mail, pulled me out of the story. Could it be from Pastor Paul? Probably not. He had not bothered to contact me all week, so there was no reason to think he would start now.

Still, I could focus no longer on the book. Putting it down, I went into my bedroom to see who had e-mailed me.

When I saw the address, my heart beat faster. It was from Bible-Man32, Paul's address. Throwing myself into the chair, I grabbed for the mouse and double-clicked on his name to open the message:

> Hi, Mayla. I got a call today from Mrs. Van Meter asking for prayer for your trip tomorrow.

Drat Mrs. Van Meter anyway! Naturally, she was one of Mama's Tuesday night ladies.

> I was surprised to hear you are going to Florida—

Ha! Surprised him, did I? Good.

> —but on reflection, I think this is a very good idea. Your grandmother will undoubtedly be happy to see you, and you can begin to heal the old wounds.

What nerve that man had, to speak to me of wounds!

> When you return, I would like to discuss our conversation of last week. I hope you have been praying, as I have been.

God Bless Your Travels,
Pastor Paul

I read it again and then a third time. Definitely not the conversation I had hoped for. Not one bit of apology was hidden in there, not even a hint of regret. And no matter how hard I looked for it, I saw no evidence that he had realized he might be just the tiniest bit attracted to me.

My first instinct was to click the Reply button and fire off a snappy response telling him I didn't appreciate his constant reminders that I should pray. But then the verse in Psalm 39 came to mind, the one that says we should watch our tongues and muzzle our lips. In today's world, computers get me in at least as much trouble as my tongue. I realized I needed to carefully consider what I would say, so I got up and paced the floor.

Of course he knew all about my relationship with Grandmother. He knew practically everything about me, thanks to what Sylvia refers to as my diarrhea of the mouth, which I obviously got from my mama. But it rankled that he felt free to give his approval for my visit. What business was it of his anyway? None at all. Did I ask for his opinion? Absolutely not. Did he think I would care at all what he thought of my travel plans? I didn't, not in the least.

I paced over to the computer and read the last part again. Well, he could just forget talking about last week's conversation. As far as I was concerned, our relationship was over. Done. History. When I got back from Florida, I would have a new perspective on life. I would focus on finding a new job, and I might even work on finding a new church, too. I certainly did not need to drive all the way to Salliesburg every Sunday when there were plenty of churches right here in Lexington. I might even start going to Sylvia's church. Of course, I would go back to Salliesburg on special occasions like Mama's birthday or Mother's Day. And then I would go to church with her and talk to all the people who had been nice to me and nod coolly at him as I left. I might even bring along my new boyfriend, the nice Christian man I expected to find shortly after finding the new church. And we would just see how the preacher of Salliesburg Independent Christian Church liked that.

I would not respond to his e-mail. It was beneath me, not worthy of my notice. Pastor Paul's opinion meant less than nothing to me.

But as I pressed the Delete key, I had to fight down a most unreasonable urge to cry.

Chapter 6

Friday morning, finally! At six o'clock my eyes popped open, and I came fully awake like a kid on Christmas morning. For one second, I even thought I could hear reindeer prancing on the roof. Then I realized the sound was coming from the floor beside my bed. I sat up, flipped on the light, and caught Harvey in the act of throwing himself against the side of the box, trying to turn it over.

"Stop that, you little monster." I reached in and pushed him gently back to the center of the box.

He looked up at me with his sweet little nose twitching, and a feeling of dread settled in my stomach. The Day had arrived, and Harvey's family had not called. I reached into the box and lifted him onto my lap. He nosed around my legs, investigating this new place, then sat still as I stroked the soft fur on his back.

"What am I going to do with you?"

His ears twitched at the sound of my voice, and I scratched them.

Completely unaware that fate was about to deal him a harsh blow, Harvey hopped off my legs and began a slow but thorough investigation of the bed. Watching him closely for any sign of nibbling, I propped my pillows against the headboard and reached for my Bible and the little daily devotional booklet I liked to read in the mornings.

By the time Sylvia stumbled out of her bedroom at ten o'clock, I had eaten breakfast, showered, dressed, put fresh bedding and food and water in Harvey's box, packed my hairbrush and toothbrush and all the stuff I had saved until the last minute, repacked them again after rummaging through the clothes to make sure my cutoffs were in there, and put my snacks and books into the backpack I would carry on the plane. My laptop was going along, too, so I could keep in touch through e-mail, and its case sat on the bed beside the backpack. I'd also checked the classified ads in the Friday *Herald-Leader* and gotten myself thoroughly depressed. Every job that sounded even halfway interesting required a college degree.

Sylvia poured a mug of coffee and came into the living room wearing a knee-length white nightshirt with a giant picture of Tweetie Bird on the front. She sat on the couch and watched as I gave my remote-control finger a workout surfing through the channels, something I rarely did. I had already come to the opinion that daytime television had absolutely no worthwhile purpose for existence.

I gave my roommate a cheery, "Good morning," to which she replied with a grumble and something close to a glare. Sylvia was not a morning person. I went back to surfing, knowing it was in my best interest to let her get a little caffeine down her throat. She's much nicer after her first cup of coffee.

Usually. But that morning, she had something on her mind, and she decided to hit me with it while she still had some morning growl left in her.

"Is the rabbit ready to go?" She glared at me through the steam rising from her mug.

I hung my head. My shoulders drooped. My lower lip may even have inched out a little bit. With my gaze fixed on the floor between my feet, I answered quietly in my best Eeyore imitation, "I suppose so."

Sylvia set her mug down on the coffee table with a bang.

"Don't start that, Mayla. We've already talked about this. We can't have a pet in this apartment."

Not looking up, I answered in a voice so low I almost whispered. "I know."

She stared at the television screen for a few seconds, picked up her mug, and took a sip.

"So," she said without looking at me, "we'll drop him off on the way to the airport. That means we need to leave in about an hour."

I drooped further and nodded again.

She spent a few minutes not looking at me, but I saw her eyes move in my direction a few times. I held my mournful pose, staring at the carpet.

"He'll be fine," she said finally.

I heard it then, the faintest hint of hesitation in her tone that I had been waiting for. Careful to maintain my dejected expression, I asked, "Did you have pets when you were a kid?"

She hesitated before nodding. "Cats."

"I never had pets, you know."

Her lips tightened. "I know. Your mother was allergic. You told me."

"What was your cat's name?"

Settling back in a corner of the couch, she curled her legs up, tucked her bare feet beneath her nightshirt, and took another sip of coffee before answering.

"We had lots of cats. There was one, a calico we called Mama Kitty because she kept having kittens. My mother always said she was going to have Mama Kitty fixed. But every time she went to the vet, Mama Kitty was pregnant again, and Mom just couldn't let them abort the kittens. So she'd come home saying, 'After *this* litter, I'm taking that cat straight down to have it done.' She never did, though."

I managed a smile. "You must have loved having all those kittens around."

Sylvia nodded, a faraway look in her eyes as she remembered. "Mama Kitty always tried to sneak off when the time came for her babies to be born. My brothers and I kept a close watch on her when the time got near, and I'll never forget the day I finally saw a kitten being born."

Picturing all those kittens, a thought occurred to me. My hopes rose, but I carefully maintained my bland expression. Keeping my voice as quiet and steady as possible, I asked, "What happened to the kittens? You must have had dozens of cats running around."

"Oh no," Sylvia shook her head, her tousled dark hair floating around her head like leaves in the wind. "We weren't allowed to keep any of them. We put up signs all over the neighborhood advertising free kittens, and people would come and take them one by one. It was so sad because I'd get attached to them, and then I had to say good-bye—" She jerked upright, coffee slopping onto Tweetie's head as she shot me an angry look. "Oh no you don't, Mayla Strong. This is not the same at all."

I drooped again. "It is for me. I never realized how attached people could get to animals until I found Harvey. I saved his life, just like your mom saved the lives of those kittens. And now I have to give him away."

Sylvia heaved a sigh with such force I almost smelled the coffee on her breath all the way across the room. Her shoulders drooped in a perfect imitation of mine, only hers drooped with resignation.

"Oh, all right. I'll watch the stupid rabbit for you while you're in Florida."

I sat up straight, unable to keep the smile off my face. "You will?"

"Yes, but only for a week. When you get back, you have to go talk to the apartment manager. If she says we can't keep it, then we'll find another home for it. Agreed?"

I flew out of the chair and threw myself onto the couch so I could hug her. "Agreed! Thank you, Sylvia."

She hugged me back with one arm, then stood. "Yeah, yeah. Now let me get a shower so we can get you to the airport on time."

While Sylvia showered, I had a stern talk with Harvey about his behavior during the next week with Aunt Sylvia. His ears twitched once or twice, but for the most part I was fairly certain he ignored me.

You can't fly directly anywhere from Lexington, Kentucky. That makes sense, because even though Lexington is the Horse Capital of the World—there are signs all over town proudly proclaiming that little-known fact—it isn't exactly the biggest circle on the map. The airport terminal is so small it would fit inside a football field and still leave room for the bleachers. I guess Lexingtonians should feel lucky that big airlines like Delta and United bother to fly there at all.

But what doesn't make sense to me are the routes you have to take. If you're going south, you have to first fly north to get on a bigger plane. Seems like a waste of airplane fuel to me, but what do I know?

I was so excited I didn't care if they flew me to Alaska first. But they didn't; I only had to make a short hop up to Cincinnati in a little plane, and from there I got on a huge one. Every seat was taken, but I was on an aisle, so it was no trouble to get absorbed in Mama's romance novel, keeping my face turned away from the man in the center who had eaten onions for lunch. But I did feel sorry for the guy by the window.

The Orlando airport, now *that's* a big one. I got off the plane and filed along with the rest of the crowd to a tram like the one I remembered riding at Disney World as a kid. My watch read just after five o'clock, and the sun was still shining in the west surrounded by the bluest sky I had seen in months. I plastered my face against the tram window, drinking in the sights of palm trees and spraying fountains on the short ride to the main terminal.

When the doors opened, I flowed out with the crowd and allowed myself to be swept past the security checkpoint for incoming passengers and into the huge terminal. This place was a vacation in itself. Besides restaurants and coffee stands, there were shops from Disney World and Universal Studios and even one from SeaWorld with a big 3-D Shamu over the entrance.

"Mayla! Over here!"

I turned and saw hands waving above the crowd and a woman rushing toward me. The next thing I knew, arms wrapped around me and hugged the breath right out of me. I hugged back, my feet doing a happy little dance of their own.

"Aunt Louise!"

She held me at arm's length to look at me, grinning from ear to ear.

"I would know you anywhere," she told me. "You're the spitting image of your father."

"And you look just like the pictures I have from my last trip here. You haven't changed a bit in fifteen years."

She really hadn't. In her fifties, Aunt Louise looked just like she had in her thirties. If there was gray in her honey-colored hair, I couldn't see it. She was about the same height as me and only a few pounds heavier, primarily in the chest area, which puts her in the same category with almost every female past puberty. She must have come straight from the bank where she worked as a branch manager, because she was dressed professionally in a dark blue suit and a white silky blouse, making me acutely aware that my jeans and plaid cotton shirt were in serious need of an iron after hours on the plane. Her makeup was perfect, like she had just applied it. I knew she was a few years older than Mama, but if I met her on the street, I would have guessed she was closer to my age than Mama's. I would never tell Mama that, though.

"Well, you've certainly changed." She looped her arm through mine and guided me toward the escalator. "You're all grown up. Just wait until Mother sees you."

"How is Grandmother?" I asked, looking sideways at her as we glided downward. "I mean her health."

Aunt Louise's face grew serious as she shook her head. "Not good. She has spells with her heart, and sometimes she seems so frail. But she is seventy-seven years old, and I know she won't be around forever."

Something in her tone made me look more closely at her. She

stared straight ahead, her mouth drawn tight with worry. But the faraway look in her eyes held a hint of something else. A wistful look. Of longing? Or of hope, maybe?

I shook my head. It had been a long day, and my mind was full of the story I had finished a few minutes before touchdown. Romance novels always left me dreamy-eyed for days.

"I hope my visit won't be too much for her."

She turned a wide smile on me. "Are you kidding? She's had more energy this week than I have seen in years. She's got a full agenda planned out for you, young lady. And I'm afraid some of it won't be fun. She plans to use your young muscles for yard work."

I put back my head and laughed. "Good! I want to spend as much time outside in the Florida sunshine as I possibly can and bake the cold out of these young muscles."

Grandmother lived only a few minutes' drive from Orlando International Airport, in the same house where my father and Aunt Louise had grown up. Daddy used to tell me that he was a "natural-born Floridian." He was proud of the fact because there weren't many, what with all the transplants from elsewhere in the country. He said he never dreamed in a million years that he would move out of Florida until he met Mama on the beach during spring break his senior year in college. Unable to forget what he called, "that captivating Kentucky accent," he had followed her home like a lost puppy. After he graduated, he found a job in Lexington so he could be near her. I loved hearing him tell that story when I was a little girl and loved watching Mama's cheeks turn pink when he spoke of winning her heart.

Riding beside Aunt Louise in her tan Buick Century, I drank in the sights outside my window. After the stark winter of Kentucky, it felt so good to see lawns of deep green grass, and to drive along tree-lined streets where the leaves rustled full and green above the car. I had forgotten how many different kinds of palm trees there were—tall giants with thin bare trunks and big green fronds at the top; short, round, bush-shaped ones with leaves that looked like they

could be used by slaves to fan Cleopatra as she lay on her barge; orna-
mental garden palms with round trunks like a giant basketball half
buried in the ground and long spiky leaves sticking out of the top.

When we pulled onto Grandmother's street, I drew a sharp breath.
I vividly remembered driving with my father down this same street.
The memory flashed so lifelike into my mind that my throat tightened painfully, and I swallowed against tears. The last time I had
been here, I was eight years old, coming with Mama and Daddy to
celebrate my birthday at Disney World. That trip was the last vacation we took as a family before Daddy's death.

Aunt Louise must have known, because the look she gave me as
she drove slowly down the shady street was full of sympathy.

"Are you okay?"

I nodded, looking at the single-story, concrete-block houses
painted the vivid colors I would always identify with Florida—dark
pink, deep yellow, bright blue, even a wild violet. Aunt Louise pulled
into a sandy driveway on the left, and I got my first eager glimpse
of Grandmother's house. This was the house my grandfather had
built for his young family just a year before he died of a heart attack
and left Grandmother to raise their two little ones alone. It was still
bright yellow with black wooden shutters and a tiled roof, and to the
left of the front door above a metal mailbox hung the same giant
butterflies I remembered so well from my childhood.

"But it's so small!" I looked toward Aunt Louise in surprise.

She laughed. "It's the same size as always."

The front door opened, and Grandmother stepped out onto the
tiny cement stoop. I opened my door and leaped from the car before
it had come to a complete stop, running across the grass and into her
outstretched arms.

I'd been warned, so I wasn't surprised to see that she had aged.
But I was surprised to see that she had shrunk. The last time I saw
her, I remember looking up at her face. Now I had to bend over to
hug her, and it wasn't just because I'd grown. Her back hunched over
like some of the older ladies I saw at church. But she returned my

embrace with surprising strength, then held me at arm's length to look me over.

If Aunt Louise's fifteen years were hidden from view, they hung heavily on Grandmother, along with a few more besides. Her hair had gone completely gray, and deep furrows creased her cheeks and forehead. The hands that clutched my arms were spotted with age, the skin wrinkled and thin over dark blue veins.

But I would recognize my grandmother anywhere. Bright hazel eyes moved in her oval face as her gaze swept over me. Her still-straight nose crinkled as her thin lips curved into a grin that was more than familiar; it was my own. If I looked into a mirror and asked for a glimpse fifty years into the future, I would see Grandmother's face looking back at me.

Tears sprang into her eyes, and my own followed suit as she pulled me toward her again for another hug, this one gentle.

"It has been too long," she whispered.

Then she released me and stepped back. Her gaze went directly to my nostril stud, and her eyelids narrowed. "But what in the world is *that* thing?"

I laughed and shrugged. "Oh, just my rebellious youth. Did you see these, too?"

I pushed my hair behind my left ear to show her the four earrings on that side, then the ones on the right. She pressed her lips together.

"Hmmm. I can't say I approve, but the young people do seem to look like that everywhere I go these days." She gave me a hard stare. "You haven't pierced your tongue, have you? I hate it when they pierce their tongues."

Thankful that I had taken the stud out of my lower lip last year, I said, "No, ma'am," and stuck my tongue out to prove my claim.

Grinning playfully, she brought her fist up to tap my chin, just like she used to do when I stuck my tongue out as a little girl. I laughed out loud with delight as Aunt Louise came up beside me, carrying my suitcase.

She put an arm around me and squeezed. "Doesn't she look great, Mother?"

Grandmother grinned again and nodded. "She does. But let's get her inside and let her unpack while we get dinner on the table."

The inside of the house was exactly as I remembered, only in miniature. I walked into a living room stuffed with furniture and immaculately clean, the slight scent of bleach hovering in the air. There was the couch I had slept on as a child, and I half expected to see it covered with freshly laundered sheets and a pillow. Instead, I followed Aunt Louise down the hall to the first room on the left, the tiny bedroom my parents had shared when we visited years ago, and I fought a wave of sorrow as I stepped through the doorway.

There was the dresser I remembered with the big oak-framed mirror, the oak bed with its white bumpy bedspread, and the matching nightstand with a shiny brass lamp and frosted glass lampshade. On the wall hung a framed picture of my father as a little boy beside one of Aunt Louise all dressed up in a frilly dress. The only other piece of furniture in the room was a green peacock chair in the corner, where I remembered sitting to watch Mama get dressed in the mornings while Daddy and Grandmother drank coffee in the kitchen.

Aunt Louise put my suitcase on the bed and turned around, smiling. "The top two drawers are empty, and there's room in the closet if you have anything to hang. I'm going to go help Mother with dinner."

I dropped my laptop and backpack on the bed beside my suitcase. "I'll help, too."

She shook her head, smiling, and patted my arm. "You get unpacked. Tomorrow you can be family and work right along with us, but tonight you're going to relax and be a guest."

"If you say so," I told her, "but I'm helping with the dishes, guest or not."

She left the room, chuckling, and I upended my backpack to spill the contents onto the bed. I dug my cell phone out of the small purse I had stuffed in there and pushed the button to turn it on. As I placed stacks of almost-folded clothes into one of the dresser drawers, I heard the familiar beep telling me I had a message.

I figured it was Mama reminding me to call her and let her know I had arrived safely. But the display said I had two messages, and my heart gave a traitorous little flutter. Could Paul have called, too?

Dropping into the green chair, I dialed the voice-mail number and punched in my code. Sure enough, I heard Mama's voice in the first message.

"Hi, baby, I hope you had a good trip. Call me when you get there. Love you."

I pressed three to delete the message, and listened eagerly for the next one. But it wasn't a man's voice. It was a girl's.

"Mayla, this is Lindsey. I'm in Lexington, and I wondered if I could spend the night with you. Actually, I need a place to stay for a couple of nights, because I have an appointment here on Monday. I'm at a pay phone, so could you call me back when you get this message, and maybe come get me? Here's the number." She rattled off a phone number and then hung up.

Lindsey in Lexington and waiting for me to call! What time had she left that message? I pressed the number to play the message header and heard the tinny voice tell me the call had come in at 3:47. It was 5:50 now. I played her message again, listening for the phone number, then hung up and dialed.

She picked up on the second ring. "Mayla?" Her voice was tight with anxiety.

"Yeah, it's me. Lindsey, where are you?"

She heaved a deep sigh. "I'm glad you finally called. I'm at the Cracker Barrel at exit 115, and I've been here for hours. Can you come get me?"

"That's going to be a little hard since I'm in Orlando."

"You're where?" Her voice broke with what sounded like a sob. "Oh that's great, just great."

"Lindsey, what is going on? Why are you in Lexington with no place to stay? Do your parents know where you are?"

She took a shuddering breath, and I was sure she was fighting tears. "No, and I can't tell them, either. I'm not going home."

"You ran away?"

"Yeah. I hitched a ride up here figuring I could stay with you for a few days until I make some plans. Guess I was wrong," she added bitterly.

I bit my lip. I don't deal well with kids, even teenagers. I don't like them much as a rule. But Lindsey was different. I had only spent a short time with her last year when her brother Alex died, but during that time, I recognized a lot of myself in her. Both of us cared for Alex, and that created a sort of bond between us. I wanted to help her, I really did. But she was a sixteen-year-old runaway.

"You've got to go home, Lindsey," I told her in my sternest voice. "A sixteen-year-old girl on the road alone is not safe."

"I can take care of myself," she shot back. "I'm not a child."

Oh, I recognized that defiance, and my heart went out to her. But I had to be the grown-up here.

"I know you're not a child, but you're not an adult, either. You can't even get into an R-rated movie by yourself, much less rent a decent hotel room. Where are you going to sleep tonight? On the street? Under a bush? Maybe in a rocking chair on the porch there at the Cracker Barrel? You haven't thought this through."

There was a moment of silence. When she spoke, her voice was more subdued. "I *thought* I was going to stay with you, but I guess I'll find someplace else."

"Just go home. I'll be back in a week, and we'll talk then. You can hang in there for ten days, can't you?"

She sniffed and drew a shuddering breath. "I can't go home, Mayla. You don't understand."

"I do understand; I really do. But you've got to—"

"Good-bye, Mayla. Don't worry about me. I'll figure something out."

"Lindsey! Don't you hang up on me, Lindsey!"

But I was talking to dead air. Lindsey was gone.

Chapter 7

reat. Just great."

Throwing myself into the chair, I redialed the number for the pay phone and listened to it ring and ring. Lindsey didn't pick up. Snapping my cell phone closed, I heaved a heavy puff of frustration.

"Lord," I directed quietly toward the ceiling, "what should I do? I can't stand the thought of her running around Lexington by herself. If only she had called last weekend instead of—"

I stopped. She *had* called last weekend. Guilt washed over me.

"But I didn't know she was going to run away. If I had . . ."

What? Would I have helped her? Let her come to my apartment against her parents' wishes? I was pretty sure I could get into a boatload of trouble for harboring a runaway.

"Well, I would have figured out something," I muttered.

With another wave of guilt, I admitted to myself that I hadn't wanted to help her even if I could have helped. I had been too wrapped up in my own problems, and her call had been an annoyance, one more thing to worry about. If only I had taken the time to talk to her, to hear her out, instead of pushing her back toward the father she was having problems with in the first place.

Flipping open my phone, I speed-dialed Mama.

"Hi baby," her cheery voice said. "How was your flight, and how's Louise?"

"Fine, Mama, and Aunt Louise looks great, exactly the same." Though she hadn't asked, I went on in a lowered voice, "And Grandmother looks so *old!*"

"Well, she oughtta, seein' she's over seventy-five by now."

There might have been a touch of satisfaction in Mama's voice, but I ignored it. "Listen Mama, I have a prayer request for your Tuesday night ladies."

I told her briefly about Lindsey's phone call.

"Dear Lord," she said immediately, "we hold this girl up to You. Reach her for us, Lord, and show us how to help her. Amen."

"Amen."

I felt a weight lift with Mama's brief prayer. God would find a way to help. If He could handle me, Lindsey Markham would be no problem for Him at all.

"Do you have the number to call her parents?" Mama asked.

Squirming in the chair, I said, "No, not anymore. But I know they live down in Pikeville. My neighbor Stuart could look it up, though. He's the one who introduced me to Lindsey's brother last year."

"Well, give him a call, and then you call those poor people and let them know where their baby is. They're prob'ly worrying themselves half to death."

Me call the Markhams? The mere thought made me cringe.

"Uh, Mama? Do you think you could do it? I mean, I'd feel like a snitch if Lindsey found out I called her parents, and I'm sure you'd handle it better than me anyway."

I could almost feel Mama's glee through the phone. She loved this stuff. Asking her to embroil herself in someone else's problems was like inviting her to Disney World.

"A'course I will," she responded instantly. "How do I call this Stuart?"

I gave her Stuart's phone number and hung up feeling much better. I had handed Lindsey into two pairs of capable hands—God's and my mama's.

Dinner was fried chicken with mashed potatoes and gravy, green beans, tomatoes, homemade biscuits, and sliced cantaloupe, Grandmother's signature meal. She had fixed that meal for me every time I saw her for the first eight years of my life, and I'd eaten it right here in this same kitchen, at this same table, sitting in these same straight-backed wooden chairs with padded green polka-dotted cushions tied in the seats. I ate until I couldn't stuff one more bite into my poor bloated tummy, relishing the tastes and smells of my childhood.

"Now, Mayla," Grandmother said, eyeing me over her coffee cup while I mopped gravy from my plate with half a biscuit, "is there anything you'd like to do while you're here?"

Aunt Louise added, "I heard there was a new baby dolphin born at SeaWorld the other day. Or you could visit Mickey Mouse like the rest of the tourists."

Pushing my plate away and sitting back with a sigh, I shook my head. "I'm here to spend time with you two. Whatever you have planned is fine with me."

Aunt Louise stacked the bread dish in the center of her empty dinner plate. "Surely you'll want to take a drive over to the beach. You can't come to Florida without visiting the ocean."

The ocean! I could almost smell the salt in the air already. "I'd love that."

Grandmother stood and reached across the table for my empty plate. "We might do that tomorrow after you get home from work, Louise." She looked at me. "The bank's open until noon, so Louise gets home around one o'clock on Saturdays. We could take a picnic and have a late lunch over at Cocoa Beach."

An odd expression came over my aunt's face. Guarded, or secretive maybe. "Actually, Mother, I made tentative plans for tomorrow after work. I thought you and Mayla might like to spend the day together, just the two of you."

Grandmother's face wore a look of surprise for one brief moment, and then a change came over her features. I saw it come, like she had suddenly been hit with a wave of weariness or a deep, aching pain. Her skin went gray as she put my plate down on top of hers with a clatter and then lowered herself slowly to her chair.

"Grandmother!" I shouted, startled, at the same moment Aunt Louise said in a voice steeped in concern, "Mother?"

Grandmother leaned heavily against the high wooden back of the chair, her hand rising with a tremor to rest on her chest in the vicinity of her heart.

"I'm fine," she said, and I grew even more alarmed at the sudden weariness in her tone. "Just one of my spells. Give me a minute, and it will pass."

Aunt Louise leapt up from the table and ran in the direction of Grandmother's bedroom, leaving me to stare in horror at the frail old woman across the table. It had happened so quickly! One minute she was fine, and the next, she was gray-skinned and struggling to get a deep breath. Aunt Louise returned in a flash with a brown medicine bottle, twisting off the top and shaking a tiny white pill into the palm of her hand. She thrust the pill in front of Grandmother.

Grandmother looked at it, then shook her head.

"It's passing already. I'll be fine."

"Mother," Aunt Louise said sternly, "you know what the doctor said. Hold this under your tongue."

But Grandmother insisted that she was fine, that she only needed a second to rest. Aunt Louise looked torn, then slowly put the pill back in the bottle and lowered herself into her chair. We both sat there, throwing helpless stares toward each other across the table as Grandmother took slow, shuddering breaths with her eyes closed. Finally, she raised her head and gave each of us a quavering half-smile.

"There, I'm feeling better now. That was an easy one." She turned to Aunt Louise. "Now, what were you saying about our picnic tomorrow?"

Still shaken, Aunt Louise answered in a tentative voice. "I wanted to go out with . . ." She stopped and shook her head. "But never mind, Mother. If you're not feeling well, perhaps we should all stay home."

"Nonsense," Grandmother said, her tone a touch stronger. "Mayla wants to see the ocean. I'll be fine."

"No, really," I jumped in, "I can see the ocean any time. I'll be here a whole week. Let's just stay home tomorrow, you and me, while Aunt Louise goes out after work."

But Grandmother shook her tightly curled gray head. "No, tomorrow will be the best day for a picnic at the beach." She stole a look at Aunt Louise. "If you just tell Mayla what to do in case . . . well, you know."

Panicked, I looked toward Aunt Louise, begging her with my eyes to do something to change her mother's mind. She sighed quietly before giving me a reassuring smile.

"I didn't have anything important to do, and a picnic on the beach sounds great. The weather's supposed to be gorgeous. I'll try to get out of work a few minutes early and we can leave by twelve thirty. How's that sound?"

Tossing Aunt Louise a grateful glance, I relaxed in my chair. Grandmother seemed to relax, too. I guessed she felt as nervous as I did at being left in the care of her untrained granddaughter who was really more like a stranger. She smiled at me, then stood and started to clear the dishes.

"Hey, let me do that." I scrambled out of my chair and took the stack of plates from her. "Why don't you go rest for a while, and let me and Aunt Louise clean up?"

She patted my hand, obviously grateful. "If you're sure you don't mind."

"Of course not. I insist."

Aunt Louise nodded, and Grandmother walked slowly in the direction of the family room. In a few minutes, we heard the sound of *Wheel of Fortune* coming from the television.

"How often does that happen?" I whispered to Aunt Louise as we stacked dishes on the counter beside the sink.

"More often than it used to. Some are worse than others, and that was one of the easier ones. But she refuses to take her medicine most of the time." She shot a glance toward the doorway. "I'm really worried about her."

"I can see why."

I looked toward the doorway too, hearing Pat Sajak's voice clearly as he chatted with the evening's contestants. I had been right to come to Florida. In fact, it seemed I hadn't arrived a moment too soon.

By the time we had the dishes washed, dried, and put away, *Wheel of Fortune* had ended. We joined Grandmother in the family room in time for the beginning of the first round of *Jeopardy*. She seemed fully restored, and we made a friendly competition out of seeing who could answer the questions first. Aunt Louise won hands down, amazing me with her quick intelligence. She was one smart cookie. No wonder she had such an important job at a bank.

Thoughts of her job reminded me of my own employment sorrows. How long would it take me to find a job? And what sort of job was I qualified for? The depressing answer was, of course, not much. I thought longingly of the job at Midstate Insurance and Investments, but without a college degree, I was pretty sure I didn't have a shot at that one. There were a few other construction companies around Lexington, competitors of Clark and Hasna, and one of them might provide an opportunity. But the industry didn't do much hiring during the winter. Spring seemed like a long time away, much longer than my severance pay would stretch.

When the returning champion missed the final *Jeopardy* question and lost twenty-five thousand dollars, Grandmother turned off the television.

"I have something you might like," she told me with a grin. "Louise, will you get the box?"

Aunt Louise left the room for a moment, then returned with a good-sized cardboard box in her arms. She placed it on the floor in front of me. As she joined me and Grandmother on the sofa, I opened the lid eagerly.

The box contained pictures, hundreds of them. Some had been put into albums, but many were loose or in rubber-banded bundles. The tiniest whiff of musty air prickled my nostrils as I shuffled through the contents. I pulled out an old album and wiped a thin layer of dust off its blue, cardboard cover before opening it.

"Oh, look!" I exclaimed. "That's Daddy and you, Aunt Louise."

Two little kids in bathing suits grinned at me from the front yard of this very house, a sprinkler spraying high into the sky behind them. My father, the younger by two years, had both hands resting on his hips, his grin punctuated by a gap where his front teeth should have been. Aunt Louise stood beside him in a suit with a ruffled skirt, dimpling for the camera, her hair hanging in wet ringlets around her shoulders.

"I remember that picture," Aunt Louise said. "Right after it was taken, Charles unplugged the sprinkler and doused me with the hose. I was so mad at him."

Grandmother chuckled at the two tykes in the picture. "You certainly were. You cried for twenty minutes." She sighed. "He was such a handsome little boy."

I looked at her out of the corner of my eye and saw a wistful expression cross her wrinkled features. How hard it must be to lose a child, much harder than losing a father. I wondered for a moment if looking at these pictures might not be such a good idea after her episode at the supper table. But when I turned a thick leaf to reveal another page with photos of the two happy children, she laughed with delight.

"Oh, look Louise. It's your seventh birthday. Remember how Charles wrapped up a box of fishing worms and let you open them at the party?"

Aunt Louise shuddered. "I'll never forget that as long as I live."

Listening to Grandmother's giggle, I realized maybe looking at pictures wasn't a bad idea after all.

❀ ❀ ❀

Before I went to bed that night, I called Mama to find out how the call to the Markhams had gone.

"They were beside themselves with worry. Sandra couldn't do a thing but cry, so Alexander got on the phone to get the details."

"Was he nice to you?" I remembered how cold Mr. Markham had been to me last year.

"A'course he was nice. I was calling about his baby, wasn't I? They said they was gonna call the police right then and have them look in Lexington. I gave them your number, in case the police had any questions."

I didn't like Mr. Markham having my cell phone number, but I could see it was a reasonable thing to do. Since I hadn't received any calls, I hoped that meant the police had already found her and she was safely at home. Or maybe it meant he didn't want to talk to me any more than I wanted to talk to him.

"Okay, Mama. Thanks for taking care of that. I really appreciate it."

"Sure, baby. Oh, and your friend Stuart is such a nice boy. He was surprised to hear from me, said he didn't know you'd left town."

"Yeah, I didn't see him before I left."

"He sounded a little miffed, truth be told. Said something about deserting him in his hour of need."

I rolled my eyes. That sounded like Stuart. First he won't speak to me; then he's mad because I didn't get his permission to visit my grandmother. Sheesh!

"He'll get over it," I told Mama. "Is everything else all right?"

"Everything's fine." She paused, then went on cautiously. "How 'bout there?"

"Everything's fine here, too. We looked at old pictures tonight. Grandmother had a whole box full of them."

"Hmmph. Bet there weren't none of me in there."

"Actually, there were. There were lots of me when I was a baby, and you were in some of those."

I didn't see the need to tell her that Grandmother's lips had tightened angrily every time we came upon one of those pictures.

"Hmmph," she repeated, whatever that meant.

I yawned. "I'm going to bed now, Mama. We're going to the beach
tomorrow. Love you."

"Love you too, baby. Have fun at the beach. Wear sunscreen."

As I drifted off to sleep, I thought of Lindsey. Guilt niggled at the
back of my mind, but there really wasn't a thing I could do to help
her from Florida.

Except pray. And that's what I did, my last conscious thought
lifted to the Lord on behalf of that unhappy girl.

Chapter 8

I awoke the next morning to bright sunshine pouring through the window. Though sunlight was better than waking to the sound of a snowplow, I moaned when I caught sight of the alarm clock on the nightstand—7:18.

"No fair, I'm on vacation!"

Pulling the pillow down hard over my face to block out the early rising Florida sun, I thought I might actually drift back to sleep. But then I remembered Lindsey, and I wondered if she was safe at home in her own bed. My thoughts turned to worries—had she been found? What did her father say when the police brought her home? He wouldn't get rough with her, would he? Was that why she ran away, because she was afraid of him?

With a sigh, I jerked the pillow aside and surrendered to wakefulness. I heard the clatter of dishes from the kitchen. Swinging my feet over the side of the bed to the soft carpet, I heaved myself up and followed the eye-opening aroma of fresh coffee down the hallway to the kitchen.

Aunt Louise stood at the sink, drying a cereal bowl with a tea towel. She turned with a smile as I sank into a chair at the table.

"Good morning, Mayla," she said quietly. "Did you sleep well?"

"I slept great, thanks. Is Grandmother up yet?"

I looked through the family room to her bedroom door, which was still closed.

Aunt Louise snorted. "Are you kidding? Sleeping Beauty won't bat an eye before nine. Would you like some coffee?"

Invitingly, she held up a nearly full coffee pot, and I nodded. I had forgotten my grandmother was a late sleeper. Must be where I got it from.

"Sweet? Light?"

I shook my head. "I take it black, thanks."

She grinned as she placed a full mug in front of me before pulling out a chair for herself. "Just like Mother. She always says I shouldn't be allowed to call what I drink coffee because, by the time I finish doctoring it up, what's left doesn't resemble the real stuff."

"Grandmother and I seem to have a lot in common." I blew through the steam to ripple the surface of the dark liquid in my mug. "It's kind of neat, discovering there's someone else so much like me."

"Charles was a lot like Mother, too, more than me. She always said I took after my father, though I don't remember enough about him to say for certain."

"He died when you were little, didn't he?"

She nodded. "I was four and Charles was two. Mother hadn't gone to work at the bakery yet, so she stayed home with us while my father worked. But when he came home in the evening, my world revolved around him. I can't picture him clearly, but I have a vague memory of a big man with dark hair and a huge laugh, tossing me into the air. I remember the way my stomach felt like it was floating, and Mother scolding him to put me down."

Her eyes took on an unfocused look as she stared at a point somewhere beyond my head, a smile hovering around her lips.

"I didn't realize you were that young," I told her. "At least at eight, I had time to form some good solid memories before I lost Daddy."

She patted my hand. "He was a good man, your father. And he loved you so much."

We each took a sip from our mugs, the silence between us easy. Outside, I heard a bird chirping and a more distant sound that might have been a squirrel chattering. Drawing in a deep breath, heavily scented with coffee, I leaned back contentedly in my chair. If this was what getting up early was like, maybe I should try it more often.

After a moment, Aunt Louise stood. "I've got to get going. I'll be home by twelve thirty, and we can leave for the beach then. I hope you brought your bathing suit."

"Of course I did. But I'm really sorry you're not going to get to go out after work."

She paused in the act of rinsing her coffee mug, and her expression changed. Disappointment? Irritation? Before I could identify the emotion that flickered across her face, it was gone. She turned to me with a one-shouldered shrug.

"Believe me, I'm used to it. Mother seems to have these episodes whenever I have plans that don't include her. The doctor says they can be brought on by stress or anxiety, and I guess she's anxious about being left alone."

I shook my head. That didn't make sense. "But she's alone all day while you're at work."

She shrugged again, this time with both shoulders. "I guess she feels like all day is long enough."

"What's wrong with her, anyway? I assume that was a nitro pill you tried to give her last night."

"That's right. The doctor calls her condition stable angina. Her arteries are narrowed, though not enough to cause problems during normal activity. But when she exerts herself or gets upset, her heart starts working a little harder and she has an attack."

"Can't they do something for it?"

Aunt Louise shook her head. "If her condition worsens, they can, but the recommended treatment is nitro. Personally, I think it is worsening, but she refuses to even discuss surgery. No one can make my stubborn mother do something she doesn't want to do."

"I know how that is," I told her, thinking of Mama. Then I said good-bye as she picked up her purse and headed for the front door.

After she left, I refilled my mug and returned to my chair. A sense of sadness penetrated my early morning tranquility. How hard for Aunt Louise to be the only person Grandmother could rely on. Aunt Louise never married, so she had no husband or children to help her. And since my father's death, she had no close relatives, especially since they had lost touch with me. There was no one to share the burden of care for her aging mother. She couldn't even plan an evening out with friends. Even though she loved Grandmother, at times she must feel smothered.

Would I one day be in her place? An image of Mama flashed into my mind—lively, active Mama who was rarely sick and never a burden to anyone. Would she one day become old and weak and require constant attention and care?

I shut that thought out of my mind. First of all, Mama would never allow herself to become a burden to me or anyone else. And even if she did, I didn't intend to be single my whole life. I would be married, and my husband would help me care for her when, and if, the time came.

Husband. That thought instantly transmuted itself in my mind to Paul Rawlings, and I shook my head violently to dislodge the image of Paul in a black tux waiting for me at the end of the aisle in the sanctuary of Salliesburg Independent Christian Church.

Forget it, Mayla. It ain't happening. Get over it, and get on with your life!

Shaking myself again, I went to my bedroom and brought my laptop into the kitchen. When it finished booting up, I plugged the modem into the phone jack and entered the toll-free number I had gotten from my ISP before leaving Lexington. Though I didn't relish the idea of a painfully slow dial-up connection, going a whole week without e-mail was unthinkable.

I skimmed through the list of new mail, deleting the spam unopened. My heart gave a heavy thud when I came to one from

BibleMan32. Willing my racing pulse to calm down, I hesitated, not allowing myself to double-click on the e-mail until I could do so with composure.

When I did, a message popped up on the screen: *The message sender has requested a response to indicate that you have read this message. Would you like to send a receipt?*

"Why, you sly dog," I whispered, chuckling.

So he wanted to be sure I read his e-mail, did he? Well, we'd just see about that. I clicked the No button, and Outlook opened the e-mail anyway, as I knew it would.

> Dear Mayla,
> I am praying for Lindsey. Your mother said she is the sister of a friend of yours who died. I assume that was Alex?

Okay, so I had known Mama would alert the prayer chain about Lindsey. And since I wanted her to have as much prayer as possible, I supposed it was okay that Mama called the preacher, too.

> I never received a response to my last e-mail. Did you get it?

So he noticed, did he? Good. He could just keep wondering. Smiling with satisfaction, I read on.

> I hope so, because I want to make sure you're praying about our last conversation, as I am. When you return, we need to have a serious talk.
>
> Sincerely,
> Paul

I stared at the signature. *Sincerely.* I had never seen him sign an e-mail that way. Usually he used some variation of *God bless you.*

What did *sincerely* mean? On the one hand, he might be trying to tell me that he *sincerely* wanted to talk to me. Or that he has been *sincerely* praying about our last conversation. Or even that he has *sincere* feelings for me.

On the other hand, *sincerely* is a common way to close letters, especially impersonal ones. Business letters almost always close with *sincerely*. And since I was a member of his congregation, he probably considered this nothing more than business correspondence.

Stop it, Mayla! I scolded myself. *You will not obsess about this.*

Sighing, I moved the e-mail to my Saved folder, as I did with most that came from him, then read absently through the rest of the new ones. But I had to admit I felt a deep satisfaction that he wouldn't get a receipt from me. He would never know I had read it.

I felt my mouth widening into a smile when I realized one other thing. He had signed this one simply *Paul*.

As Aunt Louise predicted, Grandmother didn't get out of bed until a few minutes after nine o'clock. By then, I had read all of my e-mail and disconnected my laptop, taken a shower, and was in the process of gelling my hair. She immediately put me to work assembling our picnic lunch.

By the time Aunt Louise got home from work, we had a cooler loaded with cold fried chicken, potato chips, deviled eggs, carrot sticks, and cans of Diet Coke. Piled beside the front door ready to be put into the car were our towels, an old quilt, short-legged beach chairs, a big beach umbrella, and a bottle of sunscreen, SPF 45— from Grandmother's medicine cabinet.

The drive to Cocoa Beach took less than an hour on Florida's Beeline Expressway, and it was truly a perfect day for the beach. Mid-seventies and only a few puffy white clouds high up in a bright blue sky. We rolled down our windows when we drove across the causeway over the intercoastal waters in Cape Canaveral and turned right onto

A1A, the road that runs down Florida's east coast. I leaned as far out the window as I could, drinking in the sight of the deep blue ocean with inviting white-capped waves splashing up onto the beaches.

Cocoa Beach wasn't crowded, and we planted our beach umbrella several yards away from the line where the surf had packed the soft sand into a surface firm enough to walk on comfortably. We spread out our feast on the quilt, all of us hungry by now, and ate serenaded by a flock of seagulls that hovered nearby, beady black eyes fixed hopefully on our lunch.

Then Grandmother parked herself in the shade of the umbrella with a book and declared that she didn't intend to budge all afternoon. Aunt Louise and I walked a long way up the beach and back again; then she greased herself up with suntan lotion and spread an oversized beach towel on the soft sand. I went to stand at the edge of the water, the surf sucking the sand out from under my feet. I breathed deeply of the salty ocean air, fresher than any air I had ever breathed at home in Kentucky, and thanked God for making this day I was so thoroughly enjoying.

As we drove home, the setting sun directly ahead of us, my cell phone rang. I fished it out of my purse and glanced at the number. Area code 859, so it was from Kentucky, but not a number I recognized.

"Hello?"

"Mayla, it's Lindsey."

Lindsey! I had almost forgotten her in my enjoyment of the beach.

"Lindsey, where are you? Are you at home?"

"No, I'm still in Lexington, but not for long. I've decided to come to Florida."

"What?" I shrieked, and Aunt Louise shot an alarmed glance toward me from the driver's seat.

"I know I'm horning in on your vacation, and I'm sorry, but I really need to talk to you, Mayla. I won't stay long, I promise. Is it okay?"

My heart twisted in my chest when I detected a strain of desperation in her voice. But she was just a kid. I couldn't let her come to Florida to see me. I didn't know exactly what laws I'd be breaking, but taking a minor across a couple of state lines was sure to mean trouble.

"Lindsey, I can't let you do that. I could get in big trouble for this."

"No, you can't. I'm coming on my own; you're not kidnapping me."

"But you're a runaway, and your parents know you called me. The police are probably watching me to see if you'll contact me again." Though I hoped that was an exaggeration, it wasn't out of the question.

There was a pause on the other end of the phone. "You called my parents?"

I ignored the accusation I heard in her voice. "I didn't, but my mother did. We had to, Lindsey. And you should call them, too. They're worried sick."

Another pause, and then I heard her sigh. "I'm sure they are. And I guess I'm glad they know I'm not dead or something. But that doesn't change anything. I'm still coming to Florida whether you like it or not. If you won't talk to me, then I'll just hang around on the beach or something. It's got to be warmer there than here."

"Is everything all right?" Grandmother asked from the backseat.

I nodded at her, trying to look calm so she wouldn't get anxious and have an attack.

What should I do, Lord? I silently prayed. *I need some help here, and quick!*

"Why do you want to talk to me so badly, anyway?" I asked, stalling.

"Because you were nice to my brother. Alex liked you, and he told me how you became his friend when he was in the hospital dying of AIDS and nobody else would even come visit him. And besides, I don't have anybody else."

Now she sounded like a lost little girl. I closed my eyes, remembering Alex as I last saw him, leaning back in the hospital bed on a pillow just a shade whiter than his skin, rejected by his parents and completely alone in the world. Here was his kid sister, sniffling on the other end of the phone, wanting to talk to me because she didn't have anyone else. I sighed.

"Okay, Lindsey. When and how are you getting here? And don't say you're hitchhiking, or I'll call the cops myself."

"No, I'm not, but the less you know, the better. And I want you to promise that you won't call my parents again, that you won't tell them I'm coming. Because if you don't promise, I'll disappear, I swear I will."

"I'll promise not to call them on one condition," I told her. "You call them instead. Let them at least hear your voice."

She considered that a moment, then agreed. "I'll get one of those phone cards so it won't register on caller ID and they won't know where I'm calling from. And I'll call you tomorrow when I get to Orlando."

"Be careful, Lindsey. Please."

"I will. Bye, Mayla."

I waited until I heard her hang up, then slipped my phone back into my purse.

"What was that all about?" Grandmother asked, leaning forward so her chin nearly rested on the back of my seat.

I told them about Lindsey.

"I'm really sorry," I finished, looking at Grandmother. "My plan is to let her tell me whatever it is she's upset about, then put her on the next plane home."

When Grandmother shook her head, her gray curls, from which the wind had removed any hint of hairspray, floated freely around her skull. "There's nothing to be sorry about. If that girl is upset enough to run away from home, she must be in serious trouble. The least you can do is listen to her. And the least we can do is give her a couch to sleep on."

"Maybe she's pregnant," suggested Aunt Louise.

"Maybe," I agreed. "I've wondered about that."

"In that case," Grandmother concluded, "she can't sleep on the couch." She sat back in her seat with a nod. "She can have Louise's bed."

My phone rang that evening while I helped Grandmother assemble a light supper of tomato soup and ham sandwiches. When I saw Mama's number on the screen, I slipped into the bedroom to talk to her.

"They haven't found Lindsey yet," she announced when I pressed the Talk button.

"How do you know?"

"Because I just hung up the phone with Sandra. Lindsey called home and told them she'd call back in a day or so and they shouldn't worry. Imagine that, a sixteen-year-old girl running away from home and tellin' her parents not to worry!"

"Teenagers are clueless," I agreed. "But at least she's safe. That had to make them feel better."

"A little, but a'course they want her home. And Sandra said she wouldn't tell them why she ran away, either. And she made them promise not to call the police anymore, or she said she wouldn't call back."

"But she's safe," I repeated. "That's what counts."

Mama went on as though I hadn't spoken. "Funny how she knew they called the police. Sandra asked me if you had talked to her again, but I told her you hadn't 'cause you surely woulda called us."

God, please don't let her ask me! I can't lie to Mama, and I don't want to break my promise to Lindsey!

"Uh huh," I mumbled evasively before charging on to another subject. "Do they have any idea why she ran away? Any clues? Have they had a fight recently?"

"I asked, but Sandra said they didn't, that Lindsey is a good girl and never gives them no problems. Good in school, too, and popular. Plays on the volleyball team."

"I didn't know Lindsey played volleyball."

"Must be pretty good too, 'cause Sandra says she might get a scholarship to college. And she's missing practice, too."

"Listen, Mama, I need to go help Grandmother with supper. Thanks for the update. Keep praying for Lindsey."

"Okay, baby. Love you."

"Love you too, Mama. Bye."

I pressed the End button with a sigh of relief. Thank goodness Mama hadn't actually asked me if I had heard from Lindsey.

Instead of going back to the kitchen, I dialed Sylvia's number. I knew she would be at work, but I wanted to check on Harvey.

"Mayla, hey," her voice shouted into the phone. The background noise made it nearly impossible to hear her. "Hold on a sec."

I heard her shouting at someone that she was taking a quick break, and then the noise gradually dimmed. I pictured her walking away from the bar area at The Max and into the server's alley. Arranging my pillow against the headboard, I stretched my legs out on the bed and leaned back.

"Okay, now I can hear you," she said a couple of seconds later. "How was your trip? What's the weather like? Have you been working on your tan today?"

"Fine, great, and yes. We spent the day at the beach, and it was awesome, seventy-four degrees and sunny. The ocean is unbelievable."

"I'm so jealous," she moaned. "We got another couple of inches of snow last night, and today the high was twenty-eight. I borrowed your down jacket, by the way. It's warmer than mine."

"Not a problem. How's Harvey?"

"Oh, *him*." Her tone dripped disgust. "That rabbit pees more than any creature has a right to. He stinks, he chews, and he poops in his own food bowl."

"He's one of God's creatures," I reminded her.

"God never intended him to live in a box in my apartment," she shot back. "He should be out in the wild, hibernating or something."

"Well, thank you again for taking care of him. I really appreciate it."

"Remember our deal, though. When you get back—"

"—I'll go talk to the office. I remember. Hey listen, I wanted to run something by you. I need a fresh ear."

I told her about Lindsey, from the first call right up to the latest development.

"I just feel terrible not telling Mama the truth, but Lindsey needs a friend, and it looks like I'm it."

"So are you wanting me to tell you it's okay to lie to your mother and Lindsey's parents?"

"I'm not lying." I sat straight up on the bed while my face heated at her accusation. "I'm just keeping my mouth shut for a little while."

"Yeah, right. You can make the distinction if it makes you feel better. But actually, I think you're doing the right thing. If you make her mad, she'll split, and then she could get into some serious trouble. This way, at least you're giving her someone to trust. I know I could have used a friend and a safe place to go when I was her age."

I leaned back against the pillow, relieved. Sylvia had been raised in an abusive situation far worse than any I could imagine. I doubted Lindsey's home life was anywhere close to as terrible as Sylvia's, but if it was, I wanted to make sure she knew she could confide in me.

"That's what I thought, too."

"Listen, I've got to get back to work. Enjoy the weather down there."

"Oh, I will. Tell everyone I'm thinking of them as I lie on the beach, baking my body in the hot Florida sun."

"You rat," she said before she hung up.

Chapter 9

Sunday morning dawned just as beautiful as Saturday. This time when my eyes fluttered open at seven thirty, I didn't hesitate. I got out of bed and headed for the kitchen with my laptop.

Aunt Louise had already showered and dried her hair. She sat at the kitchen table in a bathrobe and fuzzy blue slippers, sipping coffee and reading the newspaper.

"Good morning," she said with a wide smile. "I forgot to ask what time you wanted to get up. Mother and I usually go to the early service at nine and then Sunday school at ten. But there's a later service at eleven o'clock if you prefer."

I set my laptop on the counter and turned it on, then poured myself a cup of coffee while it booted up.

"Nine's fine with me. Will Grandmother be up in time?"

"I'm just getting ready to wake her. The church is only a few minutes from here, so we'll leave about a quarter till. Are you going to check your e-mail?"

I nodded. "If that's all right."

"Of course." She folded the newspaper and put it in a neat stack in front of Grandmother's chair before standing. "I'm going to get dressed. Our church is pretty casual, so feel free to wear whatever you want. Jeans and a T-shirt, even shorts, anything except a bathing suit is acceptable."

Grinning at the thought of anyone showing up at Salliesburg Independent Christian Church in shorts, I clicked on the icon to start a connection. The laptop dialed, then squawked its computer language, and I heard an answering squeal through the speaker as I made contact with my ISP's server in Lexington.

My inbox proved disappointing. Nothing from the preacher. The only new messages I received were spam and forwarded jokes. I deleted the spam and saved the rest unread to my hard drive, trying not to feel depressed. Maybe I should have answered his last e-mail.

An hour later, dressed in slacks and a short-sleeved blouse, I slid into the passenger seat of Aunt Louise's Buick. Grandmother insisted on sitting in the back so she could talk to us both without getting a crick in her neck from turning around. In just five minutes, we pulled to the side of the road on Orange Avenue in front of Belle Isle Methodist Church. Grandmother and I got out, and Aunt Louise left to park her car in the gravel parking lot across the street.

At first glance, the church appeared no bigger than my own church back in Kentucky. Its walls were of brown brick and concrete, with half-a-dozen stained-glass windows along the sidewalk beside Orange Avenue. A marquis in the front announced the title of today's sermon. But a closer look showed me that the main building covered the entire block and wound around the far corner in an L-shape. Somewhere behind that building rose another one three stories tall, with regularly spaced windows lined with white concrete ledges. I saw the fronds of palm trees off to the left and pictured a garden courtyard within the labyrinth of the church complex. Above the big glass entryway loomed a giant cross atop a towering bell tower.

"How many people go to church here?" I asked as we walked up the sidewalk toward the front doors, feeling a little like the country mouse visiting her rich city relatives.

"About twelve hundred," Grandmother replied, "but we have three services. Louise and I like this one because only about four hundred people come."

"Four hundred. Wow."

Pastor Paul would flip out if four hundred people came to a Sunday morning service at Salliesburg ICC. Heck, he'd flip out if half that many showed up.

"Does your preacher even know your name?" I asked, trying not to sound intimidated.

Grandmother laughed. "Of course he does. And he'll know yours before the morning's over."

I looked closely at her. She certainly looked chipper this morning, wearing a blue print dress with matching shoes and purse, an ornate silver cross dangling from a chain around her neck, and blue-and-silver buttons on her earlobes. Her eyes sparkled above cheekbones that blushed with a peachy glow and lips carefully colored with dark pink lipstick. She smiled at me, and I caught sight of a becoming dimple, a twin of the one that creased my own cheek if I smiled widely enough. Getting dressed up for an outing obviously appealed to my grandmother.

We followed a stream of churchgoers up the sidewalk and toward a set of wide shallow stairs. Before she put her foot on the first one, Grandmother looped one hand through my arm for support. At the top of the four steps, she didn't let go, but continued to clutch my arm, steering me toward the greeters standing inside the wide-open glass doors.

"Hello Mrs. Strong," a sixty-ish woman said, smiling first at Grandmother and then at me. "This pretty young woman must be related. She looks just like you."

"This is my granddaughter, Mayla. She's visiting from Kentucky. Mayla, this is Mrs. Selbe. She's in Louise's Sunday school class."

Mrs. Selbe took my hand in hers, but before I had time to do more than smile Grandmother tugged me farther inside the entry hall.

"Oh, Mayla, there's the music minister. I want to introduce you."

"Nice to meet you," I mumbled to Mrs. Selbe as Grandmother, with more strength than I would have given an old lady credit for, practically jerked me across the room toward a man who had almost disappeared down a set of stairs to the right of the sanctuary entrance.

"Oh, Reverend Thomas," she shouted. "Reverend *Thomas!*"

Heads turned; thankfully Reverend Thomas's was one of them. His lips spread into a wide smile when he saw Grandmother. He bounded up the steps and crossed the floor in a couple long strides.

"Good morning, Mrs. Strong," he boomed in the deep, rich voice of a trained baritone. "You look even prettier than usual today."

I got a kick out of seeing my grandmother blush at the compliment. Then I looked into Reverend Thomas's face when he turned his smile on me and found my own cheeks heating as well.

"And who is this? She must be related, because she's almost as pretty as you are."

My mouth went dry as I looked up into a pair of deep blue eyes fringed with curly dark lashes. Reverend Thomas was drop-dead gorgeous. I've always been a sucker for blue eyes, but his were startlingly deep turquoise and sparkled at me from a richly tanned face beneath a full head of almost black hair. His nose could have been described as chiseled but strong, and his lips were full around perfectly straight white teeth.

But what caught my eye and would not let go was a tiny gold ball shining in his left earlobe. This preacher had a pierced ear!

"This is my granddaughter, Mayla, visiting from Kentucky. She's here for a week."

Grandmother's smile widened as he took my hand, his grip firm. I tore my gaze away from his ear and looked into his eyes in time to see him notice my nostril stud. His smile widened conspiratorially.

"We're so happy to have you here at Belle Isle Methodist. Mayla— what a beautiful name. I don't think I've heard it before."

"Me, either." I was glad I managed not to stammer. "I'm one of a kind, as far as I know."

He threw back his head and gave a deep-chested laugh. "I'm sure you are. Welcome, Mayla. I hope you're ready to worship the Lord today, because we've got some great music planned."

"This is the contemporary service," Grandmother said. "Reverend Thomas leads the praise band. We have drums and everything." Her eyes twinkled as she bragged.

"That's right. And all the young people prefer this service and leave the old folks to the traditional service at eleven. Isn't that right, Mrs. Strong?"

He shot Grandmother a flirtatious grin, which set her to blushing again, then smiled once more at me before turning away with a quick wave of his fingers.

"He is such a nice young man," Grandmother said as we watched him disappear down the stairs. "And just wait until you hear him sing. A voice like an angel."

I tore my eyes away from the stairwell where I could see the last glimpse of that gorgeous dark hair and let her steer me into the sanctuary, trying not to stare like a bug-eyed hillbilly. It wasn't as big as Sylvia's church in Lexington, but far more ornate. Four rows of polished dark pews were lined with red velvet cushions, and when we slipped into one midway up the center aisle, I saw padded kneeling rails tucked beneath each one. A vaulted ceiling arched high above me, and a balcony ringed the room on three sides. Stained-glass windows lined both long walls, the sun shining through the ones on my right and casting dazzling, rainbow-colored rays into the room.

At the front of the sanctuary, behind a large altar draped with gold cloth, stood a huge, lighted cross behind the empty choir loft. To the left of the cross was an organ, and opposite it, looking incongruous in such a formal setting, the praise band had set up their instruments in a mish-mash of disarray. A giant drum set dominated one corner, and three shiny guitars rested upright in stands scattered around a big keyboard. Wires laced the floor leading from black speaker cabinets to the various instruments, and when I scanned the ceiling, I saw big speakers placed strategically around the sanctuary.

"Wow."

Grandmother smiled and settled back into the red cushion as Aunt Louise joined us. I scooted over to let her sit and watched as eight people filed onto the stage, led by Reverend Thomas. On the way to the center of the stage he picked up a guitar, the wire trailing behind him like a tail. The people in the sanctuary who still stood talking in little clusters hurried to take their seats.

"Good morning," he boomed, and the congregation answered with a hearty, "Good morning!" I saw a mic extending from his left ear to hover near his mouth, and the two men and two women who arranged themselves in a line behind him picked up handheld cordless mics from a stand. Man, these folks really took their sound system seriously!

"Welcome to Belle Isle Methodist on this beautiful morning. We're here to lift our voices in praise to our glorious Father today, and I invite you at this time to stand if you're able."

A big screen descended from the ceiling behind the organ, and the title of the first song projected onto it. The song was one I recognized from my favorite Christian radio station at home, K-LOVE, and though I don't have much of a singing voice, I joined in with the rest of the congregation as we worshipped. As Grandmother had promised, Reverend Thomas did have an awesome voice, rich and full of warmth. But what I noticed most was his face as he sang. That man really worshipped. He loved the Lord, and his love radiated. I closed my eyes and focused on singing to my Father.

The last song was one I didn't recognize, a beautiful worship chorus that everyone else in the congregation knew. At the end of the song, I noticed in small letters at the bottom of the screen, "Copyright © 2004 by Robert Thomas Jr." I shifted my gaze to Reverend Thomas as he placed his guitar on its stand and sat with the rest of the praise band in the choir loft. I was impressed. Good looking, a great voice, and he wrote music, too.

An older man in a long black robe with a purple stole stepped up to the pulpit. Grandmother leaned over to whisper, "That's Reverend Farrow, our senior pastor."

I nodded and glanced sideways toward Aunt Louise. Instead of looking at the pulpit, her eyes were focused on something across the center aisle to our right. I looked that way and saw a man two rows ahead of us turn in his seat. He scanned the people around us and then fixed his gaze on Aunt Louise. His face lit, and he nodded briefly before turning back toward the front of the church. I saw a spot of color appear on Aunt Louise's cheek as she, too, smiled and then switched her gaze to the pastor.

As I turned back, I saw that Grandmother had also seen the man. Her lips pressed into a hard, disapproving line, and she wadded a tissue into a ball in the palm of her hand.

Reverend Farrow's message was good, but I couldn't help comparing him with Paul. He didn't have the same fire, the same conviction that I saw in Paul every time he preached the Word of God. My mind wandered a couple of times, and my gaze kept sliding toward the choir loft and the handsome Reverend Thomas sitting there. He was the kind of man Paul would enjoy meeting. Their shared passion for the Lord would make them instant friends.

When the service ended, Aunt Louise mumbled something about seeing us after Sunday school and slipped out into the center aisle. I saw the man from across the aisle join her and caught a glimpse of her face as she smiled up into his. She positively glowed. His expression looking down into her face matched her radiant smile exactly.

Ah! Aunt Louise has a boyfriend. Interesting. I wonder if Grandmother knows.

One look at my grandmother's tightly disapproving mouth and narrowed eyelids gave me the answer. But why would she not want her daughter to have a boyfriend?

"Is everything all right?" I asked.

She shook her tight gray curls, not in answer to my question but in refusal to answer it. Exhaling a short breath in a huff, she took my arm. "Let's go to Sunday school."

I allowed myself to be led through the labyrinth of the church to

Grandmother's Sunday school room, where I sat for the next forty-five minutes listening to the most boring old woman I've ever heard read from a book I never caught the title of. But I did enjoy meeting Grandmother's friends, and she shook off her sour expression as she proudly introduced me to them all.

We returned to the narthex to wait for Aunt Louise to come out of her Sunday school class. The place was even more crowded than before as people leaving Sunday school encountered people arriving for the second service. Grandmother introduced me to dozens more people I would never remember, and I got to meet Reverend Farrow as well.

As I stood pressed against the back wall while Grandmother talked with a woman about her age, I heard my name.

"Mayla! Mayla, over here."

I turned to find Reverend Thomas walking toward me, a friendly smile on his face. My heart gave a little flutter as he came close and took my hand in his warm one. He covered it with his left hand, and I couldn't help but notice that there was no wedding ring on the third finger. I had never been smiled at by anyone as gorgeous as him before.

"I'm glad I caught you." He stepped to one side to lean against the wall beside me. "I don't know how long you're staying with your grandmother, but if you're here on Wednesday night I want to give you a personal invitation to our young adult Bible study."

"Gosh, thanks," I told him, proud that I didn't stammer as I gazed into those turquoise eyes. "I'm here until next weekend, actually, but I don't know what Grandmother has planned for me."

He grinned. "I understand. But if you can, I think you'll enjoy yourself. We have a cappuccino machine, and the praise band plays a few songs while everyone sits around and talks. Then I lead the discussion. There'll be lots of people your age there, and we'd love to have you join us."

"Thanks. If I can work it out, I'll be there."

"Good. And if not, then I hope to see you whenever you visit in the future."

As he walked toward the sanctuary, Aunt Louise arrived with the man I had seen earlier.

"Mayla, I want you to meet my friend Bill Manson. Bill, this is my niece, Mayla."

Bill's mostly gray hair still had a bit of its original dark brown in it, and he shook my hand with a strong grip. His brown eyes smiled kindly into mine, the creases at the corners crinkling with greeting. "Nice to meet you, Mayla."

"And you too, Mr. Manson."

He shook his head. "Call me Bill."

Aunt Louise, her eyes fixed on his face, said to me, "Bill is an electrician, originally from Georgia. He's in my Sunday school class."

"From Georgia, huh? How long have you been in Florida?"

"About a million years, since I was in high school," he responded with a laugh. "It's home to me, but I'll never get to claim it. There aren't too many native Floridians like Louise here, and they guard the honor jealously."

She dimpled at him, and I suppressed a smile at her unabashed flirting. Just then, Grandmother stepped up, and she was not smiling.

"Louise, are you ready to go? I need to get home and lie down for a while."

Louise's expression became serious. "Of course, Mother. You wait here with Mayla while I get the car."

She tossed an unreadable look toward Bill and left. He hovered uncertainly for a moment, then said, "Mrs. Strong, perhaps you'd like to sit in one of those chairs against the wall while you wait."

"I would not," Grandmother snapped, refusing to look at him directly. "I'm perfectly capable of standing here for the few minutes it will take Louise to get the car."

Shocked, I gave her a wide-eyed look. She stared out the window, her mouth drawn and hard. Clearly she didn't like Bill, but she was actually being rude. I shifted my gaze up to his, and he smiled awkwardly.

"Louise tells me you're from Kentucky. Nasty weather you're having up there right now."

"You know it. Getting away from all that snow has been a real treat."

"I'm sure it has. While you're here, are you going to get out to any of the theme parks?"

I shrugged. "I haven't decided, but I'm really just here to visit with Aunt Louise and Grandmother. The beach yesterday was nice, though."

"Yes, that's what Louise said."

I detected a hint of disappointment in his tone and looked more closely at him. Was he the friend Louise had wanted to go out with last night? He avoided my gaze, but the set of his jaw made me think I was right.

At that moment, Aunt Louise's car pulled up to the curb.

"Here she is." Bill sounded the tiniest bit relieved.

He followed us through the open glass doors and offered his arm to Grandmother at the top of the concrete stairs. She ignored him and grabbed for my arm instead. Taking long strides, he arrived at the car ahead of us and opened both the front and rear doors for us. I helped Grandmother get into the back, and he closed the door. Then I stuck my hand out toward him.

"It was nice to meet you, Bill. I'm here a week, so maybe we'll run into each other again."

"I hope so," he responded with a smile. "Enjoy your visit."

I slipped into the car, and he closed the door firmly. Distracted, Aunt Louise pulled away from the curb without a word, her gaze repeatedly drawn to the rearview mirror. Displeasure radiated from the backseat in nearly palpable waves, whether at Aunt Louise or me or both of us I didn't know. But we rode home in an uncomfortable silence.

❀ ❀ ❀

My cell phone rang a few minutes after two o'clock, the familiar *Flintstones* theme song breaking through the chatter of birds in the backyard where Aunt Louise and I sat on lawn chairs, relaxing in the sun while Grandmother took a nap. The number was one I didn't recognize.

"Mayla? It's Lindsey. I'm here."

Odd, but my stomach relaxed with relief in one moment and tightened with tension in the next. She was safe. But she was *here*.

"Where are you?"

"I'm at the Greyhound bus station. Do you know where that is?"

I put my hand over the mouthpiece and asked Aunt Louise, "Is the bus station close?"

She looked up from her book and eyed me over the top of her black-rimmed reading glasses. "Not far. It'll take about thirty minutes to get there."

I spoke back into the phone. "Okay, Lindsey, hang tight for a half hour or so, and I'll come get you."

"Thanks, Mayla."

I pressed the End button and swung my feet off the chair and onto the grass. "Can I borrow your car to go get her?"

Aunt Louise nodded. "Sure, but do you want me to drive you there?"

I thought a moment, then shook my head. "I'd like to have a few minutes alone with her, if you don't mind."

"Not at all."

I followed her inside and got my purse while she fished the keys out of hers. Then I wrote down directions to the bus station and left.

Aunt Louise's Buick Century was the nicest car I had ever driven, way different from my clunky old Honda. I sank into the soft driver's seat and enjoyed the smooth ride down Orange Blossom Trail to I-4. Fiddling with the radio, I discovered Z88.3, a station similar to the one I listened to at home, and cranked the stereo when the latest song from Third Day came on.

When I arrived at the bus station, I found Lindsey perched on a metal bench outside the building, a bulging green JanSport backpack on the ground at her feet and a hot pink ski jacket on the seat beside her. Dressed for winter in a thick turtleneck sweater and jeans, her cheeks were flushed with heat. She had pulled her dark hair into a thick ponytail at the back of her head, and though her hair looked like it could stand a prolonged encounter with a shampoo bottle, she still exuded a healthy, wholesome, high-school-cheerleader quality. She hadn't changed since I had last seen her, the day after her brother died last summer.

I stopped the car directly in front of her, and she leaped up from the bench when she caught sight of me, gathering her things as I leaned across the seat and opened the door. She tossed them into the backseat before sliding into the car and shutting the door.

Then she turned and looked at me. "You look different."

I touched the tiny scar midway between my chin and my lower lip. "Yeah, I dropped the freak look a few months ago."

Smudges darkened the skin beneath her hazel eyes. Her gaze swept my chocolate brown hair, but she didn't comment on the change in color. "Well, thanks for letting me come. I'm glad to finally see you."

I let out a deep sigh and shook my head. "I'm glad to see you, too, Lindsey, but I have a feeling this isn't going to be a fun visit for either of us."

She looked away, then straightened herself in the seat and fiddled with her seatbelt. "Probably not."

Putting the car into gear, I pulled out of the parking lot and back onto the parkway. "Do you want to tell me why you've run away?"

Lindsey turned her head to stare out the window. "Not real bad, no."

I clamped my teeth shut on the angry retort that threatened to lash out. If she didn't want to talk to me, why had she tracked me across the southern half of the United States? Not trusting myself to speak until I had taken a few deep breaths, I waited until I was sure I could keep my tone reasonable. "Then why are you here?"

"Because I thought it would be . . . different."

"Different? How?"

She turned to level a reproachful glare on me. "I thought you'd be nicer."

As I looked away from her, I caught sight of myself in the rear-view mirror. My lips were pressed into a thin line almost exactly like Grandmother's had been that morning. Holy cow, I could even see creases around my mouth like hers. Quickly softening my expression, I checked to make sure the lines disappeared, then forced myself to speak in a kinder tone.

"I'm sorry, Lindsey, but I've been worried about you. I've been imagining all sorts of terrible things, and it put me in a bad mood."

She watched me a moment, then nodded. Out of the corner of my eye I saw her bite her lip and take a short breath as though gathering courage. When she spoke, she stared directly ahead through the windshield. "Have you imagined that I'm pregnant?"

So that was it. My anger deflated even further. No wonder she was afraid. The thought of her father's reaction when he found out his little girl was pregnant was enough to make any teenager quake in fear. But what would the man who refused to acknowledge his son because he was gay do to a pregnant daughter?

I navigated the car into the right lane and drove up the ramp to the expressway. "I did wonder, but I hoped it wasn't true."

"Well, it is."

She sniffed, and though I couldn't look away from the expressway traffic, I reached into the floor of the backseat and grabbed my purse, tossing it into her lap. "There's a tissue in there."

I'm not the type of woman who normally carries tissues in her purse, but Mama had insisted I carry some on the airplane.

"Thanks." She fished out the little travel package of Kleenex and extracted one to dab at her eyes.

"Is Dirk the father?"

Dirk had been Lindsey's boyfriend last summer. I met him when he drove her up to visit her brother in the hospital.

Lindsey nodded.

"And what does he say about it?"

"He gave me the money for an abortion."

"He did what?" The car swerved as my grip tightened on the wheel. "That jerk!"

She shot me an angry glance. "He's not a jerk. He cares about me. He knows I want to keep playing volleyball and go to college, and I can't do that if I'm pregnant."

I looked away from the road for a moment to level her with a stare of disbelief. "Are you saying you want to have an abortion?"

"What choice do I have?" she shot back.

"I can think of several off the top of my head," I snapped, "and none of them involve murder."

She turned away. "I guess you won't be going with me to the clinic, then, will you?"

Forcing myself to watch the traffic, I shook my head, dumbfounded. She had come all the way to Florida on a Greyhound bus so I could take her to an abortion clinic? Unbelievable!

The radio quietly played a song into the silence between us, though I had turned the volume down so low that it was almost drowned out by the sound of the air conditioner. I forced myself to remain quiet until I could think of a response that wouldn't totally alienate Lindsey. But how could she think I would help her get an abortion?

On the other hand, I realized it was probably a reasonable assumption on her part. The last time she saw me I'd been sporting a five-millimeter labret stud in the shape of a cross beneath my lower lip, and my hair had been dyed purple. I had only been a Christian for a couple of months and had struggled to figure out how to adjust my old surroundings to my newfound life in Christ.

Actually, if she had come to me before then, I would have helped her get an abortion. But becoming a Christian changed me thoroughly. My new faith made me reevaluate everything I believed before, and abortion was one of the things I had reevaluated. Me, formerly the most radically liberal woman in the world, had become hopelessly conservative and proud of it.

"Lindsey," I asked, pleased that my tone was even, "are you a Christian?"

She shot me a suspicious look. "I go to church."

Interesting answer, but I wasn't about to get into that at the moment. "Then you must know what Jesus thinks about abortion."

She rolled her eyes and turned away again. I sighed. Man, I must be getting old if a teenager was rolling her eyes at me.

"Listen, Mayla, if you're gonna preach at me you might as well stop the car and let me out. I just can't take that right now."

I realized she was right. She didn't need a sermon at the moment. She needed someone to help her figure out what to do. The last thing I wanted was to force her into a desperate act because she felt she had nowhere else to turn.

Lord, I need some help here. There's a life at stake, and I don't want to say the wrong thing.

"I'm sorry, Lindsey. I won't preach. I really do want to help you."

Her shoulders relaxed as some of the tension left them. "Thanks, Mayla." She looked around. "Nice car. Is it a rental?"

"No, it's my aunt's."

"Your aunt's? You have an aunt in Orlando?"

I nodded. "And a grandmother. In fact, you'll meet them in a minute. We're going to their house."

Her mouth hung open, and her hazel eyes became two rounded ovals. "I thought you were here on vacation. I didn't know you were visiting family. I'm sorry. I shouldn't have come."

Shrugging, I said, "Forget it. No big deal. They're happy to have you."

"They know about me? That I've run away and all?"

"Sure. I had to tell them something when you told me you were on your way here."

She shot me a reproachful look. "Gosh, Mayla, you told your mother and your grandmother and your aunt. Is there anyone you haven't told?"

I ignored the accusation in her voice and answered lightly.

"Hmmm, let's see. Nope. In fact, Mama put you on the prayer chain at my church, so you've got a whole congregation full of people praying for you."

She slid down a fraction in the seat and crossed her arms, mumbling, "Terrific."

I hid a grin. I knew how she felt. I couldn't count the times my personal troubles had been spread throughout the church on the prayer chain. "Look at it like this—at least those are all strangers. I'll bet you're on the prayer chain at your church as well, and those are people you know."

"Oh, I doubt that," she said bitterly. "Daddy would have a fit if anyone knew his personal business. The Markhams are too perfect to need anything like prayer."

Since that fit everything I knew about her parents, I didn't have an argument. I kept quiet as we got off the interstate and drove down Orange Blossom Trail, trying to keep from glancing at the back of Lindsey's head as she stared out the window.

When I pulled into the sandy driveway, the front door opened, and Grandmother stepped out onto the concrete stoop. She stood watching as we got out of the car, me shouldering Lindsey's backpack while she clutched her ski jacket in front of her in both arms like a security blanket. Lindsey followed me uncertainly to the steps.

"Grandmother, this is a friend of mine, Lindsey Markham."

Deep dimples pierced Grandmother's cheeks as she smiled a warm welcome before opening the door and holding it wide to let us in. Her hazel eyes twinkled pleasantly as we approached.

"Lindsey, I'm pleased to meet you. Welcome to Florida."

"Thank you," Lindsey mumbled, ducking her head to avoid Grandmother's gaze as she edged past her into the house.

Once we were inside the living room, Grandmother swept by us, grabbing the jacket from a surprised Lindsey and the backpack from me, and heading down the hallway with them.

"We decided to put you two girls in Louise's room." She spoke over her shoulder, obviously expecting us to follow. "There's a double bed in there, so you'll be more comfortable."

"We can't kick Aunt Louise out of her bedroom," I protested, trailing after her down the short hallway with Lindsey on my heels.

"Oh, no ma'am," Lindsey agreed. "I won't stay. I just came to talk to Mayla for a little while."

"Nonsense, it's all worked out."

Sure enough, my suitcase had been repacked and moved from the small guest room to rest atop a cedar chest at the foot of the double bed, my laptop case beside it. Grandmother tossed the backpack on the bed and opened a pair of bifold closet doors to hang Lindsey's jacket as Aunt Louise stuck her head through the doorway.

"I've already moved everything I'll need into your room, Mayla. Hi, Lindsey. I'm Louise Strong. Nice to meet you."

Lindsey, looking dazed, nodded and managed a weak smile as Grandmother put her hands on her hips and studied the girl with a speculative stare. She shook her tight gray curls.

"Wearing that sweater, you'll roast in this heat," she announced. "Mayla, do you have anything the girl can put on?"

I eyed Lindsey myself. We were close to the same size except for the bust area. She actually had one. "I've got a T-shirt that might do."

"Good." Grandmother nodded, satisfied. "Lindsey, why don't you get cleaned up and changed and maybe even take a nap before dinner? How does that sound?"

Hesitantly, Lindsey admitted, "I could use a shower."

Grandmother patted her on the arm as she headed toward the door. "Take a long one, and if you need anything, just let us know. Come on, girls, let's let her rest."

Tossing a helpless shrug in Lindsey's direction, I followed my grandmother out of the room, feeling almost as stunned as Lindsey looked. A moment ago, I had been in charge. But the situation had been taken out of my hands.

❀ ❀ ❀

While Lindsey showered, I got my laptop and powered it on in the kitchen. Grandmother bustled about, getting a pork loin and potatoes ready to put into the oven. I stayed out of her way as I typed an e-mail to Mama.

Out in the yard with Aunt Louise earlier, I had been thinking about church that morning. I got to wondering what Paul would think of Reverend Thomas. I wondered if he would be just the tiniest bit jealous of such a good-looking, talented pastor with a big church. I've had a bit of experience with men, but that was before I became a Christian. Even then, I wasn't much for flirting or acting coy or any of the things girls do to attract a guy. Back then, I never saw any reason to make a guy jealous—either he liked me, or he didn't. Still, I've seen how it's done. I figured I could play the game.

I wished Paul and I were on speaking terms, because I would give him a call and casually mention meeting Reverend Thomas at church this morning. But a phone call was out of the question, and since I had been ignoring his e-mails, I couldn't figure out a way to send him one now without appearing as though I wanted him to be jealous. Even someone as new to this game as me knew that wasn't smart.

Then I had a brainstorm. I would e-mail Mama, and if I made Reverend Thomas sound juicy enough, she wouldn't be able to stop herself from telling her friends.

Hi Mama,

I wish you could have gone to church with me today. I met the most incredible man. His name is Robert Thomas, and he's the music minister at Grandmother's church. Mama, you should hear that man sing. What a voice! He leads the praise band and plays the guitar. And he writes music, too. The church sang one of his songs in the worship service, and it was beautiful.

You should see him, Mama. Gorgeous black hair and turquoise eyes. And a Florida tan, of course. He must work out, because he's got muscles like you wouldn't believe. And get this—he has a pierced ear! With that dark hair, the gold stud gives him a pirate-type look that must have women everywhere swooning over him. He invited me for coffee and to listen to some music later this week, so I must have made a good impression on him. I hope so!

Is everything okay with you? How's the weather? Tell everyone there I said hello.
    Love ya!
    Mayla

    There. I knew my mama, and that was sure to get a reaction out of her. Smiling, I clicked the Send button. She'd have that gossip line buzzing before nightfall.

Chapter 10

"Y ou snore," Lindsey accused the next morning.

I sat up in bed and stretched, glancing at the clock on the bedside table beyond her—8:17. Darn! I had enjoyed getting up early the past two mornings and spending a few minutes alone with Aunt Louise.

"Yeah? Well, you toss and turn and kick," I shot back. "I dreamed I was sleeping with the Karate Kid."

Lindsey grinned and swung her feet over to the floor. She looked better this morning, well-rested.

"I gotta go to the bathroom so bad it hurts." Aunt Louise's frilly nightgown fluttered around Lindsey's knees as she scooted out the door.

I started to call after her, "Yeah, that's what happens when you're pregnant," but I stopped myself. That probably wasn't the most diplomatic way to bring up the subject.

During the evening, we had avoided discussing her situation. I was proud of Grandmother and Aunt Louise for the way they acted—like Lindsey was an invited guest and they the gracious southern hosts. I took my cue from them and didn't grab her by the shoulders and shake her while shouting, "What are you going to do?" Halfway through the meal, I realized such behavior wouldn't solve anything and would only alienate her further. Still, my stomach had remained so tight I could barely choke down my dinner.

Not so, Lindsey. She ate like a starved teenager, which, considering she'd been on the run for a couple of days, she probably was. Then she fell asleep in front of the television an hour later, and I had to shake her awake to send her to bed. When I joined her at ten, she was in log mode.

"So what do you want to do today?" I asked when she returned from the bathroom.

She picked up her backpack and rummaged in it, avoiding my eyes. "I dunno. Make some phone calls, I guess. I need to find a clinic."

I felt my lips tightening in disapproval. "Then you'll have to find your own way there, because I'm not helping you get an abortion."

Shrugging, she tossed her backpack onto the floor. "I know. I'll figure it out."

Her offhand attitude irritated me no end, but I bit my tongue and got out of bed. She stepped to the other side and helped me straighten the comforter while I struggled to get my temper under control. Picking up a pair of shorts and a T-shirt, I headed to the bathroom without another word.

When I came out, I found Lindsey at the kitchen table, the Orlando Yellow Pages opened in front of her. I got two bowls out of the cabinet and put a box of Wheaties on the table while she went to the refrigerator for milk. We ate in an uneasy silence, avoiding each others' eyes, but I crunched my Wheaties with all the disapproval I could muster.

Grandmother got out of bed as Lindsey finished eating. Her short gray hair looked exactly the same as it had the night before, held in place with a helmet of hairspray. Obviously in a good mood, she practically sang her morning greetings.

"Good morning, girls. Did you sleep well?"

"Yes, ma'am," Lindsey replied, taking her bowl to the sink. "Must have been that delicious meal and the comfortable bed. I slept like a rock until around six, when Mayla's snoring woke me up."

I glared at Lindsey's back as she rinsed the bowl. Grandmother patted my shoulder. "She must get that from her mother. No one in the Strong family ever snored."

Her tone sounded a bit snide, but when I looked up at her, she smiled and turned away to get a cereal bowl.

"I'm going to get dressed," Lindsey announced.

I shook my head as she left the room.

"What's wrong?" Grandmother sat at the table across from me and reached for the cereal box.

Wordlessly, I pushed the Yellow Pages toward her. The book was opened to the As, with a whole list of entries beneath the heading Abortion.

Grandmother nodded. "I thought so."

"She wants me to take her to get an abortion." I kept my voice low. "I'm not going to do it."

"Of course not. But maybe you can talk her out of it."

"I'd like to, but I don't know. She doesn't want to listen to me. Which is pretty weird, considering she came all this way to talk to me."

Grandmother took a bite of cereal and chewed thoughtfully for a moment. "She's frightened right now. Maybe she needs a little time to calm down and think. We can give her that."

"Grandmother, she's a runaway," I whispered savagely. "The police could come barging through the door any minute and arrest us for kidnapping."

She chuckled. "You certainly have your father's flare for the dramatic. For one thing, we didn't kidnap her. And for another, I'm going to make her call her parents and get permission to stay."

I sat back in my chair, crossing my arms across my chest. "Can't wait to see that. If there's anyone more stubborn than that girl, it's her father."

She smiled. "I've had experience dealing with stubborn people. Watch me."

As we finished drying the dishes, Lindsey returned, dressed in her jeans and my T-shirt that she had put on after her shower last night. Her hair, clean now, bounced and shone in its ponytail, and the dark circles under her eyes had disappeared. In fact, her cheeks looked rosy and healthy. I wondered if it was that "glow" I always heard pregnant women have but decided in Lindsey's case it was just because she was a healthy teenager.

"All right, girls," Grandmother said as she hung the dish towel on a hook beneath the sink, "I'm going to take advantage of having two young people here this week." She turned a dimpled smile on us, her greenish eyes guileless. "I've got some yard work that needs to be done."

I pretended to groan while Lindsey grinned.

"Sure, no problem," she said. "Just show us what you need us to do."

The dimples in those wrinkled cheeks deepened. "That's the attitude I like. But first, Lindsey, I think we should call your parents and let them know where you are."

Ah, Grandmother had decided on the direct approach.

Lindsey's back straightened, and she shot me a poisonous look. "I don't think that's a good idea."

"Nonsense," Grandmother insisted, picking up the telephone receiver. "They must be worried sick about you. I'm sure you don't want them to think you're dead on the side of the road somewhere."

Lindsey crossed her arms. "I called them the day before yesterday and told them I was okay."

Grandmother smiled sweetly. "And that was good, but believe me, I know how parents are. In the past two days, they've convinced themselves that you've been picked up by a maniac on the road, and they're jumping up to run to the door every time they hear a car go by, afraid the police have come to tell them your body has been discovered. They haven't slept a wink in days for worrying about you. Think how much better they'll feel knowing you're safe with a nice family."

Lindsey shook her head. "You don't know my father. He hasn't lost any sleep over me, I guarantee it."

My grandmother actually chuckled and reached out to pat Lindsey's shoulder. "Honey, if you think that, you don't know men as well as you think you do. Trust me. He's losing sleep over his little girl."

For a moment, Lindsey appeared to soften while I struggled to bite my tongue and stay out of Grandmother's way.

"I'll tell you what," Grandmother said, her tone reasonable. "I'll talk to them first and tell them you're okay and convince them to let you stay on a few days. Then you can talk to them to reassure them. They won't argue with *me*."

That little old lady who could look so frail at times managed at that moment to look like a giant. I believed her—even Mr. Markham didn't stand a chance against her. Lindsey's eyebrows lowered almost imperceptibly as she considered what Grandmother said.

"Well," she began uncertainly.

"And then," Grandmother went on as though the conclusion was certain, "you can actually relax and enjoy your trip to Orlando. Won't that be nice?"

Grandmother thrust the telephone gently into the girl's hands. Lindsey stared at it, an unreadable expression on her face.

Grandmother spoke in a voice so quiet it was almost a whisper. "You have to call them sometime, you know. Why not now?"

"Well." She gave the hint of a sigh. "All right."

As Lindsey dialed the phone, Grandmother turned to me.

"You'll find a plastic watering jug in that little shelf out in the family room. Would you mind watering the plants out there? You can get water from my bathroom. And pinch off the dead leaves, too."

In other words, *Clear out and give us some privacy.* She pointed me firmly toward the family room, and I had no choice but to go. I shot Lindsey a final look, but she was staring at the phone, hesitating as her finger hovered over the last number. My shoulders tight with tension, I filled the water jug and set about watering the zillion and one plants, straining to hear what Grandmother said into the phone. No luck. I could hear her voice, her tone level and reasonable, but couldn't make out any words.

After a few minutes, Grandmother came into the family room with a satisfied smile on her face. I rushed to her side.

"You did it? You convinced them to let her stay?"

"Of course." She spoke as though there had never been any doubt. Looking at her composure, I realized that to her there never had been. "Mrs. Markham couldn't stop crying long enough to talk to me, but then Mr. Markham got on the phone. He seems to be a reasonable man, and when I explained to him that Lindsey would only run away again if he forced her to come home before she was ready, he agreed. I flattered his ego, telling him she had a will of iron that she must have gotten from one of her parents. Of course, I think part of the reason he agreed was because he's relieved that she's with a responsible adult instead of on the street."

"Did you tell him why she ran away?"

She shook her head. "That's not my place. I simply explained that teenagers today are faced with some very stressful situations that didn't exist when he and I were younger and assured him that Lindsey was healthy and in no danger."

I shook my head, full of admiration. "I'm impressed. I wouldn't have thought anyone could convince Mr. Markham of anything."

She smiled and patted my arm. "You just have to know how to handle people. You'll learn."

Just then, Lindsey appeared in the doorway, teary and sniffling. She ran to Grandmother and threw her arms around her.

"Thank you," she sniffed. "I can't believe you did it, but you did."

Grandmother's smile widened. "Of course I did." She pushed Lindsey playfully toward the back door. "Now you can pay me back by clearing out that mess of weeds along the fence row. You, too, Mayla."

Shaking my head, I followed Lindsey out into the yard. We still had to deal with the abortion issue, but at least it didn't look like I was going to jail for kidnapping anytime soon.

❀ ❀ ❀

Jail or not, I found out I was in serious trouble that afternoon when Lindsey and I finally finished clearing out every single weed in Grandmother's backyard. I came into the bedroom to find that I had missed four calls on my cell phone—all from Mama.

"I'm going to jump in the shower," Lindsey said, picking up her backpack from the corner of Aunt Louise's bedroom. "I don't suppose you have some clean underwear and another shirt I could borrow? I have another pair of jeans that are still pretty clean."

Both of us were hot and sweaty, and my legs had been scratched in about a million places from the scrub bushes we'd pulled out of the corner in the backyard. I fished out a pair of underwear and another T-shirt.

"We need to do some laundry tonight," I said, tossing them to her. "I didn't pack enough for both of us."

"Thanks." She left the room as I dialed Mama's number.

"Mayla Strong, what in the world do you think you're doin' down there?" Mama's voice shouted as soon as she answered.

"What?" I asked, though I knew full well what she meant. "Do you mean Lindsey?"

"A'course I mean Lindsey," she snapped. "Here I am getting the whole town praying for her when all the time you had her hiding down there with you."

"I did not have her hiding down here the whole time. She didn't get here until yesterday. Late yesterday," I added defensively.

"And did you call me? No! I had to hear it from Sandra, who could barely talk for crying, and I couldn't understand half of what she said. And then you didn't answer your phone, neither."

"I've been busy. I was going to call you later, Mama. I promise."

"You shoulda called as soon as you knew she was safe."

"I know." I added a hint of apology to my tone. "But she made me promise. She said if I told anyone she would run away again. I'm sorry, Mama."

"You coulda trusted *me*," she said, her voice the tiniest bit calmer. "I wouldn't a'told nobody."

The thought of Mama keeping something like that to herself was so ludicrous I almost laughed. But I had no doubt she believed she wouldn't have told anyone, so I kept quiet.

"Anyway," she said, "at least she's safe. Has she told you why she ran away?"

I paused, then answered cautiously. "She has confided a little, but she made me promise not to discuss her reasons with anyone."

A long pause answered me. Mama hates to be left out of anything.

"So," I went on before she could start trying to pry information out of me, "did you get my e-mail about church yesterday?"

Her voice suddenly took on a new level of interest. "I sure did. Tell me about Robert."

"There's not much more to tell, really. He's only the handsomest man I've ever seen—and talented, too. And a Christian, even. What more could anyone want?"

"I'm not sure I like you going out with some Florida man. I'd hate for you to get ideas about staying down there." She sniffed. "Especially for someone with an earring."

I laughed out loud. "Mama, outside of Salliesburg lots of men wear earrings."

"Not in my church, they don't. But really, Mayla, are you thinking about going out with this man?"

She sounded concerned, which made me squirm uncomfortably as I struggled with how to answer. I didn't want to lie to anyone, especially my mama.

Suddenly Lindsey shouted from the bathroom. "Mayla! Come here quick!"

I heard a touch of panic in her voice.

"Hey, Mama, I've got to go. I'll talk to you later, okay?"

"You call me back, you hear?"

"I will. Bye."

I disconnected and ran to the bathroom, where Lindsey stood

clutching a bath towel around her, watching helplessly as the toilet overflowed like a waterfall onto the floor.

"Quick, grab some towels," I ordered, reaching for the two hand towels hanging on the rack beside the door.

"Where are they?" She stood rooted in one spot, her eyes wide.

"Hall closet." I dropped the towels onto the large puddle around the base of the toilet before I lifted the tank lid. I reached inside and raised the lever to stop the water flow just as Lindsey came back with a stack of towels.

"Get down there behind the toilet and turn off the water," I ordered.

She backed up, a look of horror on her face. "I'm not bending down there in that puddle."

"It's *your* puddle," I snapped. "Now turn off the water."

She put the towels on the sink and approached cautiously. Finding a dry spot to stand in, she bent down toward the bowl and suddenly retched.

"Don't you dare throw up!" I shouted.

She swallowed hard. "I can't help it. There's pee on the floor!"

My stomach gave a dangerous little flutter as well, but I kept my face stern. "Fine. You hold this, and I'll turn off the water."

She leaned over to take hold of the lever, standing as far away as possible. When she had a grip on it, I dropped the stack of towels on the floor and knelt on them to reach behind the toilet and turn the handle, trying not to think about what I was kneeling in. The water finally off, Lindsey quickly backed into the hallway and watched as I spread the towels out, sopping up the smelly liquid. Grandmother came up beside her.

"All I did was flush," Lindsey told her. "Honest."

"I've had trouble with that toilet before." Grandmother shook her head. "It gets clogged up over nothing. Louise had a plumber here a couple of weeks ago. I'll call and ask her to get him back."

She turned away, leaving us to clean up the mess.

I looked at Lindsey, who continued to stand in the hallway looking green, and sighed. "Do me a favor, would you? Find a laundry basket and some more dry towels. And I think I saw some spray cleaner under the sink in the kitchen."

Obviously relieved, she left to do as I asked. I bent to my nasty task with another long sigh. At least I'd been rescued from an uncomfortable conversation with Mama.

At five thirty, Aunt Louise's car pulled into the driveway, followed by a blue van with white lettering on the side.

"The plumber's here," I called to Grandmother in the family room. "And Aunt Louise is home, too."

Grandmother came through the kitchen door into the living room, followed by Lindsey. The man who got out of the blue van looked familiar, and as I watched, Aunt Louise closed her car door and walked toward him, smiling. Looking more closely at the van, I read *Manson Electric* on the side.

"He's no plumber," Grandmother said in a pinched voice, and I looked at her in surprise. "I told her to call the plumber back."

I swallowed anything I might have said at the sight of Grandmother's narrowed eyes and angry expression.

"Maybe he can fix the toilet, anyway," said Lindsey innocently behind us.

Grandmother turned and stalked into the kitchen without a word. Bill Manson followed Aunt Louise across the front yard and up the stairs. I noticed a pretty pink flush on my aunt's cheeks and a happy smile playing around her mouth as she opened the door. Mr. Manson looked a little more apprehensive when, reaching over her head to hold the door open for her, his gaze swept my face and Lindsey's. I saw something that might have been relief ease his features when he realized there were only two of us standing there.

"Mayla," Aunt Louise said, a little breathlessly, "you remember Bill from church yesterday?"

I nodded, smiling. "Hello, Mr. Manson."

"Call me Bill." His smile twitched nervously.

Aunt Louise gestured to Lindsey. "And this is Mayla's friend Lindsey."

"Hello," she said, and he smiled in her direction, too.

"Let me show you where the bathroom is." My aunt took Bill's arm and beamed up at him.

They walked together down the hallway, and Lindsey looked at me with arched eyebrows. "Your aunt has a thing for the plumber," she whispered.

"Yeah, I know. But I don't think my grandmother likes him much."

She shrugged. "Parents never do."

Bill worked on the toilet for twenty minutes, Aunt Louise hovering nearby and handing him tools. Grandmother refused to come out of the kitchen, though she banged enough dishes to let everyone know how she felt about the situation. I decided the wisest course of action was silence, but I helped her get leftovers out of the refrigerator and heat them one at a time in the microwave. Lindsey went back and forth, giving us progress reports.

"He's got it unclogged," she said finally. "Said the guy who was here before left part of the clog in there, whatever it was."

Grandmother didn't even look up from the bowl of carrots she stirred.

"Hey, maybe we should ask Bill to stay for dinner," I suggested. "It's almost ready."

The spoon slammed down onto the counter as Grandmother whirled on me. "We'll do no such thing. We don't have enough to go around."

Lindsey's eyes widened, but she wisely kept quiet as my gaze swept the half-dozen or so bowls on the counter. When I looked back into Grandmother's eyes, the protest died on my lips. The fury I saw there didn't leave room for argument.

Just then, Aunt Louise came to stand in the doorway, Bill hovering hesitantly behind her. Grandmother whirled around to the counter, turning her back on us all. Oblivious, Aunt Louise gave us a wide smile.

"Everything's fine now, thanks to Bill."

After an awkward pause during which Grandmother kept her back turned, I spoke up. "Thanks a million, Bill. Four women in the house sharing one bathroom isn't my idea of a relaxing vacation."

"Yeah, thanks," echoed Lindsey, with a cautious glance thrown toward Grandmother's rigid back.

"Glad I could help." He dipped his forehead. "You ladies have a nice evening."

"I'll just see him out," Aunt Louise said, and they left.

Lindsey looked at me, then at Grandmother, and back at me. I shrugged.

"Grab some silverware out of that drawer over there." I broke the heavy silence with what I hoped was a normal tone.

Relieved to have something to do, Lindsey helped me set the table for dinner.

Grandmother had another angina attack that evening during *Jeopardy*. Lindsey looked a bit freaked out, but Aunt Louise reacted with such composure that I wondered if she had expected it. The more I thought about it, the more I figured she probably did. The attacks were brought on by stress, she had said. I couldn't figure out why, but Grandmother obviously didn't like Bill, and having him in the house had been stressful for her.

When the attack was over, we all sat in the family room in front of the television, Grandmother sitting weakly in her chair. Aunt Louise seemed distracted by her thoughts and kept throwing covert glances toward Grandmother. I had been thinking all evening of Lindsey and what I could do to convince her not to go through with the abortion. I had come up with a couple of ideas.

"I was thinking," I said casually, "that we should do something tomorrow, something special."

"Like what?" Lindsey asked.

"When I was a little girl, I loved to go to SeaWorld. I'd kind of like to go there tomorrow."

A huge grin crept over Lindsey's face. "I've never been to SeaWorld."

I turned to Grandmother with a worried look. "But I don't want to leave you alone."

"Leave me alone?" She shook her head, sitting up straighter in her chair. "I'll go with you."

"But Mother," Aunt Louise said, "you might not feel up to it."

"Nonsense." Grandmother swept us with a look that dared us to disagree. "By tomorrow, I'll be fine."

I gave Aunt Louise a concerned look, to which she responded with a very slight shrug. "You can take my car if you like," she said, "and if you stop by the bank on the way, I can get discount tickets from the employee club at work."

"Oh, goodie!" said Lindsey, clapping her hands. "We're going to SeaWorld!"

I sat back against the couch cushion, satisfied. We would certainly pay a visit to the dolphin nursery to make sure Lindsey got a good look at the new baby dolphin.

I put the second part of my plan into motion a little later that evening when Aunt Louise said good night and headed for bed. Following her down the hallway, I whispered, "Can you find a pregnancy resource center in town? One that doesn't do abortions."

Her gaze shifted briefly in the direction of the family room, where Lindsey sat with Grandmother. "I'm sure I can."

I nodded. "Thanks."

❀ ❀ ❀

Before I went to bed that night, I hooked up my laptop to check my e-mail. I had a gazillion junk e-mails and a couple from Mama with the subject LINDSEY IS THERE WITH YOU???? which had obviously been sent before we talked. But scanning the list, I saw the one name I hoped to see: BibleMan32. When I double-clicked, the notification message came on the screen again, but I bypassed it. I noticed that he began right in, without typing *Dear Mayla* or even *Hi, Mayla* or anything.

> I'm glad you're going to church while you're in Florida. I'm also glad you enjoyed the music there. I heard there was a praise band, so I assume you went to a contemporary service. I've been thinking about asking Ted Davis to add some contemporary music at our church, so if you have a minute, please send me an e-mail and tell me what songs they sang.

Aha! He wanted to know what songs they sang, did he? Well, I didn't believe that for one minute. He was trying to get me to break my virtual silence, but I couldn't be fooled that easily.

> I do want to caution you, though. I've heard the preacher there is a nice looking man, and that he asked you out. After our last discussion at your mother's house, I am worried about you. I hate to point out the obvious, but apparently he has dark hair like me, and he is a preacher like me. Please be aware that you might be on the rebound.

"Aaahhh!" I screeched, which brought everyone in the house running into the kitchen.

"Mayla, what's wrong?" Aunt Louise asked, tightening the belt of her housecoat around her waist, a look of alarm on her face. Grandmother and Lindsey both peered at me with concern from the family-room doorway.

I took a deep, fortifying breath. "Nothing," I snapped in a voice angrier than I intended. "Just . . . nothing."

I turned my back on them and pressed the Delete button savagely, then punched the Shut Down command with such force that my laptop scooted across the counter. I jerked the plug out of the outlet and turned around to find them all still staring at me.

"Men," I announced with my chin in the air, "are scum."

I stomped out of the kitchen toward the bedroom, leaving them to stare after me with dumbfounded expressions.

Chapter 11

When I was a little girl, I went to SeaWorld with Mama and Daddy during one of our summer vacations. I remember it as a magical place, full of dolphins and whales and penguins and pink flamingoes. I have a vivid memory of the stingray tank and Daddy showing me how to hold the smelly dead fish between my fingers and place my hand flat on the bottom of the tank. A group of stingrays swam over it, and one sucked the fish up in its mouth.

The stingray tank was the first place I wanted to visit on that sunny February day when we parked Aunt Louise's car in the parking lot. Excitement tickled my stomach as we walked toward the end of the row to the waiting open-air shuttle, and Lindsey bounced on her toes with enthusiasm. She wore one of my short-sleeved shirts and a pair of my stretchy shorts, which I had to admit looked better on her than on me. Her legs were firm and muscular and made me think maybe I should take up volleyball.

Even Grandmother seemed excited, chattering as we walked about the last time she and Aunt Louise had visited the park.

"And they have a roller coaster." She stopped abruptly and threw a sideways glance toward Lindsey. "Not that I'm allowed to ride it, at my age."

I realized that Lindsey wouldn't be allowed to ride it either, because pregnant women couldn't ride roller coasters. Lindsey must have thought of that, too, since she stopped bouncing for a few minutes and her face took on a pensive expression. But when the shuttle lurched forward, her excitement returned, and we all laughed in anticipation of the day we would have.

It was a great day. SeaWorld had lost none of the magic, though the stingray food was smellier than I remembered, and the stingrays scarier and hungrier. We fed dolphins, too, and I snapped pictures with a disposable camera I bought in one of the gift shops. Grandmother refused the offer of a wheelchair with disdain, and not only kept up with us but led us energetically from one show to the next. We saw Shamu and Baby Shamu, Clyde and Seamore, and the most amazing circus show I've seen anywhere.

At the end of the day, we stopped by the Dolphin Nursery, a big tank surrounded by a wall of tall bushes with fluorescent pink flowers blooming throughout. A wooden stand on one side held signs with all sorts of interesting facts about baby dolphins, and a big awning provided shade for part of the nursery tank. We leaned against the chest-high concrete wall surrounding the dolphin pool and watched half-a-dozen dolphins swimming around and around, including several small ones. A sign told us the birth dates of the three babies in the water. The newest calf, we were told by a friendly woman in a SeaWorld uniform and holding a microphone, had weighed forty-eight pounds at birth.

"Man, that's a big baby," muttered Lindsey, watching the adorable little rubbery guy swim around the tank in nearly perfect unison with his mother.

I looked up at her from where I leaned as far over the concrete side of the tank as I could without getting yelled at by the attendant, who stood nearby. "Yeah, but that mother weighs a lot more than a human mom."

The baby veered off on its own just then, wobbling like a toddler, and we watched as the mother dolphin slowed her pace to allow her infant to catch up.

"She sure keeps close tabs on him," Lindsey observed.

"Oh yes," the friendly attendant told us, overhearing Lindsey's comment. "In the wild, mother dolphins keep their babies close by their sides, and some of them nurse for up to four years. In captivity they rarely nurse beyond eighteen months, though. By then, the babies weigh as much as the adults."

Lindsey watched the pair intently, and I did my best not to look at her or make pointed comments about the cuteness of babies and what good mothers the dolphins were. After a few minutes, I noticed Grandmother shifting from one foot to another, and I realized she was ready to go. I stood up.

"Time to head home."

Lindsey nodded and followed us away from the nursery tank. I saw her look back once, and tried to keep a smug grin off my face.

The sun had set by the time we got home at almost seven o'clock that night. The house was dark and deserted looking as we turned into the driveway.

"Looks like Aunt Louise isn't home from work yet," I commented, shifting the car into Park.

Grandmother remained silent. She fiddled in her purse to find her house keys and walked with a quick, purposeful step to the front door. Lindsey and I followed her inside as she flipped the switch and flooded the living room with warm light from a pair of table lamps. Just then, a car turned into the driveway, its headlights flashing onto the wall through the front window.

"I think she's home," Lindsey announced.

Ignoring us both, Grandmother went into the kitchen while we stood by the front door watching Aunt Louise get out of a dark van.

"Hey, that's the plumber's van," Lindsey said, her voice low so Grandmother wouldn't overhear.

"Electrician," I corrected quietly.

"Whatever. It's the toilet guy."

We stood gawking as Aunt Louise shut the van door, then turned to say something through the open window before walking away. She approached the house with a springy step and nearly skipped up onto the porch before turning to wave good-bye. The van waited until she was inside with the door closed behind her before backing out of the driveway.

"Hello, girls," she nearly sang, her eyes sparkling above flushed cheeks. "How was SeaWorld?"

"Great," I replied. "The weather was perfect."

"Yeah," Lindsey said as we followed her into the kitchen, "you should have seen the Chinese acrobats on these long silky ropes hanging from the ceiling. I couldn't believe the stuff they did."

"Oh, I love them," Aunt Louise said. "They were there the last time Mother and I went. Weren't they, Mother?"

Grandmother stood at the refrigerator with her back to us and did not answer.

Aunt Louise looked toward me with a silent question. "Mother," she prompted, "did you have a good time today?"

Grandmother turned. As I watched, she changed before my eyes. Her shoulders sagged, her face wilted, and even her eyes seemed to lose their sparkle and take on a gray hue in the space of a single breath. She wavered, as though standing was suddenly too much effort. Alarmed, I took a step forward, ready to catch her if she fainted, but Aunt Louise got there first.

"Mother, you've overexerted yourself." Her calm voice belied her troubled expression. "Here, sit down for a moment, and I'll make you a cup of hot tea."

"I suppose I did." Grandmother shuffled like an invalid over to the kitchen table, leaning heavily on Aunt Louise's arm.

I leaped to pull her chair out and hovered anxiously as Aunt Louise helped her to sit. Lindsey watched from the doorway, eyes wide and forehead creased with worry.

"I can't sit for long, though," Grandmother managed to say. "I'll need to get supper. I hoped you'd have it ready when we got home, but I guess you had something more important to do."

I saw Aunt Louise's shoulders tense almost imperceptibly. Crossing to the stove, she picked up the teakettle and turned to fill it at the sink. She placed it on the burner before answering, her tone flat.

"I'm sorry, Mother. Since the park didn't close until seven, I assumed you would get something to eat there."

"We were going to," Lindsey said, "but she was worried that you'd have to eat alone, so we came home instead."

I saw Aunt Louise take a deep breath before nodding. "I'm sorry," she repeated. "I didn't know."

"It's not a problem," I said, throwing a cautious glance toward Grandmother. "We had a good lunch at the restaurant with the big shark tank and then ate junk all afternoon. I'm sure none of us are very hungry. I can whip up some tomato soup or heat up leftovers for everyone."

Aunt Louise nodded absently, her attention focused on opening a tea bag, putting it into a mug, and getting a spoon from the silverware drawer. But looking at her face, I knew she wasn't really thinking about tea. She was beating herself up for not being there when we got home.

I switched my gaze to Grandmother and saw her watching Aunt Louise. For one moment, I thought I saw her eyelids narrow speculatively before her gaze slid across the room to lock onto mine. The look she gave me was hard, not at all an expression of weakness. But in the next instant, I thought I must have been mistaken, for she once again exuded frailty and weariness.

If I didn't know better, I'd say she was faking. I shook my head. Surely not. The doctor said she had angina, even prescribed medicine for it. But when I was a kid and didn't want to go to school, I had faked enough illnesses to be suspicious now. I even made myself throw up once to get out of dodgeball in PE class. The sight of my spaghetti lunch all over the girl's locker room would have convinced any doctor that I was sick with the flu. It sure worked on Miss Wiley, my PE teacher.

"Mother," Aunt Louise said, "why don't you rest in the recliner and watch *Wheel of Fortune* while the girls and I get dinner?"

"What about my tea?" Grandmother asked weakly.

"I'll bring it to you when it's ready."

The old lady nodded and allowed herself to be helped out to the family room, where she sat quietly for the next half hour, watching television and sipping tea. When our dinner of canned vegetable soup and ham sandwiches was ready, we took hers to her on a lap tray. We set up TV trays for ourselves so she wouldn't have to eat alone.

I couldn't help but notice she ate every last crumb.

My cell phone rang as Lindsey and I were putting away the last of the supper dishes. Seeing Sylvia's number on the display, I pressed the Talk button with a touch of unease, wondering what Harvey had done this time.

"Mayla, you'll never believe it," Sylvia shouted into the phone.

"I'll never believe what?" I asked, relieved that her voice sounded excited and not angry.

"Michael accepted the Lord last night! He became a Christian!"

"That's fantastic," I nearly yelled, drawing a sharp stare from Lindsey. "Praise the Lord!"

Lindsey rolled her eyes and turned back to her task of wiping the sink with a dishrag.

"How did it happen?"

"Well, you know Lou has been talking to him for a couple of weeks, and last night they both came over to the apartment—"

"Our apartment?"

"Yeah, they were helping with the rabbit cage. Anyway, at first Michael was really quiet, distracted-like. I was actually kinda surprised he wanted to come over, because for the past few days, he'd been avoiding me and not taking Lou's calls. But I guess he's been thinking about everything Lou has been telling him, because out of the blue he popped out with 'I want to ask Jesus into my heart.' Just like that! So the three of us knelt by the couch, and Lou led him in the sinner's prayer. You should have seen him, Mayla. Tears streamed down his face, and he kept saying, 'I feel different. He's real, and He really has saved me.' We all cried. It was so awesome!"

"That's terrific." Tears sprang to my own eyes. "This is unbelievably wonderful news, Sylvia." Then I stopped, remembering Michael's roommate. "What did Stuart say about it?"

Sylvia sighed. "I don't know. I haven't seen him. But you know he's not going to like it."

"Maybe this will make Stuart realize he needs the Lord, too." I allowed a touch of hope to steal into my voice.

"Maybe." Sylvia's tone told me she didn't think so. "We can pray for him, anyway."

"Yes, we can. And we will."

"Listen, Mayla, I've got to get back to work. I took a quick break when I realized you didn't know yet. I wanted to be the one to tell you."

"Thanks, Sylvia. That's the most fantastic news I've heard since Lou became a Christian."

She giggled. "I know. Later, Mayla."

"Bye."

I set the last dish to dry in the rack and started to put away the dish towel when my brain caught up with me. Did Sylvia say something about a rabbit cage? What rabbit cage? Harvey lived in a box.

As I came out of the bathroom to head for bed, Aunt Louise stopped me in the hallway. She handed me a folded slip of paper.

"This is a Christian women's center specializing in unplanned pregnancies," she whispered. "A friend from church told me about it and said you don't need an appointment."

I opened the paper and saw an address, phone number, and directions in her neat script. "Thanks, Aunt Louise."

"You can take my car. I've arranged for a ride in the morning."

I stood there hesitantly, wondering whether or not to mention my suspicions about the timing of Grandmother's angina attacks. Before I made up my mind, she smiled and slipped past me into the bathroom.

Sighing, I went into the bedroom, where Lindsey had already arranged herself on her side of the bed, the comforter tucked snugly under her chin.

"Hey," I said, sitting on the edge of the bed. "I don't want to start an argument or anything, but have you thought any more about what you're going to do?"

Her face took on a wary expression. "I haven't changed my mind if that's what you mean."

"I see." I stood. "In that case there's a place in town you might want to go to tomorrow."

She sat up. "Is it a clinic?"

I looked down at the paper. Written at the top was *Women's Health Clinic*. "Yeah, it's a women's clinic, but I don't know much about it."

Her eyelids narrowed. "What made you change your mind?"

"I didn't," I said firmly. "I'm taking you to talk about your options. I intend to go along and make sure you're given *all* the options."

She stared at me a moment, then gave a slight nod, satisfied. Settling back onto the pillow, she pulled the comforter up around her shoulders before turning on her side to face the wall. "Try not to snore tonight."

"Keep your legs on your side of the bed," I shot back, slipping between the sheets.

I turned off the lamp on the bedside table and laid down on my back, settling myself for sleep. A few moments later, Lindsey's voice said, "Thanks for everything, Mayla."

I wondered if she would thank me tomorrow when she saw the clinic didn't perform abortions.

"You're welcome. Now go to sleep."

My phone rang at somewhere around one in the morning. I stumbled out of bed, trying to remember where I had put it the night before. Lindsey mumbled a sleepy protest as I groped on the bedside table, knocked the phone onto the floor, and dragged it to me by the charger cord.

"H'lo," I managed to whisper, mindful of Aunt Louise sleeping just across the hallway.

"I hope you're happy," a tear-stained voice accused.

"Stuart?"

"He's gone, thanks to you. Gone." A choked sob gripped me by the eardrum and jerked my eyes open.

"Who's gone? Michael?"

"Of course Michael, you idiot. Who else?"

A flash of irritation jolted me completely awake. "And just how is this my fault? I'm a thousand miles away, for cryin' out loud."

Verbal poison shot through the airwaves, caught by my cell phone and tossed into my ear. "I don't care where you are; the whole thing is your fault from beginning to end, and you know it. Don't think you can dash off to Florida on vacation and escape scot-free, Mayla Strong."

"Free from what?" I snapped back; then I heard the answering sob in his voice and forced myself to calm down. There was a hurting soul on the other end of this phone. "Listen, Stuart. Michael has made his own decision for Christ. No one is to blame. Instead, you should be happy for him. He's found a peace you can't begin to understand."

A long pause met my words, and then I heard Stuart's voice as though from a great distance. "I know. But what about me?"

My heart twisted at the agony in that voice. *Lord, give me the right words, please!*

"You can have that peace too, Stuart," I began, but I realized I spoke to dead air. Stuart had hung up.

I pressed a button to call the number back, but my call went straight to voice mail. He must have powered off his phone.

Frustrated, I snapped my cell phone shut and tossed it into the corner. Why did people keep hanging up on me?

Chapter 12

I found myself wanting to avoid my grandmother the next morning. She didn't notice. Wednesday was her cleaning day, and she kept us busy all morning stripping the sheets, dusting the furniture, and running the vacuum. She did her share of the work, too, I had to admit. And she didn't look the slightest bit tired while she did it.

Around eleven o'clock, I told Grandmother that Lindsey and I were going out and would be back some time after lunch. Aunt Louise must have told her what we were doing because she didn't question me at all, just stood on the porch, waving good-bye. She actually seemed relieved to have some time alone, and as I backed the car out of the driveway, I realized having a house full of people was probably wearing on her.

The sun glittered overhead in a light blue sky as I followed Aunt Louise's directions to I-4. Lindsey plastered her face to the window, watching the little lakes and tall palm trees we passed. From the freeway, I exited in the middle of downtown Orlando.

"Wow, look at the tall buildings," I commented, looking skyward out the windshield as we drove by one.

"Tall?" Lindsey snorted. "This is nothing compared to New York."

I glanced over at her. The biggest city I had ever seen besides Orlando was Louisville, Kentucky. I raised an eyebrow, fighting down a touch of jealousy. "You've been to New York?"

"Sure. Mom and Daddy took me last year to see a couple of plays. Now *that's* a big city. Hey, lookie there!"

"What the heck is that?" I exclaimed, trying to get a good look at a multicolored statue in the center of a plaza in front of a big building.

"It's a big lizard," Lindsey said, "and it's painted all sorts of wild colors."

I laughed. "That's hysterical."

"Hey look, there's another one on the wall!"

Sure enough, a giant, psychedelic chameleon appeared to be crawling down the side of one of the buildings.

"I'll bet you didn't see anything like that in New York," I said, chuckling.

We made several turns and ended up on a charming, brick-paved street curving gently alongside a big lake. A fountain in the center sprayed high into the air, causing the water all around the lake to ripple like diamonds reflecting the sunshine. A smooth white path ran alongside the water, and I saw a pair of joggers pass a woman pushing a stroller. The buildings across the road from the lake looked like old restored houses, with business signs out in front of several of them.

"Look for 487," I told Lindsey and drove slowly as she stared out the window at the numbers on the buildings. I noticed her white-knuckled grip on the door handle. Poor kid. She must be really scared. I couldn't begin to imagine how she felt.

"There it is."

I pulled into the driveway of an attractive yellow house with white shutters. White wicker furniture with thick floral cushions sat invitingly on a deep front porch with a swing hanging from two shiny chains. A sign on the front of the house beside the door said AA WOMEN'S CENTER.

"I wonder what the AA stands for," Lindsey asked as I pulled the car down the driveway to the back of the house.

"I don't know. Maybe they did that so it'll show up first in the yellow pages. I've seen companies do that before."

"Yeah, maybe."

Lindsey's voice sounded as though it came from as far away as her thoughts were at the moment. She stared out the window with unfocused eyes while I parked the car in a small parking lot in the back. A narrow sidewalk ran up the other side of the house to the front, alongside a tall flowering hedge. But the back door had a big WELCOME sign over it, too, so I guessed we could get inside through either one. I shifted the car into Park and turned the key to the Off position. When the engine stopped, the radio did, too, and inside the car grew quiet.

"You ready?" I asked after a few moments.

Her shoulders twitched, and she drew in a sharp breath, looking at me with wide hazel eyes. "I'm sorta nervous."

Nervous? This kid had tracked me down, barged in on my vacation, moved in with my family, and badgered me to take her to get an abortion. And now she was too nervous to go inside the clinic? Smothering a rush of irritation, I tried to make my voice soothing. "Listen, you don't have to do anything today. We're just here to talk about options. There's nothing to be nervous about."

"Yeah, but these past couple of days have been almost like a vacation. I even forgot about my problem for a long time yesterday. This makes it all, you know"—she swallowed hard—"real."

I kept my face carefully void of the frustration I felt. "Lindsey, you're pregnant. You were pregnant yesterday, and the day before, and the day before that. You can't ignore the fact and hope it goes away."

She caught her lower lip in even, white teeth that reminded me she couldn't be too far out of braces, her gaze traveling back to the house. Then she heaved a decisive breath and nodded.

"Yeah, okay. Let's go."

We marched up to the back door, and as I reached for the handle Lindsey stopped one step behind me. I opened the storm door, and when she made no move to step past me I twisted the knob of the white wooden door and pushed it open. Then I stepped back and looked at her, my eyebrows high.

Squaring her shoulders, she stepped through the door.

"Hello," said a pleasant female voice.

I followed Lindsey inside and looked around. The room was bright and cheerfully full, with bookshelves lining two of the four walls and framed pictures of giant colorful flowers on the other two. A pleasant citrus smell filled the air, and I saw a lighted jar candle on top of one of the bookshelves in front of a huge bulletin board with every square inch covered in snapshots. Though I wasn't standing close enough to examine them, I did see several close-up shots of smiling babies. In front of us was a cluttered desk. The young woman seated behind it had risen to her feet and was walking around it with her hand outstretched. Her hair shone with the warm reddish color that Mama has tried for years to find in a bottle, but this woman's red eyebrows and the spray of freckles across her nose told me hers was probably real. She couldn't have been much older than me, so I guessed her age at around twenty-five.

"My name is Amber," she said with a welcoming smile.

Lindsey hesitated for a fraction of a second before taking the woman's hand. "Lindsey."

"Hello, Lindsey, it's nice to meet you." The woman turned toward me. "And you are?"

I was quick to take the hand she thrust at me, aware that Lindsey stood watching and nervously chewing on her lip. "I'm Mayla. Nice to meet you."

"Mayla, what a pretty name. Welcome to the Women's Center. What can I do for you ladies today?"

I hesitated, waiting for Lindsey to speak up. She cast a panicky look my way, and I could see she had frozen.

I smiled awkwardly at Amber. "We're here to learn about the options available for an unwanted pregnancy."

Amber responded smoothly, not batting an eyelid in Lindsey's direction. "I can help you with that. That's what we do here. How about if I give you a little tour before we sit down and talk?"

I nodded, relieved at her matter-of-fact manner.

"Good, follow me through here." She led us through a doorway on our left where we stepped into another office, this one much smaller and the desk less cluttered. "Our volunteers use this office to answer the phones and meet with clients," she explained.

We followed her through another door into a similar office and then down a little hallway past a bathroom. Then we arrived at another open doorway. Inside, an older woman sat behind a bigger desk, a telephone held to her ear. A window in that office looked out onto the front porch, and I caught sight of the swing swaying in a light breeze. Amber stuck her head through the doorway to catch the woman's attention.

"Hold on a minute, Margaret." The woman cupped her hand over the mouthpiece and stood up behind the desk, smiling toward us. "Hello."

"Sally, this is Mayla and Lindsey. I'm giving them a tour." She turned to us. "This is Sally Travis, the director of the center."

"It's nice to meet you," Sally said from where she stood tethered to the desk by the phone cord. "When you're finished with the tour, I'll be happy to answer any questions you have."

"Nice to meet you," Lindsey mumbled, looking nervously down the hallway.

I smiled and nodded, then turned to follow Amber as she continued through another doorway.

"We're really quite proud of this house," Amber told us as we walked through what had once been the living room and now held a couch and a couple of big, overstuffed easy chairs. "The center opened over twenty years ago, and at that time was located in a deserted drugstore in an old strip mall. About five years ago, a patron donated this house, and we've been slowly fixing it up ever since. Still a lot of work to do, but it's coming along. Watch your step here."

We followed her down a set of narrow stairs to a huge basement with old-fashioned fake wood paneling tacked over cement walls. The place was stuffed full with racks of clothing and overflowing boxes piled along the back wall. On the left side were deep shelves made of wide planks and concrete blocks and covered in all sorts of things from children's car seats to pots and pans.

"We store donations down here," Amber explained, "so if our clients need anything, they can get it. Through that door are washers and dryers where we wash all the donated baby and maternity clothing when it comes in."

I looked around the room. "You must do a lot of laundry."

Amber laughed. "We do, and a lot of mending, too. But thankfully, we have lots of volunteers, and our clients do most of the work themselves. During some of the group sessions, we all sit around a pile of torn clothing with sewing boxes open beside us, mending while we talk."

"Group sessions?" Lindsey asked. "What are those?"

"That's one of the services we offer. Most of our clients find it helpful to talk to others who are in a similar situation, and the support they draw from one another is invaluable. We establish the groups by age, and we also have sessions where you can talk to someone one-on-one."

"Talk about what?" Lindsey shot me a suspicious glare before turning her attention to Amber, her eyelids narrowed to mere slits. I suspected she had just realized that this was no abortion clinic.

"All sorts of things," Amber answered calmly. "We talk with women who find themselves in an unplanned pregnancy situation about their options and about the feelings they're going to experience with each one. We partner with them throughout the pregnancy and help them find the resources they need—things like medical referrals, or adoption agencies, or private adoption attorneys, or housing facilities, whatever. And we also offer post-abortion counseling for women who have chosen that route." Lindsey relaxed a fraction at that. "But our volunteers aren't therapists or even trained as counselors, for the most part. We do receive training in crisis counseling, and most of us are former clients ourselves. Like me."

I could almost see Lindsey's mind working as Amber listed the services this center had to offer. "Do you do abortions here?"

Amber countered the question unexpectedly with a direct one of her own. "Are you pregnant, Lindsey?"

The question took Lindsey by surprise. She opened her mouth to answer, then shut it again. Turning away from us, she looked toward the back wall while Amber threw a knowing glance in my direction.

Just as I was beginning to get impatient, Lindsey turned back to us, and my irritation melted away. Tears glittered in her eyes as she nodded. In the next moment, she threw her arms around Amber and dissolved into a sobbing mess.

I am uncomfortable around hysterically crying people, but Amber didn't seem to have that problem. She comforted Lindsey like it was the most natural thing in the world to have a sobbing teenager wiping snot all over her shoulder. Heck, maybe for her it was. While I stood feeling awkward and wondering if I should pat Lindsey on the back or something, Amber caught my eye and nodded toward the shelves. I saw a box of Kleenex there and rushed to grab it, glad for something to do.

When the torrent of tears finally slowed and Lindsey had pushed away to blow her nose, Amber said, "Why don't we go upstairs where we can sit and talk?"

Lindsey nodded and followed Amber up the stairs. She did not look at me, and I trailed along behind them feeling like an outsider. At the top of the stairs, Amber led us through the kitchen, pausing to open the refrigerator.

"Mayla, you can sit in here while Lindsey and I talk. Help yourself to water or juice, and there are some magazines in that rack over there."

Lindsey threw me a panicked look. "Can't she come with us?"

I didn't know whether to feel relieved or apprehensive. On the one hand, I wanted to hear what Amber had to say. But Lindsey seemed to take the opposite side of any argument we found ourselves in, and we certainly weren't in agreement on this one.

My uncertainty must have shown on my face, because Amber gave me a reassuring smile. "Of course she can."

Amber took three bottles of spring water from the refrigerator and led us into the living room, closing the door for privacy. Lindsey sat on the couch, and Amber sat beside her, leaving me to take one of the chairs beside a sealed fireplace.

Setting a bottle of water on the coffee table before each of us, Amber relaxed against the side of the couch, turned slightly on the cushion so she faced Lindsey.

"Before we begin, would you mind if I lead us in prayer?"

Lindsey sat upright, startled. She glanced at me before nodding.

Amber closed her eyes, and I did, too. "Father, I thank You for bringing Lindsey and Mayla here today. I pray that You will guide our conversation and our feelings, and that You will give Lindsey the wisdom she needs to make her decision. I know how much You love her, Lord, and I ask that You'll let her feel that love as we talk today. In Jesus's name, amen."

"Amen," I echoed.

Amber smiled at Lindsey, whose expression had become wary. Clearly, she hadn't expected to be prayed for.

"Before we begin, would you like to take a pregnancy test? We provide them free of charge."

Lindsey shook her head. "I've done three already."

"Okay, and do you know how far along you are?"

Lindsey nodded. "I know exactly when it happened." Her voice trembled. "December 22, after the Christmas dance."

In a soft voice, Amber asked the question I wanted to ask myself. "Was that your first time?"

A fresh wave of tears flooded Lindsey's eyes as, swallowing hard, she nodded again.

Amber patted her hand. "You'd be surprised how often girls get pregnant during their first encounter. That's because it normally isn't planned, so they don't take precautions. That's what happened to me."

I leaned forward in my chair, ready to hear her story. I had noticed in the basement that she called herself a former client and wondered what was behind that comment. Lindsey, still wearing a guarded expression, watched Amber's face closely.

"I was fifteen and had dated the guy for about a year. We didn't plan for anything to happen that night." She paused, then went on with a wry twist to her lips. "At least, I didn't. But one thing led to another, and a month later, I realized I was pregnant. My parents had always been really strict, and I was terrified to tell them. I felt abortion was the only possible choice."

Lindsey shot an unreadable glance toward me, then looked back at Amber. "Listen," she said, her voice suddenly firm, "you're being really nice to me and all that, but I've made up my mind. I'm going to have an abortion."

Her jaw jutted forward, daring Amber to argue with her. My fingernails bit into the palms of my hands, and I clenched my teeth as tightly as my fists to keep from screaming at her. Honestly, that kid was as hardheaded as they come. How Amber maintained her composure, I didn't know. But she did. She answered in the same calm voice.

"There are other options I wish you would consider before you make a decision."

"You don't understand." Lindsey's eyes flashed an accusation across the room at me, as though this was all somehow my fault. "This will ruin my life. No volleyball scholarship, no college, all my plans down the toilet." A touch of anger crept into her voice. "Getting an abortion is my choice, isn't it?"

Amber answered quietly. "Yes, it is your choice. And it was mine, too."

I nearly wrenched my neck jerking my head to stare at her.

Amber nodded, sitting very still and holding Lindsey's gaze in hers. "I decided to take the easy way out. I found an abortion clinic right here in town. They're not hard to find. My boyfriend drove me down there, but he couldn't stay." She gave a silent snort of laughter. "He had to leave to get to football practice.

"I sat in a waiting room with six other girls for what seemed like hours. Three of us were there alone, but the others had friends or boyfriends with them. We were all terrified and didn't talk to each other. I remember one girl hugged a teddy bear and cried. They called us back one at a time, just like at the doctor's office. Everything was very clean. They put me in an examining room, and a woman came in to talk to me. She said she was a counselor, but I don't remember what she said other than asking if I knew what I was doing. She didn't stay long, but she gave me half a Valium before she left.

"The procedure itself only took a few minutes. I never even knew the doctor's name. He came in, performed the abortion, and then left. It was very uncomfortable but not unbearable. I lay there for the next thirty minutes crying because I was so lonely, until a nurse came to examine me and told me I could leave. I took the bus home."

She stopped speaking and looked down at her hands. I could hear both of them breathe in the silence and tried to sit absolutely still so as not to break into this moment Amber was sharing with Lindsey.

"They don't tell you what happens after an abortion," she said, looking up. "They don't tell you about post-abortion syndrome, or the guilt, or the anger. They don't tell you how devastating it is to grieve when you can't tell anyone why you're grieving."

Lindsey pressed the tissue against her eyes as though to hide from Amber's direct stare. Her quiet sobs floated gently on the silence like feathers on a pond.

When Amber spoke again, her voice was almost a whisper. "God knows all about your plans, Lindsey. He has plans for you, too. The Bible says His plans are to give you hope and a future better than anything you can imagine. He's not going to take that future away from you because you've made a mistake. He loves you too much for that."

"I know," Lindsey gulped, "but you don't understand. If I don't have an abortion, everything is ruined. Everything. My parents . . . my father . . ."

Sobs overtook her, and she buried her face in her hands. Because I had talked to her father, I knew a little about her concern. I couldn't imagine having to tell Mr. Markham something he didn't want to hear, something he wouldn't approve of.

"I'll tell you what," Amber said after Lindsey had cried for a few minutes. "I have all kinds of literature I can give you, and I can put you in touch with other people who've been in your situation, people who chose all of the different options. You owe it to yourself to check them all out, Lindsey. But first, I have a question for you. Would you like to see your baby?"

Lindsey looked up. Her eyes were red and swollen, and her breath came in shuddering heaves. She threw a glance across the room at me before looking back at Amber.

She nodded.

"Good!" Amber grinned. "Come with me."

We followed her to a room beyond the kitchen, one we hadn't seen before. Inside was an examining table just like a doctor's office, and beside it an odd-looking machine with a screen, like a little television set. Amber looked at Lindsey's shorts—which were mine—with a critical eye. Then she crossed to a cabinet on the far wall and drew out a white sheet.

"You'll need to slip those shorts off, but you can leave your underwear on. Then just sit up on the table, and Sally will be right in." She glanced at me. "Do you want Mayla to stay?"

Lindsey looked at me, and I held my breath. I hoped she wasn't about to kick me out of the room just when things were going to get interesting. But she nodded, and I exhaled with relief, smiling.

Amber smiled, too. "I'll be right back." She closed the door behind her.

I walked over to check out the ultrasound machine. "This is way cool. I've seen them on television, but never in person."

"I'm glad you're enjoying yourself," Lindsey said dryly.

She unzipped the shorts and pulled them off over her sneakers, handing them to me before she hopped up on the table and covered herself with the sheet. I folded the shorts and draped them over my arm, still looking at all the dials and gadgets on the ultrasound machine.

A quiet tap sounded on the door. "Ready in there?"

"Ready," answered Lindsey, smoothing the sheet over her legs.

The older woman we had met earlier entered, followed by Amber. She gave us a wide, friendly smile and covered the space between the door and Lindsey in two strides, her hand outstretched.

"Sorry for the phone call earlier. I'm sure Amber did a good job showing off our center. Was she able to answer all your questions?"

"Yes, ma'am," Lindsey said, shaking her hand.

Sally turned to me and shook my hand, too. I liked her immediately. She had a wide, toothy smile with just a touch of mischief at the corners of her lips. She wasn't as old as I had originally guessed, perhaps a few years older than Mama, and slender like Aunt Louise. Her hair was as gray as Grandmother's, though, and I wondered if she had grayed prematurely. And her glasses made her look older at first glance. She wore them low on the bridge of her nose and tilted her chin upward to look through them. Her smooth skin was free of wrinkles.

"Besides being the director here," Amber told us, "Sally is also a nurse practitioner, so she does the ultrasounds and examinations."

Sally eyed Lindsey though her glasses. "All right, Lindsey, lie back, and I'm going to put some warm gel on your tummy. Don't worry, it wipes right off. Amber tells me you're around nine weeks along?"

Lindsey nodded.

"Take a look at this then." Sally went to a cabinet and took something out. She handed Lindsey a tiny pink baby doll, soft and pliable. "This is what a baby looks like at eight weeks, so yours is a little bigger."

While Sally seated herself on a rolling stool before the ultrasound machine, Lindsey peered at the miniature person in the palm of her hand, her eyes wide. "It looks like a real baby already."

Sally laughed. "She *is* a real baby. She has ten toes and ten fingers, a nose and mouth, and all her internal organs have started developing. Now let's see if we can find her. Sometimes babies are shy and try to hide from us, the little buggers."

She folded the sheet down to expose Lindsey's stomach, then took up a squirt bottle and squeezed out a thick squiggly line of clear gel. Picking up a wand attached by a curly cord to the machine, she ran it across the gel on Lindsey's tummy, all of us watching the small television screen.

All I could see were gray splotches and black blobs. Disappointed, I squinted the way I would to look at one of those illusion pictures, trying to find anything that looked like a baby in there. Sally pressed a button and the image on the screen froze.

"There's the placenta," she said, pointing to a dark spot. "Nice and high, so that looks good."

She pressed another button and the image started shifting this way and that as she moved the wand across Lindsey's stomach. We all stared intently at the screen. A glance at Lindsey's face told me she was just as confused by the gray blobs as I was.

"I don't see anything," I finally confessed.

Amber laughed. "This machine isn't one of the fancy 3-D machines, so the picture isn't very clear. But don't worry; you'll see the baby in a minute."

Sally, moving the wand back and forth in the gel, seemed unconcerned. "Now, where is that little . . . ah! Here you are. Lindsey, meet your baby."

Lindsey and I watched, fascinated, as Sally traced the baby's outline on the screen with her finger. Suddenly, I saw it. The baby's head and body came into focus for me, and I heard Lindsey gasp as she saw it, too. In the chest, we saw a rapidly beating heart, and as we watched, one tiny arm moved in an arc as though the baby were swimming.

A verse popped into my mind, and I whispered in an awed voice,

"For you created my inmost being; you knit me together in my mother's womb."

To my surprise, Lindsey reached out and grabbed my hand.

"Can you tell if it's a boy or a girl?" she whispered to Sally, watching her baby's heart beat.

Sally shook her head. "It's a little early for that, at least with this equipment. In another few weeks we can, though."

Enthralled, Lindsey could not tear her eyes away from the screen. Neither could I. I was seeing God's miracle of life right there on the screen in front of me. As we watched, the baby seemed to move its little body like a jackknife diver and gave a gigantic leap.

Sally laughed. "He's an active one, all right."

She twisted the wand again and then pressed the button to freeze the screen just as the baby turned sideways. The image on the screen was a perfect shot of a tiny baby in silhouette. Sally pressed another button and a Polaroid picture popped out of a slot. She pulled the film out and handed it to Amber, who waved it back and forth, waiting for the image to develop.

Sally winked at Lindsey. "A little souvenir to take with you."

She reached up to flip the ultrasound machine off, then wiped Lindsey's belly with a white washcloth. "You can get dressed. We'll be in the kitchen when you're ready."

When they had closed the door behind them, I handed Lindsey her shorts. She avoided my gaze, but I noticed that her face wore a troubled expression. Exercising more restraint than I normally do, I bit my tongue and didn't ask if she had changed her mind about the abortion. Instead, I stood quietly as she zipped her shorts and adjusted her T-shirt over the waistband.

"Ready?"

She nodded, and we stepped into the kitchen, where Sally and Amber stood waiting for us. Sally had a large white envelope in her hand, which she handed to Lindsey.

"We have prepared a lot of information you might want to read, brochures and pamphlets for various agencies, as well as a Q&A

document with the most common questions we've received over the years. If you have any questions at all, or even if you just need someone to talk to, our card is in there. We answer the phones 24-7."

Staring at the envelope in her hands, Lindsey said, "I don't live here, so . . ."

Sally smiled. "We have a toll-free number. I mean it. Any time."

Lindsey nodded, still avoiding eye contact with anyone, and turned toward the exit. I fell into step behind her, followed by Amber. Sally stayed where she was, watching Lindsey with a compassionate stare. I nodded good-bye, and she raised her hand in a silent farewell, giving a sad shake of her head.

We went through a doorway into Amber's office, the one we had entered an hour before. Stopping at the back door, Lindsey straightened her back before turning to Amber with an outstretched hand.

"Thank you for talking to me."

"My pleasure, Lindsey. Really. You'll be in my prayers. Oh, and here."

Amber held out the little black-and-white picture, now fully developed. Lindsey glanced at it, and I saw her bite her lower lip before dropping it inside the white envelope.

Amber held her hand out to me. "Thank you for coming with Lindsey, Mayla. I enjoyed meeting you."

"Thanks. You, too." I paused, wondering if I should ask a question that burned in my mind. I knew I would wonder about it for days if I didn't, so I plowed ahead. "You said before that you had been a client of the center. But the center doesn't do abortions."

She grinned, nodding. "I didn't get to finish my story, did I? I ended my first unplanned pregnancy with an abortion. But a year later, I got pregnant again. I sometimes wonder if I did it on purpose, sort of like trying to get a chance to make things right. I don't know, but that time I found the center."

She reached over the clutter on her desk and picked up a five-by-seven framed picture. Handing it to me with a proud grin, she said, "That's Ashley. She just turned six."

I looked into the laughing face of a gorgeous little red-headed girl with sparkling green eyes and the same spray of freckles across her nose as her mother. Lindsey stepped closer to peer over my shoulder.

"She's beautiful," I told Amber, meaning it.

She nodded and flashed a toothy smile. "I know." She shifted her gaze to lock with Lindsey's. "I haven't had an easy time, but she's worth everything I've gone through."

With another long stare at the picture, Lindsey turned and walked through the door. I handed the photo back to Amber and followed, aware that Amber stood at the back door watching us leave.

Lindsey was silent in the car on the way back to Grandmother's house. I wanted to ask what she was thinking, but she was so distant I didn't disturb her. Instead, I prayed silently, asking the Lord to guide her to the right decision.

She didn't speak until we turned onto Grandmother's street. Then, throwing a furious glare at me, she spat, "That was a dirty trick, Mayla."

Stunned, I turned my head to give her an open-mouthed stare. "What are you talking about?"

"Watch where you're going," she snapped, and I jerked the car back onto the road, away from the mailbox I had almost hit. "You told me you were taking me to an abortion clinic, and then you took me to a place where you knew they were going to shove religion down my throat."

I could not believe what I was hearing. Pulling the car over to the side of the road, I shoved the shifter into Park and turned in my seat.

"First of all, I never said I was taking you to an abortion clinic."

"Yes, you did!"

"Did not!" I snapped my mouth shut and drew a quick breath. I refused to be drawn into a childish argument. I went on in a carefully level tone. "I told you I was taking you to a clinic and that I wanted to make sure you considered all the options."

"You knew exactly what that place was."

"That is true," I admitted, and she turned away from me with a jerk, folding her arms tightly across her chest. "But I was with you the whole time, and no one tried to shove religion down your throat. Not that it wouldn't do you a world of good."

She turned to me, her eyes blazing. "What is that supposed to mean?"

"Just that you're considering committing murder on an innocent life, and if you were a Christian, you would know you can't do that!"

"I'll have you know I became a Christian three years ago. I was baptized and everything. But that has nothing to do with this situation."

I slapped the steering wheel and threw myself back against the seat. "How can you say that? Being a Christian has everything to do with your decision, Lindsey."

Tears sprang to her eyes, and she pierced me with a reproachful look. "I wish you would quit preaching at me long enough to help me."

Before I could come up with an answer, Lindsey opened the door and got out of the car, slamming it behind her. I sat in the driver's seat, watching her stomp down the street.

"Lord, what am I doing wrong?" I nearly shouted toward the roof of the car. "Nothing I say or do seems to get through to that girl!"

Chapter 13

Grandmother sat in a wingback chair in the living room leafing through a magazine when I came into the house. I raised my eyebrows in a silent question, and she nodded toward the bedroom. A peek down the hallway showed me a closed door.

"Not a successful visit?" Grandmother asked quietly.

I threw myself onto the couch. "Not exactly."

She gave a slight shrug. "At least she hasn't done anything yet. She just needs more time and our support. She'll make the right decision in her own time."

Frustrated, I sat back against the couch with force. "But what if she doesn't? What if she goes through with the abortion?"

Grandmother turned her head with a speculative look down the hallway. "I don't think she will. I could be wrong, of course, but if she really wanted to have an abortion, she would have done it already. She wouldn't have come looking for you."

Considering that, I studied the old woman sitting in the chair across the room from me more closely. She sat serenely, her hair perfectly in order and a hint of blush on her cheekbones that matched her lipstick.

"You certainly are taking this whole thing in stride," I told her. "Some women of your generation would be horrified to have a pregnant teenager show up on their doorstep."

"I learned a long time ago that some situations are easier to control than others. Sometimes you have to sit back and wait for an opportunity to push things toward the outcome you want, but you can't force them. You must be patient. Getting yourself all worked up will only give you an ulcer."

"Or angina," I commented.

She gave me a sharp look. Suddenly her forehead cleared. "Oh, I forgot to tell you. You got a phone call while you were out."

"I did?" I'd had my cell phone with me the whole time. "Who was it?"

Grandmother shrugged, closing the magazine. "He didn't say. Just that he was a friend of yours and would call back. A polite young man, that's all I know."

Was it Paul? Had he actually called my grandmother's house looking for me? My pulse sped at the thought. I couldn't think of a single other "polite young man" who would have any reason to call me or who would know where I was. Paul could have gotten Grandmother's phone number from Mama, I supposed. But why would he call the house phone instead of my cell?

Grandmother stood. "I need to figure out what we're having for supper before church." She looked at me. "Are you going to Bible study with us?"

"Sure, I'd like that."

I remembered Reverend Thomas and his young adult Bible study and wondered if I could persuade Lindsey to go. I doubted it, but I could try. As I tagged after Grandmother into the kitchen, something niggled at the back of my mind. I felt like something had been left unsaid, something about finding yourself in a situation you can't control. But the thought never did more than niggle before getting shoved aside, because at the front of my mind was a burning question that took more than its fair share of attention.

Had Paul finally softened enough to call me?

❀ ❀ ❀

While Grandmother readied a tray of pork chops to go into the oven later that afternoon, I went into the bedroom for my laptop. Lindsey lay on the bed, facing the wall, pretending to be asleep. Biting my lip, I decided to leave her to her pretend nap. I couldn't think of a thing to say to her anyway.

The list of new e-mail proved disappointing. Nothing from Paul and only one from Mama. Opening it, I cringed when I saw what she had written.

> Mayla, you have not called me back like you promised. I am thinking all sorts of terrible things up here, like you and Lindsey are in some kind of trouble, or you drowned in the ocean, or you are getting mixed up with that man with the pierced ear, or SHE is filling your head with lies. (You know who I mean.) I don't want to call because I don't want to bother you on your vacation, but if you have a minute, please call me so I know you are okay. Or at least send me an e-mail.
> Love,
> Mama

Guilt stabbed at me. I had not even thought of Mama for days, not since Monday when she found out Lindsey was here with me. I had promised to call her back that night but never did.

My inbox held nothing else interesting, so I shut it down and slid the laptop back into its case. Taking my cell phone, I went through the family room and out to the back porch to sit in one of the lawn chairs. I kicked off my sandals and stretched out. The afternoon sunshine warmed my skin as I speed-dialed Mama's number.

"Hello?"

"Mama, it's me," I said, then went on in a rush. "I'm so sorry I didn't call you sooner. Monday night, everything was confused because Lindsey was here, and yesterday we went to SeaWorld, and then last night, Grandmother wasn't feeling well so I was worried about her, and then today we cleaned all—"

"Mayla," she interrupted, "I understand. You're busy down there."

I heard relief in her voice and a touch of hurt, too. "Mama, I'm never too busy for you. You're the most important person in my life next to Jesus; you know that."

That must have brought a smile to her face, because she sounded happier when she asked, "So how's Lindsey?"

I sighed. "She's okay, I guess. But moody. Let me ask you a question, Mama. Was I really annoying when I was a teenager?"

"Sure you were, but you've almost gotten over it now." I couldn't help but laugh with her. "No matter what's bothering that girl, she's got a whole bunch of people praying for her up here."

"That makes me feel better, but I don't think it means much to her."

"She's a Christian, ain't she? Her folks are churchgoing people, and they told me she goes with them."

"As you well know, not everyone who goes to church is a Christian," I told her. "And not every Christian has a close walk with the Lord."

"True, but sometimes a crisis can make people snuggle up right close to Him. I think that's happening to Sandra and Alexander."

"Really?" I shook my head, completely unable to think of critical, self-centered Mr. Markham having a relationship with the Lord. "What makes you think so?"

"Because we're talking every day. I been looking up encouraging Bible verses, and they like hearing the Word spoken over Lindsey. I told 'em how I spoke the Word over you for years 'till you finally came to the Lord." I winced. I'm sure that conversation was interesting. "And since they found out you're a Christian, they're resting easier, knowing you're gonna take care of things while she's down there."

I sat straight up and gulped. "They trust *me?*"

"A'course they do," Mama chuckled. "You're a child of God, Mayla, and they know Lindsey looks up to you. Otherwise she wouldn't have gone all the way to Florida chasing after you. And," she added with no modesty at all, "they like me, and if I say you're a good girl, they believe it.

"And now," she went on with a smooth change of subject, "tell me about this Robert person. Have you seen him again?"

"No." I hesitated. I felt guilty leading Mama on about Reverend Thomas, but I didn't want to let Paul off the hook about him just yet, and I knew she was feeding him whatever scraps of information I let drop. "But tonight is when we planned to see each other again."

"Hmmmm. Well, I can tell you right now, my Tuesday night ladies don't think much of a preacher with an earring. And Pastor Paul don't trust him, neither."

I sucked in a breath, then exhaled it slowly, surprised not to see steam jutting from my nostrils. How dare that man express his opinion about *my* date to *my* mother! I could feel my anger building, and my temples begin to throb. "Pastor Paul doesn't get a vote."

Unaware that my eyeballs were getting ready to explode on this end of the phone, Mama delivered a final word of caution. "Just you keep your head about you down there." She paused, then went on evenly. "And how's everyone else?"

I knew who she meant. "Grandmother's okay. But she has angina, so sometimes she has these mini heart attacks that are really scary."

I paused, wondering if I should mention my suspicions about Grandmother faking her attacks. But before I could go on, Mama spoke in a rush.

"Oh, there's the neighbor boy just finished with shoveling my sidewalk. I've got to go, baby, and get him some hot chocolate to drink while I write out the check. Love you."

"Love you too, Mama. Bye."

"Call me again," she ordered before hanging up.

I tossed my cell phone onto the braided plastic between my bare feet, frustrated. I had not gotten a chance to ask Mama if she had given Grandmother's phone number to Paul. Just thinking of him made my teeth clench. How dare that man! Well, if it was him who called, he would call back. And when he did, would I have an earful for him.

❋ ❋ ❋

I lay for a long time in the warm sun, willing my anger to ooze away with the gentle breeze that rustled the leaves of Grandmother's orange trees, and I calmed down enough that I actually dozed off. The door opened behind me, startling me awake, and Grandmother came outside and handed me a glass of sweet tea. She sat in the chair next to mine and took a sip from her own glass. I noticed she had changed into a plaid straight skirt, tan blouse, and low-heeled tan pumps. She stretched her stocking-covered legs out on the lawn chair and tilted her face toward the sun, closing her eyes with a sigh.

"Sometimes I have a nap around this time of the afternoon."

"Today's a good day for a nap," I answered. "Both Lindsey and I are taking advantage of it."

She turned her head to look at me with one open eye. "Lindsey's not sleeping."

"She's not?"

She shook her head. "I popped in a few minutes ago to check on her, and she's sitting on the bed reading through a stack of brochures."

"Really?" Maybe there was reason to hope after all.

Grandmother nodded and looked out into the yard. "When Louise and Charles were little, I used to sit in this very spot and watch them play in the grass. Louise would bring her Barbie dolls outside and make Charles play with her." A faraway smile hovered around her lips. "He loved her so much he would do anything she asked, even play Barbies."

I followed her gaze out into the yard, imagining a boy and a girl playing in the shade of the tree in the corner. "Tell me about when Daddy was a little boy."

Her smile widened, and she settled herself more comfortably in the chair. I did the same, and listened, entranced, to her memories of my father. As she painted picture after picture of her precocious little boy, I realized I could listen to her stories all day long. Though I thought I had come to Florida to escape the cold Kentucky winter, I knew this was the real reason. I wanted, no *needed* to spend time learning about my family. And Grandmother seemed prepared to satisfy that desire on this drowsy Wednesday afternoon.

Lindsey and I were helping Grandmother put the finishing touches on dinner at five forty when Aunt Louise got home from work. Lindsey moved around the kitchen quietly, every so often casting a sullen glance my way that I refused to acknowledge.

She seemed to know her way around a kitchen, which was more than I could claim. Still, even I can wash lettuce, once Grandmother smacked it on the counter and gouged the core out. Then she showed me how to break it into bite-sized pieces using my hands—never a knife, she insisted. I had a respectable-looking salad going when the front door opened and Aunt Louise stepped into the kitchen.

"Hello." She smiled pleasantly and hung her purse on the back of a chair.

"Hey. How was your day?" I asked, up to my elbows in tomato guts.

She came over to the sink and gave my shoulders a cautious squeeze, careful not to get anything gooey on her clothes. She looked very chic in a navy blue suit and a lime green silk blouse that complimented her honey-colored hair. *Mama really should get some newer-looking clothes,* I thought. *She could look as good as Aunt Louise with a little effort.* I suppressed a grin at the thought of Aunt Louise wearing one of Mama's floral-print church dresses.

"The same as every other work day." She picked up the stack of mail on the edge of the counter and flipped through the envelopes. "And yours? Did you do anything interesting today?"

Her gaze slipped briefly to Lindsey before giving me a look loaded with questions.

I waggled my eyebrows and gave a very slight nod, hoping she got the message that I'd tell her about it later. "We spent the morning cleaning, and then relaxed in the sun all afternoon."

She looked at me through narrowed eyelids. "I can tell. You've burned your nose."

I fingered the tip of my nose gingerly, wincing. "Yeah, I know. My legs, too."

Grandmother gave a final stir to the green beans and turned from the stove to announce, "Dinner will be ready in five minutes."

Aunt Louise nodded. "I'm going to get changed. Oh, and before I forget—" She turned to me. "Are you going to church with us to-night?" With a quick glance at Lindsey, I nodded. Aunt Louise went on brightly. "Good. After our Bible study I'm going out with a friend for ice cream, so if you can drive Mother home, I'd appreciate it."

She left the room quickly, as though she had just dropped a bomb and didn't want to wait around for the fallout. I cast a cautious glance toward Grandmother. Her eyes were wide, and her lips parted in surprise. Emotions played across her face as she stared at the empty doorway where her daughter had stood a moment before. Her expression reminded me of Mama's the first time she saw me with my labret stud. Then I saw Grandmother's eyelids narrow before she turned her back on me to give the green beans one more vicious stir, and in that fraction of a second, I could almost hear her thinking, *We'll see about that.*

She turned the burner on the stove to its lowest setting and left the room without another word, heading through the family room to her bedroom beyond. Lindsey and I exchanged glances before continuing with our individual supper chores. The atmosphere in the little house seemed to thicken like when the air gets heavier on an early spring evening right before a thunderstorm hits. Maybe I had too active an imagination, but as I chopped the final chunk of tomato, I had a feeling Aunt Louise wouldn't be going for ice cream that night, after all.

Ten minutes later, Aunt Louise returned to the kitchen dressed in slacks, loafers, and a short-sleeved sweater. She glanced through the doorway into the family room. "Where's Mother?"

"In her bedroom." I kept my voice carefully empty of any of the opinions that spun through my mind.

She nodded and went that way, and I was not surprised a moment later to hear her exclaim in a voice full of fear, "Mother!"

Silverware clattered to the table as Lindsey and I dropped what we were doing and ran after her. Grandmother lay on her side on the floor at the foot of her bed, her face pale, and her breath coming in short gasps. Aunt Louise knelt beside her, looking up to throw me a panicked glance as we entered the room.

"Grab that medicine bottle on her bedside table," she ordered, pointing.

I did and twisted the top off of the bottle of tiny white pills before handing it to her. I dropped to my knees beside her, searching Grandmother's face. Doubt tugged at me as I saw her slack jaw and heard her labored breathing. This did not look like a faked attack. It looked like the real thing.

Aunt Louise grasped a pill between her thumb and forefinger and held it in front of Grandmother's lips. "Mother," she said in a stern voice. "Open your mouth."

Grandmother shook her head weakly.

"Mother you are going to take this pill, and I mean it. Open your mouth."

"I just need to rest a moment," Grandmother said, her voice faint. "Let me lie here a while, and I'll be fine."

"If you don't take the pill," Aunt Louise told her, "I am going to call 911."

There was a brief pause before Grandmother finally opened her mouth. Aunt Louise breathed a sigh of relief.

"Good. Now hold this under your tongue."

We all hovered anxiously, listening as Grandmother's breathing slowed and, after what seemed like hours, returned to a normal, if shallow, pace.

"I'd like to get up now," she said, opening her eyes.

Aunt Louise and I each slipped a hand beneath an arm and helped her into a sitting position. She sat on the floor, leaning heavily against the footboard of her bed with her eyes closed. Her forehead creased, and she spoke in a cross voice.

"I'm dizzy. Those pills always make me dizzy."

"That's because they open your blood vessels and increase the blood flow to your heart."

"They give me a headache, too," she complained.

Aunt Louise glanced at me with a relieved smile that made my tension begin to ease. "That's better than a heart attack."

Grandmother grumbled, "Sometimes I wonder." She opened her eyes and looked at me. "Did someone remember to turn off the oven?"

"I'll do it," Lindsey volunteered, then whirled and practically ran out of the room.

I stood. "I'll help her." I paused, looking down at her. "Are you sure you're all right?"

She managed a weak smile and a nod. "I'll be fine."

In the kitchen, I found Lindsey standing over the stove, stirring the green beans absently.

"You okay?" I asked, concerned by her worried expression.

She nodded, then looked up at me with wide eyes. "I've never seen anything like that before. I was about ready to call an ambulance. I thought she was going to die."

"Me, too." I felt a rush of guilt. I had known that attack was coming, had predicted it as soon as Aunt Louise told us about her plans for the evening. And sure enough, looking at Aunt Louise's face in the bedroom as she knelt over her mother, I was positive there was no way she was going anywhere tonight.

But Grandmother's symptoms had been so terrifyingly real, her collapse so dramatic. That couldn't possibly have been a fake attack. Could it?

Dinner, when we finally sat down with TV trays in the family room, was overcooked. We had turned off the oven but left the pork chops inside, and the extra forty minutes in the heat cooked them to pieces, literally. Grandmother had laid them on top of a dish of cornbread stuffing and covered them with gravy, and the meat disintegrated as we dished up big gooey spoonfuls of the stuff. The green beans were mushy, too. But at least the salad was good. I noticed with a touch of pride that Lindsey had two helpings.

Grandmother sat in her recliner and picked at her food listlessly. She was too weak from her episode to even think about going to Bible study, and I could tell Aunt Louise had resigned herself to staying home, too. Grandmother refused the offer of aspirin for her headache, grouching that it wouldn't help. Caught up in her own thoughts, she ignored Pat and Vanna on television completely. Lindsey did too, and ate her dinner silently. Aunt Louise stared at the television as she chewed, but I doubted if she was paying much attention. We were a pretty introspective group that night.

We had nearly finished eating when the doorbell rang.

"I wonder who that is," Aunt Louise said, pushing her tray back and leaving the room.

We heard a man's voice in the hallway, but not Bill the electrician's. Though I couldn't hear the words spoken in response to Aunt Louise's questions, the tone sounded familiar. That was someone I knew, someone from home. Realizing with a start whose voice it was, I jerked my head up at the same moment Aunt Louise led Stuart Hortenbury into the room.

"Mayla, look who's here," Aunt Louise announced, gesturing toward Stuart as though presenting me with a tremendous surprise.

And she was. My jaw dropped open wide enough to shove an orange into my mouth as Stuart waltzed into the room, a devilish glint in his eyes when he looked at me. He went straight to my grandmother and held out his hand.

"Hello, Mrs. Strong, I'm Stuart Hortenbury. We spoke on the phone earlier today."

Grandmother sat a little straighter in the recliner, actually perking up enough to flash a flirtatious dimple as Stuart reached out and grabbed her hand. I swear I saw her blush when he executed an exaggerated courtly bow over it.

"It's nice to meet you, Mr. Hortenbury," she said in the perfect imitation of a southern belle greeting a potential beau.

Stuart waved his hand expansively. "Oh, please, call me Stuart. I won't answer to anything else." He turned and took a step toward Lindsey with an outstretched hand. "Hello?"

She glanced my way before extending her hand hesitantly across her tray. "Hello, I'm Lindsey Markham."

Stuart froze, his eyes flying wide open as a look of delight lit up his face. "Markham? You mean like Alex Markham's little sister?"

Lindsey brightened with surprise. "You knew my brother?"

"Baby girl," Stuart exclaimed, waving his arm dramatically in the air, "he was a dear friend. Come here and let me hug you."

Lindsey stood, and Stuart swept her into his arms, giving her a brotherly bear hug. Releasing her, he put his hands on his hips and turned to me.

"Why are you still sitting? Get over here, girlfriend!"

Stunned, I stood and stepped out from behind my TV tray to be swept into a hug. Stuart actually picked me up and whirled me around before setting my feet down on the carpet.

"Are you surprised to see me?" he asked, flourishing his arms wide.

I eyed him with a touch of apprehension. "Surprised doesn't begin to describe it. What are you doing here, Stuart?"

"I had a few vacation days I needed to use." His gaze swept the room to include everyone in his explanation. "I said to myself, if Mayla can spend a week lying around on the beach, then so can I! So I hopped in my car and drove right here. I got out of the wretched state hours before another winter storm was scheduled to hit." He shuddered expansively.

"You just hopped in your car and drove right here," I repeated dryly. "A thousand miles."

"Eight hundred and twenty-two," he corrected. "And I did it all at once. I left at five thirty this morning."

"My goodness," Grandmother exclaimed, "you must be exhausted. And hungry. Louise, fix Stuart a plate."

"Oh, no, ma'am." Stuart turned toward her. "I couldn't impose when I wasn't expected for dinner."

"Nonsense," Grandmother insisted. "I always make more than enough, so Louise has plenty of leftovers to take for lunch."

"Well . . ." Stuart inspected my plate. "It does smell delicious."

"Good." Grandmother nodded, satisfied. "Louise?"

"I'll do it," I said, giving Stuart a hard stare. "Come help me."

"Of course." He smiled sweetly at everyone as he followed me into the kitchen.

Once out of sight, I turned on him with a glare and whispered, "What are you doing here?"

"My life is in ruins, and it's all your fault," he hissed. "Why should you be down here vacationing in the sunshine while I'm suffering alone in the frozen north?"

I took a calming breath. "Listen, I know you're upset, but I don't have time for this right now. I'm down here to spend time with my grandmother, and first Lindsey shows up and now you. How did you find me, anyway?"

"The Internet. There are thirty-four Strongs listed in Orlando and only fifteen with a woman's name or an initial." He shrugged. "I started at the top of the list, and your grandmother answered the fourth call."

I had to admire his resourcefulness. "And how did you find the house?"

He rolled his eyes. "Duh. MapQuest." His shoulders drooped. "I really need to talk to you, Mayla. I won't stay long, I promise. I just don't want to be alone right now."

He stared dejectedly at the floor, and he really did look miserable. Even if he was the most infuriating person in the world, he was hurting.

I sighed. "All right, you can stay for dinner, and then we'll talk. But after that, you have to leave."

He smiled broadly. "Sure, Mayla. I was thinking I'd head over to Daytona and find a place on the beach to stay for a few days. The sea air will do me good."

Taking the plate I handed him, he loaded it with food and then followed me out into the family room. I set up the last TV tray and put him on the couch between me and Lindsey, and then we all watched him eat. And eat. And eat. He must not have stopped for food during his fourteen-hour drive, because he seemed determined to prove his claims that the meal was the most delicious he'd had in years. Grandmother eyed him with delight, and though her eyes still seemed dull with pain, I noticed that she looked livelier than before Stuart had arrived.

Aunt Louise, too, seemed to enjoy matching wits with him as they tried to beat each other with the correct questions to Alex Trebek's answers. Impressed, I watched them without joining in. I had no idea Stuart was so smart.

When he finally stopped eating, probably because there was not one scrap of food left for him to devour, Stuart impressed Grandmother by insisting on washing the dishes. She seemed so taken with him that she moved to a chair at the kitchen table so she could continue to be entertained by his antics.

And Stuart was certainly entertaining. Even I found myself laughing at his impersonations, especially when he did Dom Deluise as Captain Chaos. Aunt Louise laughed so hard her mascara smeared under her eyes, and the look on Lindsey's face was proof that he had succeeded in completely captivating her.

When the last dish had been put away, Stuart covered a gigantic yawn.

"Goodness, I'm tired," he said. "It's been a long time since Kentucky, and I think the drive is about to catch up with me."

"Where are you staying?" Aunt Louise asked. "Somewhere close, I hope."

"I don't know." Stuart turned to her. "Can you recommend an inexpensive hotel in the area?"

Grandmother exclaimed, "You don't have a place to stay? Well! You can just stay here." She gave a determined nod, as though the matter had been decided.

"Oh, I couldn't do that, Mrs. S.," he rushed to say at the exact moment I opened my mouth to say the same thing. "You've been too kind to me already, feeding me that delicious dinner and making me feel at home."

"There's no reason at all for you to spend good money on a hotel when we have two couches right here." She peered up at him. "As long as you don't mind sleeping on a couch."

I quickly interjected, "I'm sure Stuart doesn't want to—"

"I *love* sleeping on couches," he exclaimed. "Whenever I went to my own grandmother's house, she always made up the couch for me. But I really can't impose on you like that. A hotel is fine."

He gave her a look like a little boy insisting that he take the smallest piece of pie, knowing full well that his unselfishness would earn him the biggest. I almost snorted with laughter. No one could possibly be gullible enough to fall for that feeble protest.

Except my grandmother, apparently. "Nonsense! I won't hear another word about it. You'll stay here as long as you're in Florida."

He rushed forward to give her a grateful hug and delivered a smirk over her shoulder in my direction. "Just for that, I'll cook dinner for you tomorrow night. I'm a great cook. Just ask Mayla."

While Aunt Louise went down the hallway to the linen closet

and Lindsey showed Stuart the location of the bathroom, I helped Grandmother to her recliner in the family room.

"You don't seem pleased to have your friend stay the night," she commented. "Have you two had a tiff?"

I shook my head. "It's not that. I came down here to spend time with you, and first Lindsey shows up and now Stuart. We haven't been able to talk alone as much as I had hoped." I collapsed a TV tray and put it in the stand. "Plus, I'm worried that having all these people around will be too much for you."

"Don't worry about me." She gave a dismissive wave with her hand. "I'd rather have a house full of people than an empty one any day."

I gave a snort of laughter, reaching for another tray. "In that case, I hope you have a couple of sleeping bags."

"Why is that?"

I leveled her with a rueful look. "Because I have more friends back in Kentucky who haven't managed to make it down here yet. But judging by the way things are going, I'm sure they'll turn up sooner or later."

When the couch in the living room had been made up for Stuart and he had brought his stuff in from the car—and I had teased him about having a suitcase bigger than mine—we all trooped back out to the family room. Grandmother turned on the Discovery Channel, where we watched a pride of lions struggle to survive in the wild. Lindsey seemed to find it interesting. Stuart was asleep within ten minutes, his head leaning against the back of the couch.

Halfway through the lions' second messy meal of the evening, Aunt Louise stood.

"I think I'll take a walk." She spoke quietly, with a glance at Stuart snoozing in the corner.

I sat up. "Mind if I tag along?"

"I'd love the company."

"Take a flashlight," Grandmother advised. "It is dark out there."

I followed Aunt Louise through the kitchen, where she paused long enough to take a flashlight from a drawer. The night air was cool and pleasant after the warmth of the day. I guessed the temperature to be around seventy and spared a smug thought for Sylvia and the weather in Kentucky at that moment. We walked along the road toward the small lake at the end of Grandmother's street, which was well lit by streetlights.

"I don't think you need that flashlight." I nodded toward a tall light pole as we passed.

"No, but it's easier to do as she says." She heaved a heavy sigh. "You know, at work I'm competent and in complete control. But the minute I walk through that door, I become obedient little Louise again, doing whatever my mother says without thinking. Sometimes I feel like I'm two people."

I looked sideways at her. "I know how hard it must be on you, being the only one to take care of her."

She remained silent for a few steps, her gaze fixed on something far in the distance. Then she looked over at me with a sad smile. "You have no idea."

Ah, here was a woman who needed an ear. "Tell me about Bill," I said, hoping the request would open the right door.

It did. A genuine smile broke out on her face, and her eyes took on a dreamy, unfocused stare. "He is the most caring, compassionate man in the world. He's smart and funny and can talk to anyone. Well," she faltered and cast a brief glance backward, "almost anyone. And he knows the Bible better than anyone I've ever met. He teaches our Sunday school class one week every month."

"Is that where you met him?"

She nodded. "He moved here two years ago from Tampa, and from the first moment, I knew he was the man for me." Embarrassed, she stopped speaking.

"And he feels the same about you?" I prompted.

"Oh, yes!" Her eyes shone in the streetlight.

"So what are you waiting for? Why haven't you gotten married?" The look she gave me answered my question. "Ah. Grandmother."

"Mother can't stand Bill, though she has never spoken more than five words at a time to him. He doesn't understand why she is so much against him, but I tell him he hasn't done anything to make her dislike him. I'm the problem, not him. She's afraid if we marry I'll move away and she'll be alone."

"But all kids grow up and move away," I insisted. "That's normal. You have to do what makes you happy, Aunt Louise."

She shook her head sadly. "You've seen her, Mayla. What if she's alone when she has an attack like tonight? I can't risk that."

"She could have one while you're at work just as easily," I pointed out.

"But she doesn't. They're always in the evening."

"Listen," I said slowly, "don't you think the timing of these episodes is just a little too convenient? I mean, I've only been here a few days and I've noticed that she only has an attack when you say you want to do something on your own."

She nodded miserably. "I asked the doctor about that. They're brought on by stress. The thought of me having a relationship with someone else and leaving her is so terrifying to her that the stress brings on an angina attack." I was still pondering that when she went on in a near whisper, "I have to admit sometimes I think life will be so much easier when she's gone." She hurried on in a rush, "Not that I would ever wish anything to happen to her."

She looked at me, her eyes pleading with me to understand. I felt a rush of compassion for her. "Of course not. I'm sure those feelings are completely normal. You can't help but feel trapped."

Tears sprang to her eyes, which she quickly turned away to hide. We walked in silence for several yards before she spoke again.

"I want to show you something. Look over there."

She stopped walking and pointed to a house on the right side of the road. Though the deepening night made seeing difficult, I made out a white stucco home with dark shutters and a covered porch. Big citrus trees stood sentinel on each side of the front yard, and flowers lined a sidewalk curving from a driveway to the front door. A sign in the yard proclaimed PRIME PROPERTY FOR SALE—GREAT BUY!

Aunt Louise stood staring at the house with a wistful expression. "Bill and I have talked about how wonderful it would be if we could buy this house. It's just down the street from Mother, so we could be at her house in minutes if she needed us."

The look on her face was so full of longing my heart ached in sympathy. "I think you should. This would be perfect. Surely she couldn't complain if she knows you're only a few houses away. You should take matters into your own hands and make her accept your decision."

She stood silently, watching the house for a few more minutes before turning to look directly at me. "One lesson I've learned over the years is that you can't control other people. There are some things you just have to accept."

"Funny," I told her, "Grandmother told me just this morning that some situations can be controlled if you wait for the right timing. I think this is one of them."

She gave a little laugh. "That sounds like Mother. But I think trying to control every situation you find yourself in is a sign that you don't trust God to work things out to your satisfaction. Sometimes, you just have to put things in His hands and let Him work it out His own way."

Her words had the ring of truth, and I let them settle in my mind for a few minutes.

"Sorry," she said, shaking her head. "I don't usually lecture, but that is one of Bill's pieces of wisdom, and I think it's a good one."

My thoughts seemed frozen in that moment. Right there, standing in the street in the quiet of the night, I felt the Lord's nudging, and I knew He had just delivered a lesson He wanted me to take hold of. I needed time alone, time to think and pray. But with a house full of people, when and where would I find that time?

Chapter 14

When we returned to the house, Stuart had moved to the living-room couch and was fast asleep, breathing deeply and evenly. Grandmother's bedroom door was closed, and Lindsey sat staring at the television screen alone.

"Your grandmother decided to go to bed and sleep off her headache."

"Bed sounds like a good idea to me," Aunt Louise said, yawning. "Good night, you two."

"Good night." I dropped onto the couch beside Lindsey.

When Aunt Louise had left and we were alone, Lindsey spoke without looking at me. "I used your cell phone to call home. I hope you don't mind."

I shook my head, watching her profile. "I don't. How did the call go?"

She continued to stare at the TV. "Weird."

Struggling to suppress an almost irresistible urge to grab her by the ponytail and jerk her head around to face me, I set my teeth together and forced myself to ask calmly, "How so?"

She shrugged one shoulder. I was about to lose the battle, and my hand was inching toward her when she turned her head to look at me.

"Mom just cried," she told me with an eyebrow shrug, "but then

Daddy got on the phone, and he said the strangest thing. He said whatever is bothering me is nothing we can't handle together, and he wanted me to know he's praying for me."

So Mama had been right. I felt my eyes widening. "Wow."

Lindsey nodded. "Yeah, that's what I thought. I don't think Daddy has ever prayed before, at least not that I know of." Her lids narrowed. "I know he never prayed for Alex."

I had spent the ten months since Alex's death thinking of Mr. Markham as the most selfish and unloving father in the entire world. But now I almost felt sorry for him. Though the thought shocked me to the core, I found myself wanting to defend him to his daughter.

"People change," I heard myself saying. "Maybe the threat of losing you on top of losing his son was too much for him to handle alone."

A wrinkle creased her forehead. "What's that supposed to mean?"

"Don't get mad at me for preaching," I warned, "but the Bible says, 'Yea, though I walk through the valley of the shadow of death, I will fear no evil.'"

She rolled her eyes. "Everybody knows that. It's in the twenty-third Psalm."

I hoped she couldn't see my gritted teeth. "Yeah, so that means God promised He'll stay with us no matter what terrible things we go through. Maybe your dad figured his kid running away and refusing to talk to him is a pretty dark valley he didn't want to go through alone."

She studied me a moment before turning away. "Maybe, but that's still weird."

I wanted to grab her by the shoulders and shake her and shout, *You're going through a valley too, Lindsey!* But I was sure she would consider that preaching at her, and my words would only push her further away. Aunt Louise's advice kept echoing in my mind. Maybe this was one of those situations I needed to turn over to the Lord and not try to control.

But an innocent baby might die if I let up on her! I couldn't live with myself if I let that happen. Plus, her parents trusted me to take care of her—Mama said so. Standing by while she had an abortion wasn't exactly taking care of her, in my opinion.

Lord, please help me figure out what to do.

Another Bible verse came into my mind just then, as though whispered by a Voice closer to me than my own. *Cast all your cares on Me.* A sense of urgency stole over me, and I turned away from Lindsey, my gaze fixed unseeing on the dark window. I needed to pray for Lindsey. I had become so engrossed in trying to figure out how to stop her from having an abortion that I had neglected to pray. In fact, I had not prayed about anything lately. But I was going to rectify that situation right then.

"I'm going to bed, too," I announced, standing and heading for the bedroom. I turned around in the doorway to look at her. "Good night."

Her gaze fixed on the television screen, she said dismissively, "G'night."

I put on my pajamas quietly and turned out the light before sliding beneath the blanket and settling back on the pillow.

"Lord," I whispered, "I want to cast my cares on You. I seem to have a lot of them lately." I glanced at the red glowing letters of the alarm clock and realized that it was only nine thirty. I couldn't remember the last time I had gone to bed this early. Even so, as I continued my prayer, I felt myself growing drowsy. "There's this thing with Paul, Lord. You know about that. And there's Grandmother and Aunt Louise, and of course there's Lindsey and the baby. And now Stuart." A huge yawn interrupted my train of thought. I closed my eyes. "Plus, I need to find a job when I get back to Kentucky. I could use some help with that, Lord. I'd sure like to have that job at Midstate, but of course I don't have a chance for that one."

Why hadn't I gone to college when I'd had the chance? Just too darn stubborn, that's why. I yawned again, and rolled over on my side, my head sinking comfortably into the fluffy pillow. If only I could afford to go to college now. But I didn't have the money for tuition and books and all that, not and pay my rent, too. And I couldn't live off of Mama. If only I had taken Mama up on her offer back when I got out of high school . . .

My last thought before I drifted off to sleep was one of mild irritation when I heard Mama's voice ringing in my mind. "You know I'm always right."

❀ ❀ ❀

"Hey, Mayla. Wake up, Mayla."

Pulled from a deep sleep by an insistent whisper and something poking repeatedly at my arm, I moaned in protest as I pulled the pillow over my head.

"Mayla, wake *up*. I need to talk to you."

The pillow was jerked roughly away as the irritating whisper repeated its vile message. Beside me, Lindsey rolled to the far edge of the bed, mumbling softly in her sleep.

I opened a cautious eye to see a fuzzy, spiky-headed silhouette hovering inches from my face. I slammed the eye shut again. "Stuart, what the heck are you doing? What time is it?"

"Shhh," he cautioned. "It's five thirty, and I'm waking you up. We didn't get to talk last night."

"Five thirty?" I repeated, outraged. "In the morning?"

"Duh," he said. "You're really dull when you first wake up, Mayla, has anyone ever told you that?"

"You don't have to insult me," I mumbled, then sat up in bed. "Okay, I'm up."

"You are not. Your eyes are still closed. Come *on*."

I felt the covers being ripped away and my legs roughly turned so that my feet were on the floor. The next thing I knew, I was hauled to a standing position, pulled forcefully from the bedroom, and shoved into the bathroom where a light blinded my sleep-darkened eyes.

"Wash your face and then come into the kitchen," Stuart ordered. "I've got coffee ready and waiting for you."

A few minutes later, I stumbled down the hallway and through the kitchen doorway. Stuart thrust a mug of coffee into my hands and guided me to a chair at the table. He seated himself next to me, and I glared at him as I blew into the cup before taking my first cautious sip.

As my mind cleared and my eyes began to focus, I realized that Stuart had been up for a while. He had shaved and fixed his hair, and his clothes looked fresh, the collar on his shirt crisp. Over the odor of my coffee, I caught a spicy whiff of his signature cologne.

"When did you get up?" I asked, wondering how in the world anyone could manage to look that good at five thirty in the morning.

"About an hour ago. I must have really been tired, because I fell asleep early and slept like a rock."

"You should have slept longer." I yawned hugely and didn't bother to cover it.

"You look terrible in the morning." He flashed an annoying grin. "I heard a joke once that fits you. This comedian said men go to bed and get up in the morning looking exactly the same. But women deteriorate overnight."

"Thanks," I said dryly. "If you're through insulting me, do you mind telling me why you dragged me out of a perfectly comfortable bed at this insane hour?"

Stuart took a sip from his coffee mug, avoiding my eyes and taking his time to answer. Finally he said, "You promised we'd talk after dinner last night, but we didn't get to."

I hid a sigh and leaned back in my chair. "I'm listening. Talk."

He cut his eyes sideways at me. "I don't know, Mayla. Maybe I should wait until you're in a better mood."

I set my coffee mug down on the table with some force. "Stuart, you chased me all the way to Florida to talk to me. You drag me out of bed before the crack of dawn, and now you freeze up? What do you want from me?"

His nostrils flared as he gave me a fierce look. "A little compassion would be good. You don't seem very receptive right now, even though my life is falling apart and it's your fault."

"My fault?" I shook my head. "You keep saying that, but I have no idea what you're talking about. Michael accepted the Lord. That's wonderful. I'm thrilled for him. Then apparently he decided to leave you. I didn't know that until you told me, and I still don't know anything about his reasons. So how is this my fault?"

"This is your fault because you're the reason Sylvia became a born-again Christian." He said the term like it tasted terrible in his mouth and he couldn't wait to spit it out. "And then she got to Tattoo Lou. And then Lou started working on Michael. He held out a while, but Lou and Sylvia wore him down. And now that he's a Christian too, he's decided to move back to Texas to figure out his life. So the whole twisted chain started with you, Mayla. If you hadn't made Sylvia turn into a Goody Two-shoes, Michael would still be with me."

He sniffed hugely and turned his head away to dab at his eyes with a napkin. I wasn't entirely sure the sniffling was real, so I decided to ignore it. Stuart had a reputation for being overly dramatic.

"First of all, I didn't *make* Sylvia do anything. She came to me and told me she wanted to know Jesus like I did. And second, you make Christianity sound like some sort of malicious computer virus and Christians like the hackers who spread it." I stopped to gather my thoughts. Stuart kept his face turned away from me. When I went on, I used a softer voice. "We're not like that, Stuart. Christianity is a relationship with a real Person, a true Friend who happens to also be God. I don't know what happened to make Michael decide he needs to move away and figure out his life, but I do know he'll be happy if he's letting God lead him."

Stuart turned back to me. I saw deep pain in his eyes. "What was wrong with his old life? Lou kept telling him that being gay is wrong. He called it an abomination. What if Michael believed him?" Real tears flooded his eyes. "Me, an abomination. That really hurts."

I reached out and took his hand, squeezing it. "I'm sure it does. I'm sorry."

He gazed directly into my eyes. "Do you think being gay is an abomination, Mayla?"

Feeling like an insect pinned to a piece of cardboard in a science exhibit, I tried hard not to let my gaze drop away from his. This was one of those questions I had struggled with since becoming a Christian. I knew the wrong answer could turn Stuart away forever. *Lord, please give me the words to say!*

I took a deep breath and blew it out slowly. "I'll tell you what I think," I said, looking Stuart straight in the eye. "Any life not completely devoted to the Lord is wrong. And that's basically every person on the face of the earth. I know that my lifestyle before I became a Christian was wrong. Some would call promiscuity and being completely self-serving an abomination, because those things are outside of God's perfect plan. That was me."

Stuart's lip curled. "And now you're perfect?"

Grinning, I said, "Sure I am." I took his punch on the arm with a chuckle, then sobered. "Nah, I don't claim to be perfect. Far from it. But what I am is happy. I feel a peace I never knew before I met Jesus." I paused, then said in a low voice, "That's what Michael has found, Stuart. And because he has, he's got to do what he feels the Lord is leading him to do. Don't be mad at him for that."

His gaze fell to his coffee mug. "I'm not mad at him," he whispered. "I'm just . . . feeling alone."

"You don't have to be," I said. "The same Man Michael met would love to welcome you, too."

He looked up quickly, his eyelids narrowed. "How do you know I'm not already a Christian? I went to church as a kid, you know, all the way through high school. I was in college before I stopped going."

I grinned. "Because if you were a Christian, you wouldn't think it's an infectious disease."

Chuckling, he nodded. "Yeah, I guess you're right about that." He paused and went on in a serious tone. "But you know, lately I've been thinking—"

"You two are up early," said a sleepy voice behind me.

Stuart seemed relieved at the interruption, and I wondered what he had been about to say. I turned to see Aunt Louise in the doorway, her eyes half closed and her hair standing out around her head like a modern-day Medusa. With Stuart's joke in mind, I realized she did look as though she had deteriorated overnight and answered with a giggle.

"Good morning. Stuart's an early bird and doesn't like to be alone." I pulled a face to show I had been an unwilling guest to this early morning party.

Stuart leapt toward the counter and had a mug of coffee poured for Aunt Louise before she had stumbled sleepily across the floor and seated herself at the table.

"Cream? Sugar?" he asked, setting the mug down in front of her.

"Both." She reached for the sugar bowl in the center of the table as Stuart went to the refrigerator for a carton of half-and-half. "So what's on your agenda today?"

"I don't know what Grandmother has planned," I answered. "Stuart, is there something you want to do?"

"Grocery shopping." He slipped into his chair and picked up his own mug. "I'm cooking chicken alfredo à la Hortenbury for dinner."

Aunt Louise smiled. "À la Hortenbury? I take it this is a special recipe?"

"Absolutely," he said with a nod. "And completely top secret. I developed it myself."

"Stuart really is a good cook," I added. "Every so often, he invites a group of us over and experiments on us."

"Then I can't wait to try your top-secret recipe." She sipped her coffee. "If you're planning on doing anything outside while you're here, the weather tomorrow is going to be perfect. Not too warm, and sunny all day."

Stuart sat up tall, his eyes shining. "Maybe we can go to the beach. What do you think, Mayla?"

I shrugged. "Fine with me. We'll see what Grandmother and Lindsey want to do when they wake up."

We chatted about nothing in particular for a few minutes before Aunt Louise left the table to get ready for work. But by then, Stuart had closed the door to further serious discussion and only wanted to plan his menu for dinner. Feeling as though an opportunity to reach him had slipped away, I refilled my coffee cup and helped him search the spice cabinet as he made his grocery list.

Lindsey and Grandmother thought the beach on Friday was a great idea. When they had both showered and dressed—Grandmother in a nice dress and panty hose, like she was going to church—we all piled into Stuart's car and drove to the Florida Mall to find a bathing suit for Lindsey. That mall was something to see, and so huge it felt like Lexington's Fayette Mall would fit inside twice with room left over.

I am not a shopper. Stuart and Lindsey, on the other hand, acted like kids turned loose in a toy store with Donald Trump's credit card. They started in Sears on one end of the mall and went in every single store we passed on the right side, working their way toward JCPenney at the opposite end. After an hour or so, I realized with horror that they intended to work their way back on the other side. I am strictly a park-at-the-closest-entrance-and-dash-inside-for-whatever-you-need shopper.

Lindsey soon discovered Stuart's flare for fashion and graduated from bathing suits to low-riders and tank tops. In fact, the two of them tried on every outfit they saw, and even convinced Grandmother to model a few.

I have to admit, the place was pretty cool as malls go, especially when we got to the food court. I decided to park myself at a table in front of a full-sized carousel and wait for the shopaholics to run out of steam. Grandmother sat with me amid a pile of Stuart's shopping bags while he and Lindsey linked arms and strolled off in search of bargains. I found a counter where they sold fresh-squeezed lemonade and bought two, and we settled ourselves in to wait.

An hour later, Lindsey and Stuart returned, both of them carrying shopping bags bulging with their purchases. Grandmother and I listened as they entertained us with tales of their shopping success. Finally, almost three hours after we had arrived, we all piled into Stuart's car, Lindsey in the front with Grandmother and me in the back.

"Now, where's the grocery store?" Stuart asked as he backed the car out of the parking place.

"There's one not far from the house," Grandmother replied.

She leaned her head against the back of the seat, and I realized she looked tired. "Hey Stuart, could you take us home first? We've had a long morning, and I'd like to lie out in the backyard for a while this afternoon."

I caught his glance in the rearview mirror and slid my eyes in the direction of Grandmother.

He nodded. "Not a problem."

Lindsey decided to ride along with Stuart to the grocery store, and they dropped Grandmother and me off at the house. After giving them directions, we waved good-bye and went inside.

I changed into a bathing suit and flip-flops and slipped a T-shirt over top. When I came out of the bedroom, Grandmother was in the kitchen, standing in front of the microwave. She turned as I came into the room and smiled.

"I thought I'd have a cup of coffee." She nodded in the direction of the microwave. "There's plenty for two."

I shook my head. "No thanks."

The bell dinged, and she took out a steaming mug. When she sat down at the table, I joined her to talk for a few minutes before going outside.

"I had a nice time at the mall," she said, taking a sip.

"Yeah. Me too. Lindsey sure seems to have taken a liking to Stuart."

She chuckled. "He is quite a character, that Stuart. I've never seen a man who loves to shop as much as he does. I wonder if he bought those new clothes for her or if she had the money to pay for them herself."

I had wondered the same thing. "If we're lucky, she spent her abortion money on them."

She fell silent and appeared to be lost in thought. Though she still looked tired, her face was a good color, and she didn't seem unwell at all. In fact, she looked no more tired than she had after spending the day at SeaWorld. Odd how stress could bring on those attacks but physical activity didn't seem to.

Even though Aunt Louise said she had spoken with the doctor about the timing of the attacks, I couldn't forget that flash of determination I had seen on Grandmother's face before the last one. Something did not seem right, and I couldn't stand to leave my question unasked. I would only be here a few more days. Now was as good a time as any.

I cleared my throat, and she looked across the table at me. "Grandmother, I've been wondering about something. You know these attacks of yours?" Her head tilted a fraction, and she paused before nodding once. "Well, I've noticed you seem to always have one whenever Aunt Louise has plans to go out with Mr. Manson."

Her face remained blank, almost too blank, as her gaze locked onto mine. "What are you saying?"

I squirmed under the sudden intensity in those hazel eyes, but now that I had started, I wasn't about to back down. "I was just wondering if there might be some connection. You know, it wouldn't be unusual for you to be a little nervous about Aunt Louise developing a relationship that might lead to her moving out one day."

She set her mug down on the table, leaned back in her seat, and crossed her arms. "Are you asking me if I am faking the attacks?"

Fidgeting in my chair, my gaze dropped away from hers. Then I looked back up. "Yeah. I guess I am."

She stared at me for a few seconds, as though considering her answer. "And what if I said that was true?"

I sucked in a breath. "Is it?"

"If it was true," she said, "I would have a perfectly good reason. I'm old, Mayla, and Louise is all I have. Especially since your mother killed my son."

I jerked back as though slapped, stunned into silence at such an outrageous accusation. Mama would be devastated to hear those words, and I would never, ever repeat them to her. What a vicious, horrible thing to say. My silence lasted only a second, because in the next second words shot out of my mouth at something short of light speed. "My mother did not kill your son. His brain was dead already, and his body was being kept alive unnaturally. I was there. I remember him lying in that hospital bed with all those tubes and wires coming out of him like something out of a horror film. Mama loved him, and it took guts to do what she did. And you know it, too."

Grandmother's voice dripped the poison of hatred as her gaze burned into mine. "She doesn't know what love is."

"You are not going to talk about my mama like that," I shot back. "She knows more about love than you ever will. You're holding Aunt Louise here as a prisoner just as surely as if you had chains around her ankles. What kind of mother would try to keep her own child under her thumb just because she was afraid to be alone?"

Two angry spots of pink appeared high on Grandmother's cheeks as she took a couple of deep breaths. I could see she was struggling to gain control of her temper. She stood suddenly and went to the sink, her back to me. I was puffing like a woman in labor, my pulse racing with hot anger. But even in the midst of my rage, I knew this wasn't the way I wanted this conversation to go. I had better get control of myself, the way Grandmother seemed to be trying to get control of herself. *Lord*, I prayed silently, *please help me cool down.*

Grandmother turned to face me, and she looked more composed.

"Do you know what kind of mother does that?" she asked in a quiet voice, staring at me from across the room. "One who won't be around much longer. I've got a few years at best, and then Louise will be free to do whatever she wants. Is it so wrong to want to keep her with me for the time I have left?"

Looking into her eyes, I realized she was being completely truthful. And the fact was, at seventy-seven and with a weak heart, she was right. My anger melted away as compassion flooded through me, and I saw her for what she was—an old woman who had never gotten over the loss of her son and who was holding onto her remaining child with every ounce of strength she had. Regretting my anger and harsh words, I crossed the room to give her a long hug.

"No," I told her, pulling back and looking into her eyes, "it's not wrong to want to keep your family close. But Grandmother, you can't do it at the expense of Aunt Louise's happiness. I hope you have a lot of years left, but when you do die, surely you don't want her to be relieved, do you?"

She looked startled for a moment, then waved a hand dismissively. "This man is nothing but a passing fancy of Louise's. She doesn't really care about him."

I shook my head. "You're wrong. She loves him. But she loves you, too, and the two loves are tearing her apart."

She searched my face. "Do you really think she loves this . . . this electrician?"

I grinned at the disbelief in her voice. "She told me she loves him."

Oops. Aunt Louise had probably told me that in confidence so perhaps I should have kept my mouth shut. But understanding was beginning to dawn on Grandmother; I could see it in her face. She shook her head and made her way slowly back to the table, seating herself once again in her chair. I leaned against the sink and watched her take a sip from her mug.

At that moment, the front door opened, and Stuart and Lindsey came into the kitchen. This seemed to be the day for interruptions at critical moments.

"Hey, Mayla, grab the other bags from the trunk," Stuart ordered, then grinned at Grandmother as he piled his load on the counter. "Mrs. S., you are going to experience the best dinner of your life tonight. You have my personal guarantee."

Grandmother smiled and stood slowly, looking suddenly older than she had a few minutes before. "I'm looking forward to it. But now I think I'll rest for a while."

She gave me an unreadable look before leaving the kitchen, but I did see a smile playing at the edges of her mouth as she turned away. Satisfied that she would be okay, I went out to do as I had been told.

True to his word, Stuart fixed the best dinner I have ever eaten. We started with a vegetable antipasto tray loaded with thinly sliced Italian peppers, artichokes, bruschetta with some sort of garlicky dipping sauce, and several kinds of olives. I can't stand the green olives Mama puts out for dinner at home but allowed myself to be persuaded to try these giant ones. Then I had to be persuaded to leave some for everyone else, because they were so good I wanted to eat them all.

Next, Stuart served a delicious salad that made mine from the night before look like leftovers from the lawn mower, alongside more bruschetta with fresh garlic and olive oil. I was stuffed even before we got to the main course, but the alfredo sauce was thick and rich and delicious, with tender pieces of chicken over perfectly done pasta. I couldn't help myself and ate a huge plateful.

When I thought I couldn't even look at one more bite, he brought out dessert—little cups of raspberry sorbet with fresh berries and a fancy chocolate cookie with a picture of the queen of England or someone stamped in the chocolate.

"Ooohhh," I moaned, pushing my empty dessert cup away and holding my bulging belly with one hand. "I hurt myself."

Stuart looked at my tummy and commented dryly, "I've never

seen anyone eat like that. You look about four months pregnant." He glanced at Lindsey with a grin. "No offense."

Lindsey laughed good-naturedly, a testimony to the relationship that had developed between the two of them throughout the day. If I had mentioned her pregnancy in public, she would have snatched me bald-headed.

Grandmother, who had been pleasant but pensive throughout the meal, patted Stuart's hand. "That was delicious. I've never had a better meal in any restaurant. You should be a chef."

Aunt Louise agreed. "You're certainly good enough. Some of those fancy restaurants pay a lot of money for someone who can cook like you."

He laughed, shaking his head. "Cooking for me is fun. I only do it when I want, and I only cook what I want. I'd hate to spoil my fun by having to cook what people tell me to."

"Well, tomorrow night's dinner won't be nearly as good as this one," Grandmother said, reaching for his empty plate to stack it on hers, "but I'm going to fix you the best fried chicken you've ever eaten. And homemade biscuits, too."

"Oh, good!" I exclaimed, clapping. "I'm going to get Grandmother's fried chicken twice in one visit!"

She smiled at me; then her gaze shifted to Aunt Louise. "Louise, why don't you ask your friend Mr. Manson if he would like to join us for dinner tomorrow?"

Silence fell around the table, along with Aunt Louise's jaw. Lindsey, Stuart, and I all turned our heads toward her as she took a moment to recover herself. I saw her swallow hard before speaking. "Do you mean it, Mother?"

Grandmother's lips tightened. "I wouldn't have suggested it if I didn't mean it. Of course, it is rather late notice. He might have other plans."

"Oh no, he doesn't," Aunt Louise said quickly, then stopped herself. "I mean, I'll ask him."

Grandmother stood and reached for Lindsey's plate, and we all got up to help her clear the table. Aunt Louise looked dazed as she gathered silverware, and I saw her give a tiny shake of her head as though trying to clear her mind. Grandmother caught my eye behind her back and gave me a very brief smile before turning toward the sink.

After *Jeopardy* had ended, Grandmother brought out an ancient Monopoly box held together with yellowing tape and asked if anyone was in the mood for a game. We all joined in, and I spent a pleasant evening beating the pants off Stuart. Finally, I had found something for which he had no talent, and I took full advantage of the years Mama had forced me to play board games with her when I was a kid.

Around nine thirty, Lindsey asked if she could use my phone to call her boyfriend, and I told her to go ahead. She went back into the bedroom and came out half an hour later as I gloated over my huge pile of Monopoly money. She looked thoughtful, and I could see she did not want to discuss her conversation with Dirk.

She handed the phone to me. "You got a call while I was talking. I let it go to voice mail."

Figuring it was probably Mama, I excused myself and headed down the hallway. In the bedroom, I flipped open the cell phone. Expecting to see Mama's number, I pulled up the Missed Call log. My heart skipped a beat when I saw the number at the top of the list.

Paul's cell phone.

I stared at it for a moment, stunned. Paul had called me. He had actually picked up his phone and dialed my number, wanting to talk to me. I pressed the keys to display the Voice Mail screen and saw that I had a new message. Was this the call I had been waiting for? Was he actually going to tell me that he realized he had feelings for me?

My pulse racing, I dialed my voice mailbox. Holding the phone to my ear with a shaky hand, I closed my eyes against the wave of emotion that surged through me when I heard his voice.

"Mayla, this is Paul. I hoped I would catch you, but you must be busy. Listen, I've been thinking a lot about you lately. In fact, I can't seem to think about anything else—"

I missed his next few words, because the blood was rushing to my head and my thoughts were going wild. *He can't stop thinking about me!*

"—because you haven't answered my e-mails, though your mother says you've sent her e-mail since you've been in Florida. I know you're mad at me after the argument we had, and I want to talk about that. But in the meantime, I'm worried you might jump into a relationship with that man down there."

Paul cleared his throat, and I felt a satisfied smile hovering around my lips. My plan to make him jealous had worked! When he went on, his voice held a touch of steel. "And let me tell you something, I do not think it is appropriate for a pastor to ask a young woman out when she visits her grandmother's church. Anyway," he said, his tone softening, "I'm worried about you. And . . . I miss you. And I want to talk to you in person. Or, uh, on the phone, anyway. So could you call me?"

There was an awkward pause, and then, "I guess that's what I wanted to say. I mean, there's a lot more I want to say but not in a message. I hope I'll talk to you later. You're in my prayers, Mayla. Good-bye."

Sinking onto the bed, I punched a button to listen to the message again. After the third time, I saved the message and closed the phone. Leaning against the headboard, I stared at the phone in my hand and tried to get a grip on my feelings.

Odd. Why wasn't I dancing for joy? My plan had worked. Though Paul had not come right out and declared that he cared for me, he had said he couldn't stop thinking about me. And that he missed me. He was obviously jealous of Reverend Thomas, as I had intended. And he wanted to talk to me in person to tell me something he couldn't leave in a message. This was *it*. The man I had professed to love was about to tell me he had feelings for me, too.

So why was I numb? Why did this feel like such an empty victory, like I had won a championship game by cheating? This man had done nothing but treat me honorably, and I realized with a start that I felt like a swindler, as though I didn't deserve him.

"Lord," I said in a quiet voice, aware that Aunt Louise had left the kitchen and was moving around in the bedroom across the narrow hallway, "what is wrong with me?"

"Who are you talking to?" Lindsey asked, coming into the room at that moment.

I shrugged, too confused to be embarrassed. "Nobody. Or rather, Somebody big. I was praying."

"Oh." She stopped just inside the doorway, looking taken aback. "You want me to leave?"

Shaking my head, I sat up and swung my feet over to the floor. "No, you can go on to bed if you want. I'm going to sit on the back porch for a while."

After hesitating a moment, Lindsey crossed to her side of the bed to pull her borrowed pajamas from beneath her pillow, watching me cautiously as though afraid I would burst into prayer at any moment. Slipping my cell phone into the pocket of my shorts, I gave her a distracted smile and left, closing the bedroom door behind me. On my way through the kitchen, I mumbled to Stuart and Grandmother that I was going outside to be alone for a while. In the family room, I snatched up a crocheted afghan from the couch and let myself out the back door.

Settling in a lawn chair, I tucked the afghan snugly around my bare legs and looked out into the yard. I held myself very still, and after a few minutes, the motion sensor above the door shut off the safety spotlight angled to illuminate the porch. I was swathed in a comforting near darkness. A three-quarter moon had risen above the treetops and cast a silvery light upon the neat square of yard inside Grandmother's privacy fence. I heard a car door shut somewhere in the distance, and after that, the only sound was an occasional rustle as a gentle wind blowing over the fence stirred the leaves in the orange trees.

Finally, I was completely alone with the Lord, with no distractions. Looking at the spray of stars glittering in the blackness above me, I whispered, "Oh, Father, I'm sorry I've ignored You the past few days. I've been so busy trying to keep things under control down here I forgot to pray. And then last night, I fell asleep almost before I started."

I paused, and in the sudden silence, a particularly enthusiastic cricket began an impressive chorus somewhere in the vicinity of the fencerow to my right. He didn't miss a beat when I continued. "And nothing's working out like I thought it would, either. You know I've been praying for a while about Paul, but now that he might be ready to admit he likes me as a woman instead of just a parishioner, everything feels wrong. And that's not the only thing that isn't working out, Lord. Even though I might have made some headway with Grandmother today, she's the most manipulating woman I've ever seen, and I'm worried about Aunt Louise. Stuart is convinced that all his problems are my fault, and I can't talk Lindsey out of an abortion."

A cloud moved slowly in front of the moon, and everything around me fell into its shadow. "And I still don't have a job, not that I've been looking this week. But that's something else I'm worrying about, because without a college degree, I don't know who will hire me. In fact, Lord, nothing is going very well for me right now, and I could really use Your help."

The verse I had heard last night while talking to Lindsey came back to me. I recognized it from 1 Peter—"Casting all your care upon Him, for He cares for you."

"Well, I'm trying, that's for sure," I whispered a touch grumpily.

But was I? Had I really cast the care of Pastor Paul's feelings for me on the Lord, or had I simply presented a list of complaints? If I had truly put the care on Him, would He have wanted me to try to make Paul jealous by pretending that Reverend Thomas had asked me for a date?

I squirmed in my chair, certain that the Almighty would have wanted no such thing. And He especially would not have wanted me to deceive Mama in order to get to Paul.

When I looked at my actions surrounding Paul and Mama, they began to look suspiciously familiar. Grandmother used different tactics to control Aunt Louise, but the motive was the same. I was beginning to realize I had more in common with my grandmother than just looks.

What had Aunt Louise said on our walk a few nights ago? Trying to control a situation was like saying you didn't trust God to work it out to your satisfaction.

"Lord, I'm sorry I've been manipulating Paul, and I'm sorry I used Mama to make him jealous. I really do trust You."

But did I really? What if God didn't want me to be with Paul? What if God had some other woman in mind for him—would I be okay with that?

Cringing, I forced myself to say, "And if You want him to be with someone else, I can handle it."

Then I remembered another recent situation where I had kept pushing until I got what I wanted. When Sylvia had not wanted to keep the rabbit, I had pouted and worked on her until she agreed. Wasn't that manipulating her? I shifted uncomfortably in my chair again, and the security light suddenly illuminated the porch, sending the cricket into a moment of silence. I really was a grade-A control freak!

"Lord, I'm doing a lousy job of trusting You lately," I admitted, looking up at the bright white moon.

The worst part was that even when I got what I wanted, things didn't turn out the way I expected them to. This trip to Florida, for instance. Instead of being a quiet family time, half of Kentucky had packed up their problems and followed me.

"Well, I'm going to stop trying to control Lindsey right now,

Lord," I vowed. "I've tried, and I probably only made things worse. So I'm casting the care of her and the baby on You, okay?"

Silence answered me, but in the silence I felt a sense that maybe I had finally done the right thing, the best thing I could do for Lindsey. Encouraged, I turned my prayer focus to the next problem on my list.

"And about Stuart, Lord, I have no idea what to do for him." I felt relief admitting that. I really didn't know what to do, and suddenly I realized that was all right. I didn't need to. "I trust You to work things out for Stuart. If there's something You want me to say, please let me know. Because I really do love him, Lord. He's a good guy, and he needs You even if he doesn't know it."

Again, I felt peace. Maybe I was finally making progress in this "casting all your care on Him" business. The security light went out again, and I tilted my head back, gazing at the stars above me.

"And Lord, if You see me trying to control someone again, please whack me or something. I'd rather let You handle things." I closed my eyes and relaxed, feeling more peaceful than I had felt in what seemed like weeks.

But I was not finished for the night. I had some apologizing to do. The thought of calling Paul made me squirm in my seat—I was not quite ready for that conversation. And since it was after ten o'clock, I knew Mama was already in bed. But there was one person who would still be awake. I fished my phone out of my pocket and dialed Sylvia's number.

"Hey, Mayla," her voice said when she picked up on the second ring. "What's up?"

"Oh, lots. You'll never believe who showed up here yesterday." I told her about Stuart and our early morning conversation.

She gave a low whistle. "I can't believe he drove all that way just to talk to you. I mean, I know you guys are friends and all, but I never got the idea you were *that* close."

"I know. But I'm kind of thinking this might be a God thing. Stuart is asking some pretty deep questions, and for some reason, he seems to think I have the answers."

"You do," she said. "Or at least, you know the Man who does. Whether he knows it or not, what Stuart wants is an introduction."

"Pray about it, would you? But I actually had another reason for calling." I stopped, searching for words. I was unaccustomed to this apology business.

"If it's about Harvey," she offered, "he's fine. At this moment, he is chewing on a piece of wood Lou brought over for him in hopes of preserving the table legs."

"Actually, it is about Harvey. I wanted to apologize for badgering you into watching him for me. You really didn't want to, but I wouldn't take no for an answer. I feel lousy for taking advantage of a friend like that."

There was a moment of silence on the phone, and when Sylvia spoke again, her voice was thoughtful. "Thanks for realizing that, Mayla. I have to admit I was feeling pretty taken advantage of for the first few days."

I winced. "I'm really sorry, Sylvia. As soon as I get back, we'll take Harvey to that rabbit farm you told me about. If you want to go ahead and do it tomorrow, that's okay."

"Actually"—she chuckled—"I've kind of gotten used to the little fiend. He has a pretty strong personality for a rodent, but we seem to have come to an understanding. I'm sort of hoping the apartment complex lets us keep him."

I grinned, my mood flying high. "Thanks, Sylvia. You're about the best friend anyone could have."

"Just don't get the idea I'm going soft on animals," she warned. "Next thing I know, you'll be bringing home a possum or something, and then we'll have a real problem."

"No possum, I promise."

"Good night, Mayla. Tell Stuart I said hello."

"Will do. G'night."

By the time I got back inside, Grandmother and Stuart had gone to bed. I plugged in my laptop, determined to e-mail both Mama and Paul before I went to sleep. Feeling a little guilty for taking the coward's way out, I nevertheless couldn't force myself to call Paul. The message I was going to deliver was too painful, and I was sure I would cry if I had to say it directly to him.

I started with the easy one.

> Dear Mama,
> I have to confess something to you. You know all that stuff about Reverend Thomas asking me out? Well, it wasn't exactly the truth. I mean, he did invite me to go somewhere, but it was a Bible study he was leading for the young adults at his church. He was being a good pastor, not trying to ask me on a date.
>
> The reason I told you that is because I knew you would tell Pastor Paul about it. And I wanted to make him jealous. Now Mama, PLEASE don't go telling your Tuesday night ladies that! I'm going to be embarrassed enough already when I come back to church just having to face him.
>
> The Lord has been teaching me a lesson since I've been in Florida, and I realized I've been manipulating people for a long time, including you. I'm sorry, Mama. I love you more than anything, and I hope you'll forgive me.
> Love,
> Mayla

I knew my mama better than maybe anyone else in the world, and I knew she would forgive me. Heck, she would probably tell me she knew all along what I was doing.

The next e-mail took a lot longer to write, and more than once, tears splashed onto the keyboard before I was ready to press the Send button.

Dear Paul,

I got your message tonight. I would have called you back like you asked, but I was too embarrassed. That's because I have not been honest with you lately. In fact, I've been downright dishonest. You see, I never got asked out on a date by this preacher down here. That was a lie, and I told it to Mama knowing it would get to you, and I hoped it would make you jealous. I also have not been answering your e-mails for the same reason. I wanted you to think I was down here having too much fun to be bothered by you and that I never thought of you at all, and I hoped you would be jealous.

The truth is I realize I've been manipulating people to get what I want, and you're one of those people. I'm really, really sorry. You deserve to be treated better.

I want you to know I understand what you said to me at Mama's house that day—that I'm one of the members of your church and that's how you think of me. I was wrong to ask more from you, because that puts you in a bad position. I will not do it again. I hope we can still be friends.

I read the e-mail and re-read it. Did that say everything I wanted to say to him? No. I wanted to somehow relay how heartfelt my apology was, how desperately I hoped he would forgive me, and how I hoped we could put this whole thing behind us.

No. What I really wanted was to tell him I loved him, how I hoped he would realize he loved me, too.

But in the end, I decided all that would have to go unsaid. Maybe he would know what I felt when he read my signature:

Sincerely,
Mayla

Chapter 15

Stuart, Lindsey, and I went to the same beach on Friday that I had visited with Grandmother and Aunt Louise the day after I arrived in Florida. Grandmother decided she wanted to stay home so she could be sure to have dinner ready on time. I suspected she was pouting a little after our conversation about controlling Aunt Louise, but I didn't mention anything. She packed a lunch of sandwiches and chips and leftover antipasti for us and stood on the porch, waving as we pulled away in Stuart's red Grand Am.

The day was just as beautiful as my previous beach day, though a stronger wind had blown in some amazing waves. Sitting on a beach blanket, I laughed until my sides hurt as Stuart, with his winter-white skin and bright yellow Hawaiian print Speedo, leaped into the biggest ones, turning aerial somersaults as the waves crashed into him. He looked like one of the performing dolphins Lindsey and I had seen at SeaWorld, only clumsier.

When he got tired of acrobatics, Stuart coaxed Lindsey and me into the water—which was really cold—and taught us how to body surf. We spent at least an hour playing in the salty surf, standing a few feet apart and looking out to sea, waiting for just the right moment to leap into an oncoming wave and ride it all the way to the sandy beach.

Finally, when Lindsey's lips had turned blue and my teeth were chattering so badly I couldn't talk, we headed back to our beach blanket, dried ourselves off, and lay on the warm sand, feeling the sun bake the chill out of our bodies.

The goosebumps had disappeared and I'd stopped shivering when Lindsey asked without opening her eyes, "Stuart, when are you going home?"

"Tomorrow. I'll leave early and drive straight through, and that way I can have a day to recover before I go back to work on Monday."

"Do you think you could make a detour and take me home?"

I turned over on my side and propped myself up on one elbow so I could see her where she lay on the other side of Stuart. "Does that mean you're not going to try to find an abortion clinic here in Florida?"

She didn't answer for a long time. Stuart and I exchanged silent glances. Finally she opened her eyes, turning her head to look at me. "I've decided not to have an abortion."

My heart did a joyous pitter-patter, but I tried hard to keep my face passive. "What made you change your mind?"

She closed her eyes and turned her face toward the sky, seeming unwilling to look at me. "Last night I was telling Dirk about that women's center and the ultrasound and all that. And he said he's been thinking about the baby a lot, and if I want to keep it, he thinks we should get married."

My stomach tightened instantly. A couple of sixteen-year-olds getting married and raising a kid? I opened my mouth to tell her that idea was almost as bad as having an abortion, but then I shut it. This was not my decision. I was through meddling. Even if I thought this marriage was a colossal mistake and a disaster in the making, I would not say so.

Unless she asked my opinion, of course.

Lindsey continued. "He said I don't need a volleyball scholarship to go to college, that lots of people work their way through school even with a kid. And he said he would get a job to help with tuition and day care and all that. He sounded like he thought it could really work. I guess I hadn't thought about that."

While I wrestled my tongue into submission, Stuart sat up and reached for the sunscreen bottle. "Is that what you're going to do?"

Lindsey shrugged. "I dunno." She looked at me. "You're awfully quiet, Mayla. I thought you'd be doing backflips down the beach."

"I'm thrilled," I told her, meaning it.

She gave me a suspicious look. "But?"

I widened my eyes. "But what?"

"C'mon, I know you're dying to tell me what I ought to do."

I shook my head. "Nope. I've given up meddling in other people's lives. Whatever you do is your decision, because you're the one who has to live with the consequences. But," I added, taking the bottle from Stuart, "I do think you should go to college no matter what. I wouldn't want anyone to go through what I'm going through right now."

Stuart cocked his head in my direction. "What do you mean?"

I told them about losing my job and discovering that all the good-paying jobs I had found required a degree.

"So go to school and get one," said Stuart, shrugging a shoulder. "You can do that."

"And pay for it how? I have to work two jobs just to pay my bills."

Stuart dismissed that with a flip of his fingers as he lay back on the blanket. "With all the grants and financial aid and student loans available these days, anyone who wants to work for a degree can get one. Money is not a valid excuse. And with so many schools offering online programs, time isn't one, either. You could do it if you really wanted to."

I spread sunscreen on my legs slowly, thinking. I had never considered financial aid. Or Internet classes, either. Of course, that wouldn't help me land a good job right now, but in a few years . . .

"Now that we've solved both of your problems," Stuart said in the manner of someone who has just provided the solution to world hunger, "it's my turn."

"What is your problem, Stuart?" asked Lindsey, holding out her hand for the sunscreen. I snapped the top shut and tossed the bottle to her.

He heaved a dramatic sigh. "Only that Mayla has lured all my friends over to the dark side and left me behind."

"The light side," I corrected. "And you can stop claiming to be mad at me about that. I know better."

He opened an eye to look up at me. "What do you mean?"

I bit the inside of my lip, wondering if I should tell him what I really thought. Lindsey would accuse me of preaching, but I had been thinking about Stuart coming all this way just to tell me I had ruined his life. He might really believe that line, but I didn't think that was the reason.

Of course, I have never been known for keeping my opinions to myself, no matter how hard I try.

"What you're feeling isn't anger," I told him. "It's loneliness. You feel left out, so you decided to come down here so you wouldn't be alone."

He closed his eyes and lay in silence for a moment. Then he heaved himself up into a sitting position and sat with his arms resting on his knees, staring into the distance toward the dark line where the sky and the ocean met. "I think there's some truth to that. Just a year ago, we had a whole group of people in our apartment complex who partied and had fun together." He shifted his gaze to me. "Then you got religion, and the group dissolved."

"Hey, that's not fair. Lisa and Stan moved away," I pointed out. "Heidi went into rehab, and we never saw her again."

He conceded these points with a nod. "True, but all the others have either gotten religious or scared off those of us who didn't."

"We didn't scare off anyone," I argued, but he held up a hand.

"Lou drove them off."

I couldn't argue with him. Tattoo Lou was so excited about his newfound life in Christ that he could be a little hard to take at times, even for me. Several people had stopped coming to Stuart's Friday night get-togethers after the time he turned off the stereo, opened his Bible to 1 Corinthians, and read aloud the list of wicked evildoers who will not inherit the kingdom of heaven. People tend to get offended at being called drunkards, especially when they're sitting on the couch with a can of beer or a gin and tonic in their hand.

"Well, yeah," I admitted, "Lou can be a little exuberant at times."

"He sure can." Stuart's brow wrinkled. "How come you were never like that, Mayla? That's what got Sylvia, you know. If you'd charged in there spouting religion and telling us we were all going to hell, she would have kicked you out of the apartment and that would have been the end of it."

"Mayla can do her fair share of preaching," Lindsey volunteered. "Believe me."

I stuck my tongue out at her while Stuart shook his head. "No, you haven't seen preaching until you've seen Lou. Mayla isn't like that."

They both looked at me, their expressions demanding an answer. I shrugged. "I guess I figure I'm not any better than anyone else. What right do I have to tell someone what he's doing is wrong? Like the bumper sticker says, 'I'm not perfect, just forgiven.'"

Lindsey rolled her eyes.

"No, really," I insisted. "I'm a Christian, but I still mess up all the time. I'm impatient, and I fly off the handle sometimes—"

"That's for sure," muttered Stuart.

I glared at him and continued. "And I get really upset if I don't get my own way." I paused and took a breath before making my big confession. I looked directly at Lindsey. "And just recently I've realized I'm a control freak."

Lindsey snorted and Stuart tilted his head to give me an incredulous look out of the tops of his eyeballs. "You've just realized that recently?" He looked at Lindsey, and they both burst into uproarious laughter that I felt was completely unkind and uncalled-for. They laughed so hard Stuart threw himself to the blanket and rolled, holding his sides, while Lindsey's face turned red, and she had to gasp for breath.

"Thanks, guys," I told them dryly. "So nice to know I can have a serious conversation with my friends about my shortcomings."

"Sorry, Mayla." Stuart got himself under control and wiped a tear from the corner of his eye. "It's just that I always assumed you knew you were bossing people around and were doing it on purpose."

Offended, I tilted my nose into the air and turned away from them to rummage in the cooler for a can of Diet Coke.

"Don't be mad, Mayla," Lindsey said, still snickering. "You might be a control freak, but that's not always bad. After all, I came to you for help because I knew you'd know what to do."

I aimed the can at Stuart and popped the top, but because it hadn't been shaken, nothing sprayed on him. Darn. "But when I told you what to do, you didn't like it."

She shrugged. "I didn't want to do what *you* wanted. I wanted you to help me do what *I* wanted."

"Control freaks don't work that way."

"Let's get back to me!" Stuart insisted, thumping his chest with a fist. "Here I am with no roommate and no friends—"

"You've got friends." I gestured to myself and Lindsey.

He sighed. "No offense, but I have no *fun* friends. Nobody to go drinking with on Friday nights after work."

"So find some new friends who like to do the same things you do," Lindsey offered.

"Or," I said quickly, "maybe your old friends have found something better, and you should check it out. Instead of going to a party with me next Friday, come to church with me next Sunday."

He gave me a sharp look. "I thought you were through being a control freak."

I took a sip from the can. "I am. By inviting you to church I'm trying to help you, not control you. You see, Stuart, I know what you need."

He tilted his head skeptically. "And what is that?"

"You need a new best friend." I smiled as sweetly as I could. "You need Jesus."

❀ ❀ ❀

We passed the rest of the day in a companionable mood. If Stuart did not leap at my invitation to introduce him to Jesus, at least he didn't get mad at me. And Lindsey didn't accuse me of preaching, either. I felt maybe I had handled the situation well, and in a non-control-freakish manner. Satisfied, I lay on my back after lunch, relaxing to the sound of the waves shooshing onto the beach and the occasional wild cry of a seagull. I think we all dozed off for a while. I know I did.

I awoke when I became aware that Stuart had stood up beside me. Opening my eyes, I stretched and sat up as he fished another Diet Coke out of the cooler. The wind had blown sand up onto my legs, where it had stuck to the salt-encrusted sunscreen I had smeared on earlier. I brushed at my thighs, wincing as the movement caused some discomfort in the sensitive skin inside my elbows.

Stuart took a deep drink from the can and then held it out toward me. "This is the last one."

I took the can and gulped the cold liquid, then handed it to Lindsey, who was staring at me with a look of mild alarm. "Did you use sunscreen?"

"Yeah."

Stuart stooped to examine my face. "Are you sure? Your face looks really red."

"And your chest and arms, too," Lindsey added.

I peeled back the bathing suit strap from my shoulder and displayed a strip of winter-white skin standing out starkly on a field of red.

"Uh oh," I said, looking up at Stuart. "I might have forgotten to put it on my arms and face after we got out of the water."

He gave a low whistle, and Lindsey shook her head. "You're really gonna be hurting later on."

❀ ❀ ❀

She was right. I felt itchy and prickly all the way home, and when we got to Grandmother's house, I went straight to the shower. Though the cool water set me to shivering, any warmth touching my upper body stung unbearably. When I got out of the shower, Grandmother knocked on the bathroom door.

"Take this," she said, handing me a clear bottle of aloe gel through the doorway. She eyed my red, towel-wrapped body with concern. "Layer it on thick, and don't rub it all the way in."

"Thanks." I grimaced when my attempt to smile hurt my poor burned face. I smeared a generous amount of the slimy gel onto my chest and shoulders, then gingerly eased my loosest T-shirt over my head, wincing when the neckline brushed my nose. Standing before the sink, I peered into the steam-fogged mirror. My nose shone like an approaching train in a tunnel at midnight.

"Great," I grumbled, globbing on the aloe gel. "I look like Ronald McDonald."

When I came out of the bathroom, Stuart stood in the hallway, holding a couple of pills and a glass of water.

"What's that?"

"Ibuprofen." He thrust the pills at me.

"Will they help?"

He shrugged. "Can't hurt." He looked over his shoulder and continued in a low voice. "I don't mind taking Lindsey home tomorrow, but do you think you could come along?"

I tossed the pills to the back of my throat and took a huge gulp of water. "Why? Are you afraid to be alone with her?"

"No," he said, looking uncomfortable. "But I don't really want to take her home and have her parents think she's been with me all this time."

Considering Mr. Markham's reputation for being a mean-tempered jerk, which Stuart knew full well, I couldn't really blame him for his reluctance to show up with the man's runaway teenage daughter. Still, going with them would mean cutting my vacation short by a day.

"I don't know, Stuart. I haven't gotten to spend as much time alone with Grandmother and Aunt Louise as I had hoped. Tomorrow's my last day here."

He gave me a measured look, as though considering whether or not to beg. Instead, he nodded. "I guess you're right. But I'm not happy about this. I hope they know I'm just the delivery guy."

"I'm sure they realize that. They know where she's been." I patted his arm as I slipped past him, heading toward the kitchen.

I found Grandmother alone, attacking a chicken with a knife roughly the size of Crocodile Dundee's.

"Where's Lindsey?"

"Showering in my bathroom." She handed me a smaller knife and pointed toward a cantaloupe in the sink. "Would you peel that?"

"Uh, sure." I stared at the melon, wondering how in the world one went about peeling the thing. I picked it up hesitantly and turned it over, trying to figure out where the top was. Finally, with a shrug, I shoved the tip of the knife into it and started trying to shave off the outer layer.

Grandmother, watching from her position by the stove, came to my rescue. She took the knife and the melon from me and cut it swiftly and expertly in half.

"I think it's easier if you scrape out the seeds before you peel." She picked up a spoon and scooped the gooey insides into the garbage disposal.

I took the second half and imitated her, then followed her instructions to cut thick slices before peeling off the rind. Within minutes, I had a couple of successes in the bowl and I smiled with satisfaction that I could add yet another skill to my culinary résumé. If only I had another week with Grandmother, I could probably graduate to hard-boiled eggs.

"Lindsey said she's going home with Stuart tomorrow," Grandmother told me as we worked.

"That's right." I watched the knife as I cautiously sliced through the soft melon. That thing was sharp. "Stuart invited me to ride along with them, actually."

Without looking at me, she asked, "Are you going?"

"Do you think I should?"

Her lips tightened into a thin line before she answered, "If you want to," in a tone that told me she would not be happy if I chose to leave a day early.

"I don't really want to, but I'm wondering if I ought to."

Still not looking my way, she replied, "Whatever you think," clipping the words short.

I've never had much patience with evasive behavior. I'd much rather have someone just come right out and tell me what they want instead of trying to guilt me into giving them their way. Setting the knife on the counter, I turned to face her. "Are you mad at me?"

She looked up, her eyes round. "Why would I be mad? If you think going with your friends is more important than spending one last day with your grandmother you haven't seen in years and may never see again, then that's what you need to do."

Anger flared inside me. So this is what Aunt Louise felt like when Grandmother gave her the martyr treatment. I spoke with some heat. "I didn't say I was going, I just asked if you thought I should."

Her eyebrows rose. "Now who's mad?"

Clamping my mouth shut against a frustrated scream that threatened to lash out at her, I turned back to the sink and picked up the knife. If that cantaloupe had been alive, it would have shivered in fear. Through gritted teeth, I managed to say, "I am not mad, and I am not going with Stuart and Lindsey. So let's drop the subject."

"Fine," she said, returning to her chicken preparations.

We worked in silence for a moment, and I fumed. How did Aunt Louise stand living with her? I mean, she was my grandmother and I loved her, but this was just one more example of her manipulating behavior. Only instead of being an observer, I was on the receiving end this time. I considered pointing it out to her and wondered how she would take it.

But as I was formulating the words in my head to describe how she was acting, something occurred to me. I had done my share of guilt dispensing, even recently. When Mama hadn't wanted me to come to Florida, I had acted like I wouldn't come if she didn't want me to. But then in the next breath, I made sure she knew it would cost me a bunch of money, knowing she would insist that I go.

So this guilt thing was just one more way of controlling people. Well, I was through doing that, and now that I recognized the behavior, I was through letting people do it to me. Maybe one way to stop allowing people to behave that way was to hit them head-on with their behavior. I've always been one for the direct approach.

"You know, Grandmother," I said slowly, my eyes fixed on the cantaloupe, "instead of you trying to make me feel guilty about leaving early with my friends, I'd much rather you tell me you want me to stay because you'll miss me when I'm gone."

She turned to me with a wide-eyed stare. "I'm not trying to make you feel guilty."

I raised my eyebrows. "Aren't you?"

She looked at me a moment, but when I didn't back down, she gave a brief half-smile, which was as close to a confession as I was likely to get. "Well, I hate to see you leave, and I will miss you. I feel like we've barely begun to get to know each other."

"I know," I agreed. "But I won't wait another thirteen years before coming back. I promise."

Satisfied, she nodded. "In that case . . ." She paused, then sighed. "In that case, I think you should go with them tomorrow."

My eyebrows rose again. "You do?"

Nodding, she said, "Lindsey looks up to you, and I think she would like to have you there when she sees her parents."

That was probably true. If nothing else, I would serve as a distraction, a stranger to be met and dealt with during that awkward moment when she first arrived home. Whereas Stuart was so terrified to meet Mr. Markham he probably wouldn't get out of the car.

"You're probably right."

Grandmother turned back to the chicken, picked up a piece, and put it in a plastic bag full of flour. Without looking at me, she said,

"One other thing, Mayla. I do love my daughter. I want you to know that."

I heard such passion in her voice that for a moment I was speechless. The words I had used during our argument came back to me. *Prisoner with chains around her ankles . . . what kind of mother keeps her child under her thumb?* Wincing, I realized she had been thinking about those words all day.

"I'm sorry, Grandmother." I hung my head. "I said some pretty ugly things yesterday. I was mad because of what you said about Mama, but I had no right to accuse you of not loving Aunt Louise. I know you do."

She nodded, satisfied. Then she looked at me with a tenderness in her eyes that melted my heart. "And I love you, too, which is why I am going to hold you to your promise to visit more often."

I covered the space between us with my arms outstretched. "Those planes fly both ways, you know. You could visit me, too."

She returned my hug, and I suppressed a hiss of pain when she squeezed my sunburned skin. "I might just do that." Then she frowned. "But in the summertime, after the snow is gone."

Dear Mayla,
I want to talk to you about this e-mail you sent. Call me.
Love, Mama
P.S. Don't worry. I am not mad at you.

That was the only mail in my inbox. Nothing from Paul. With a sinking heart, I took my cell phone outside to call Mama while Grandmother and Stuart put the finishing touches on dinner. The late afternoon sun stung my skin when I walked through the back door, so I took a folding chair from the porch and put it in the deepest shade I could find beneath one of the orange trees.

"Hello, baby," Mama said when she picked up the phone.

"Hi, Mama. I'm glad you're still speaking to me."

"Oh for heavens' sake, hush! You know better than that." She paused. "Though I do wonder why you thought I would tell the preacher anything about you being asked out by that man down there." She gave a little sniff that might have meant she was offended.

"I didn't think you would pick up the phone and call him directly. I figured you would tell your Tuesday night ladies to pray, and one of them would tell him."

She was silent for a moment. "Olivia Elswick does call him ever' time somebody's dog sneezes."

"And that is exactly why I asked you not to tell them I was trying to make him jealous. You haven't, have you?"

"A'course not. Why, if I told that gaggle of geese you have a crush on the preacher, it'd be all over the church 'fore suppertime."

I winced. She said that with something that sounded suspiciously like glee in her voice.

"I wish you wouldn't call it a crush. You make me sound like a high school kid."

She ignored me. "Tell me how long this has been going on."

"Nothing is going on, Mama. He doesn't have any feelings for me, and that's the end of it."

"Is your heart broken, baby? 'Cause if that man broke your heart, I'll just give him a piece of my mind when I see him at church on Sunday, preacher or not."

Horrified, I pictured Mama laying in to Paul in the middle of the sanctuary, surrounded by a crowd of delighted church members enjoying every minute of her show. I rushed to say, "No, my heart is not broken, and *please* don't say anything to him, Mama!"

"Well." She gave another quick sniffle. "I want to talk more about this when you get home. But now tell me about Lindsey."

I gave her a quick update, including the news that Stuart was here and that we would both be riding back to Kentucky with him tomorrow. "We won't get home until late, so I won't be at church on Sunday. But I'll call you when you get home."

Actually, the thought of going to church ever again was not appealing. I couldn't imagine what I would say to Paul when I saw him. Or what he would say to me.

"That'd be fine. And Mayla?"

"Yes, Mama?"

"I'm proud of you for admitting what you done. I love you, you know that?"

"Thanks, Mama. I love you too. Bye."

Disconnecting the call, I closed my eyes and took a deep breath, aware of how lucky I was. First Grandmother forgave me for acting like a fiend yesterday, and now Mama forgave me for lying to her. The Lord had plopped me right in the middle of the best family in the world.

If only they could manage to speak to each other, life would be nearly perfect.

"They're here," called Stuart from the living room.

Lindsey and I came running to welcome Bill Manson to the house for dinner. The three of us stood before the big front window, watching as Aunt Louise emerged from her Buick and waited for Bill to get out of his van. We saw him pause to look into the rearview mirror before joining her on the walkway. He plucked at the collar of his blindingly white shirt as he approached the house, bending his head to listen to something Aunt Louise said as they walked. Lindsey swung the door open as they stepped onto the porch.

"Hello, everyone," Aunt Louise sang in a bright voice. "Lindsey and Mayla, you remember Bill." We chimed a greeting. "And Stuart Hortenbury, this is Bill Manson."

Stuart stepped forward to shake Bill's hand. "Nice to meet you, sir."

Bill nodded, then lifted his face and inhaled. "Something sure smells good."

"Where's Mother?"

"I'm here." Grandmother appeared in the doorway to the kitchen. She stood with her back ramrod straight, her gaze fixed on Bill, and her expression carefully bland.

Bill broke the silence before it became awkward by crossing the room in three steps, his hand outstretched. "Hello, Mrs. Strong. Thank you for inviting me to dinner."

Grandmother took his hand and gave a regal dip of her head. "We're glad you could join us on such short notice."

Aunt Louise had been eyeing me with mild alarm. "Mayla, that's a terrible sunburn. Didn't you use sunscreen?"

"Sure she did." Stuart rolled his eyes. "On her legs."

"Oh dear. Have you got something to put on it?"

I glared at Stuart before nodding. "Grandmother gave me some aloe."

"Dinner will be ready in a few minutes," Grandmother announced. She looked at me before heading back into the kitchen. "Find out what everyone wants to drink, and you can help me get things on the table."

I took drink orders, then left them in the living room to talk. While Grandmother whisked flour and milk into a pan for gravy, I filled six glasses with ice. Diet Coke for Lindsey and me; water for Stuart; and sweet tea for Aunt Louise, Bill, and Grandmother. We had put an extra leaf in the kitchen table to make room for six people, and Grandmother had set it with her good dishes. A white tablecloth and a candle centerpiece added a touch of elegance to the old kitchen table.

When the whole house had filled with the delicious odor of the freshly baked biscuits Grandmother piled in a bread basket, she instructed me to call our guests. Suppressing the urge to give a Kentucky hillbilly call to supper like Mama used to do to embarrass me with when I was a kid—"Grub's on the table, come and git it!"—I behaved myself and politely informed our guests that dinner was ready.

When everyone had taken their assigned seats, Grandmother looked at Bill. "Mr. Manson, would you ask a blessing?"

"Of course."

We bowed our heads, and because I was sitting at the end, I saw Aunt Louise reach for his hand under the table. My heart gave a sentimental little flutter. One day, I hoped to have a man to hold hands with while we prayed. Forcing thoughts of Paul from my mind, I closed my eyes.

"Father in heaven, I am so thankful for the people gathered around this table. You've drawn us together in this place, at this time, for Your purpose. Help us to fulfill it in a way that glorifies You. Thank You for the food You've placed before us. Bless the hands that have prepared it, and let it strengthen us to do Your will. In Jesus's name, amen."

A chorus of "amen" sounded around the table—even, I noticed, from Stuart. I raised my eyebrows in his direction, and he gave me a grin and a slight shrug.

"Mayla, Stuart was telling us that you've decided to go back to Kentucky with him and Lindsey tomorrow." Aunt Louise took a piece of chicken from the plate and held it for Bill as he selected one.

I nodded. "Stuart needs someone to read the map for him; otherwise he'll end up in California instead of Pikeville."

Stuart pulled a face in my direction. "Actually, she can't stand the thought that we might have fun without her."

Her glance sliding from Stuart to me, Lindsey giggled. "Tomorrow should be an interesting day."

"Mrs. Strong, this chicken is delicious."

Grandmother bestowed a brief smile in Bill's direction, while Aunt Louise beamed. "Fried chicken is Mother's specialty. And the biscuits, too. She makes them from scratch."

While we all agreed that even the colonel couldn't beat Grandmother when it came to chicken and biscuits, I noticed that Aunt Louise's face absolutely glowed, and not in the same way mine did. Hers radiated joy. She gushed happiness like a waterfall in a rainforest whenever she looked at Bill. And since she did not seem to be able to keep her eyes off him, we were all practically washed away in the flood surging from her direction.

My glance slid over to catch Grandmother's, and I saw she had noticed the same thing. She gave me a crooked smile before turning her attention to the man who had so obviously captured her daughter's heart.

"Mr. Manson, I'd like to know more about you. Tell us a little about yourself."

I looked down at my plate to hide my smile. I had a feeling things were going to start looking up for Aunt Louise.

Chapter 16

Stuart insisted that we leave the next morning at the incredibly uncivilized hour of six. That meant I had to haul myself out of bed at five fifteen, and I made sure he knew I was not happy about it. Being the kind and considerate friend he is, he told me to shut my trap and get over it or I would find myself deposited on the side of the road on a lonely stretch of I-75 somewhere between Valdosta and Tifton.

Grandmother and Aunt Louise both got up to see us off. Wrapped in a bathrobe and with old-fashioned curlers all over her head, Grandmother sat on the sofa in the living room, struggling to stay awake as we hefted our suitcases out the front door. I left Aunt Louise, Stuart, and Lindsey to figure out how to arrange everything inside the Grand Am and returned to the house to sit beside Grandmother.

Taking my hand in hers, she patted it and smiled. "I have enjoyed having you here this week."

I grimaced. "Even with your house bulging at the seams with my friends?"

"Even then."

I leaned my head on her shoulder. "I wish we didn't live so far apart."

"We need to make an effort to talk more often. Use that little phone of yours to call me every now and then."

"I will." I raised my head and looked at her. "Hey! You should get a computer. Then we could talk to each other through e-mail."

"Me with a computer?" She laughed. "I wouldn't know how to work one."

"Aunt Louise does. She could give you lessons."

Grandmother shook her head, chuckling. "We'll see."

Stuart came through the door and announced, "We're ready to go." He fixed a stern eye on my coffee cup. "I'm not stopping every fifteen minutes to find a bathroom, so you had better take care of that before we leave."

I heaved a dramatic sigh and stood up. "This is going to be such a fun trip."

Pressing my coffee cup into Grandmother's hand, I went down the hallway while Stuart thanked Grandmother for letting him stay. When I returned, we all piled out the front door into the morning darkness. The sky behind the houses across the street had started to lighten as the sun prepared to make an appearance.

Stuart got into the driver's seat while Lindsey hugged Grandmother. "Thank you for everything."

"Good luck to you," Grandmother replied. "Let us know how you're doing."

Aunt Louise hugged Lindsey next. "You'll be in my prayers."

Lindsey climbed into the backseat of the Grand Am, and the time had arrived for me to say good-bye. I hugged Aunt Louise and whispered, "I hope everything works out for you."

Then I turned to my grandmother. She stood in the grass beside the car, wearing her curlers and her old bathrobe, her eyes bright with tears that matched my own. I put my arms around her and stood still, wondering when I would see her again and refusing to consider the possibility that I might not. *Lord, please keep her safe and healthy until my next visit.*

"I love you, Grandmother." I wiped a tear from my eyelashes and smiled. "Please take care of yourself."

She looked up into my eyes. "Would you give your mother a message from me?" Wondering if I dared, I nodded. "Tell her she has done a good job raising my granddaughter."

Smiling through a sudden rush of new tears, I hugged her again before sliding into the seat of the passenger's Grand Am. As Stuart backed out of the driveway, I lowered my window and leaned out. I waved as long as I could see them, Aunt Louise standing close to Grandmother, one arm wrapped around her waist, both women waving good-bye.

The mood in the car for the first part of our trip was light. After an argument over the radio station—Stuart refused to listen to Christian music, and I refused to listen to techno—we settled on one that Mama would probably have approved of and surprised each other by being able to sing along with most of the songs. We amused ourselves by playing the alphabet game with license plates, just like I used to do with Mama and Daddy when I was a kid.

To Stuart's dismay, I was not the one who insisted that we stop at every rest area along the way. I had always heard that pregnant women have to go to the bathroom a lot, and Lindsey proved the point. Stuart responded like a gentleman and didn't grumble at her, as he certainly would have had I asked him to find a clean restroom every hour on the hour. And I was happy because I never once had to request a pit stop.

As we headed into Georgia, the sky clouded over and hid the sun, and when we stopped at a rest area just south of Atlanta, the air had taken on a definite chill. A few hours later, when we left I-75 to head east on I-40 near Knoxville, I lowered the window and stuck my arm out into the frigid air.

"Hey, that's cold!" Lindsey snapped from the backseat. "Close the window before I freeze to death."

Stuart gave me a sideways look as I obeyed. Our pregnant passenger's mood had definitely deteriorated since the morning and seemed to be getting progressively worse as we neared the Kentucky border.

As we merged onto US-23 North for the final hundred miles of Lindsey's trip, the mood inside the car turned downright stormy. Tension oozed from the backseat, and twilight darkened the inside of the car. Stuart clenched the steering wheel with a white-knuckled grip, and when the radio failed to produce anything we could agree upon, an awkward silence fell between us. I caught sight of patches of snow here and there in the fields lining the road.

Lindsey's voice broke into the awkward silence. "What do you think my father will say when I get there?"

I cast a look in Stuart's direction, but he kept his eyes firmly on the road and did not turn his head. I turned around in my seat to look at her in the gloomy light. "I don't know. What did he say when you called him last night?"

"Just that he was glad I was coming home and that I shouldn't worry because everything will be fine." She looked down at her hands clasped in her lap. "And that he missed me."

"You didn't tell him about the baby, did you?" She shook her head. "When are you planning to do that?"

"Probably tonight, because they're going to want to talk about why I ran away." She looked up, her expression troubled. "I wish I didn't have to tell them at all. If I had just gotten the abortion, I could make up some other reason for running away, and they'd never have to know."

I could think of several responses to that, but none that didn't sound like a lecture. So instead I asked, "What do you think they're going to say?"

She looked down at her hands again. "Mom won't say much. She'll wait to see what Daddy says, and then she'll try to calm him down if he gets really hyper. But Daddy? I don't know. He might tell me how I've messed up my life, or what a loser Dirk is, or"—she gulped— "how disappointed he is in me."

"You know, Lindsey, they might already suspect. I hate to say it, but that's one of the first things I thought when I learned you had run away. Grandmother and Aunt Louise, too."

Even in the dark, I could see the pain in her eyes. "It really isn't being pregnant, you know. It's that Daddy will know for sure that I'm not a virgin, anymore. He always calls me his special princess. I don't think he'll call me his princess anymore."

She choked back a sob, and I reached into the backseat to squeeze her hand, my heart aching for her. My daddy called me his Little Sugar Dumpling. For three years after he died, I cried whenever I realized no one would ever call me Little Sugar Dumpling again. I hoped like crazy that Mr. Markham had been doing some major changing over the past week. *Lord, can you work on him so he doesn't break Lindsey's heart?*

"I'm not afraid to tell them about the baby," she repeated, using the sleeve of Stuart's jacket in the seat beside her to wipe her tears. "But I know nothing's ever going to be the same between us."

There was not a thing I could say in response to that. She was right.

Nestled in the Appalachian Mountains in eastern Kentucky, Pikeville is a small town compared to Lexington. Because it was fully dark by the time we arrived, I couldn't see much of the town. But I could see the dark outline of mountains all around us, and the road we followed ran alongside a river for a few miles.

Lindsey had gone from tense to sullen, and stared out the window like a dog who knows he's on the way to the vet. She spoke only to give one-word directions to Stuart as he navigated over a narrow mountain road with no guardrails that made me glad I couldn't see what lay beyond the trees just a few feet outside my window. His headlights cut twin slices of light through the darkness, and I found myself praying silently that we wouldn't hit a patch of ice that would send us flying off the road as we rounded one of the sharp curves.

Finally Lindsey said, "That's it on the right."

In the center of a cozy little valley, set far back from the road, I saw a two-story house with light blazing from the windows. Stuart turned the car onto the long dirt driveway, past a mailbox shaped and painted to look like a miniature version of the house. As soon as all four tires left the road, outside lights came on to illuminate a deep front porch. Two people stepped through the doorway.

"There they are." When I'm nervous I sometimes feel the need to state the obvious. And I was nervous, whether for Lindsey or myself I didn't know.

As the car rolled slowly to a stop near the front porch, I saw Mrs. Markham clutch at her husband's arm. I had met her once before, just after Alex's death. She had not changed. Her hair hung limply from a part in the center of her scalp, and she wore an oversized sweater over baggy slacks. At the moment, she was peering anxiously into the dark interior of the car, trying to get a glimpse of her daughter.

I shifted my gaze for my first look at Mr. Markham. In some ways, he was exactly what I had expected. A tall man, I could see his muscular shoulders beneath a white, long-sleeved Polo shirt that was tucked into tan slacks around a lean waist. His dark hair was cut short, and in the dim light, I couldn't see any gray in it. He looked like someone who had an important job at a bank.

But when I studied his face, I realized he looked like something else at that moment. He looked like a worried father, anxious to have his daughter back home again.

"This is it," I said in a low voice, glancing toward the backseat. "Are you ready?"

Lindsey swallowed hard, then nodded. I opened the door and got out, turning to lift the lever that released the seatback, aware that the two people standing on the grass watched me with anxious stares. I extended my hand to Lindsey, who took it and allowed me to help her out of the car. Then I released her, and we turned together to face the Markhams.

They had eyes for no one but their daughter. Lindsey stood frozen in place for a moment, her backpack slung across one shoulder. I realized in an instant how young she really was. I saw her jaw tremble and her eyes fill with tears, and then the backpack hit the grass as she rushed forward into her mother's arms. Oblivious to me and Stuart, Mr. Markham threw his arms around his daughter and wife, and the three of them stood huddled together, the sound of muffled sobs soft in the cold night air. I realized with something of a shock that the women were not the only ones who cried.

Stuart got out of the car and walked around to my side with my jacket. I gratefully put it on and zipped it up against the frigid breeze that blew into my face. We both leaned against the front of the car to feel the warmth radiating from the engine.

The huddle broke after a moment, and all three Markhams turned toward us. Lindsey brushed at the tears on her cheeks. "Mom and Daddy, this is Stuart and Mayla."

Mr. Markham took an immediate step toward Stuart, his hand outstretched, while Mrs. Markham surprised me by grabbing me in a firm embrace and sobbing on my shoulder. She kept whispering, "Thank you, thank you," into my ear, and I gave her back a few awkward pats.

When she released me, I turned uneasily toward Mr. Markham. Here I was, face-to-face with the man who had treated me so coldly when I called to tell him his son was dying of AIDS. Aware of the diamond stud in my left nostril and the row of tiny gold rings rising up the sides of my ears, I tilted my chin and looked directly into his eyes.

But only for a moment. He grabbed me in a rib-cracking hug that threatened to squeeze the breath right out of me. I had to bite back a gasp of pain when the rough embrace chafed my sunburned skin. When he released me, I would have staggered backward except for the firm grip he had on my hand, which he pumped so hard I was afraid he might jar something loose. He looked at me like I had just won the Kentucky Derby. I half expected him to cover me with roses.

"How can we ever thank you?"

I shook my head, embarrassed. "I didn't do anything."

His glance slid first toward his daughter, then his wife, and finally back to me. "You did more than you know."

I managed to extract my hand when Mr. Markham put his arm around Lindsey again.

"You're all tired from your trip," Mrs. Markham said. "Let's go inside and get out of this cold."

They turned toward the house, clearly expecting us to follow. I glanced at Stuart, and he gave a wide-eyed shake of his head.

"We've still got a long way to go tonight," I told them, "so we're not going to stay."

They faced us again, and I saw Mr. Markham hesitate, as though wondering if he should insist that we come inside. But then he nodded.

"I expect you want to get home as quickly as possible."

Lindsey stepped away from her father's side to give Stuart a hug.

"Bye, baby girl," he said. "Take care of yourself."

"You too, Stuart. Thanks for going out of your way to bring me home." She turned to me, and we each took a step forward into each others' arms. "I'm sorry I wrecked your vacation."

"You didn't wreck anything. To be honest, I got kind of used to having you around."

She pulled back so she could see me. "Thanks for everything, Mayla."

I hugged her again and put my lips close to her ear. "I know you don't want to hear this, but when I care about somebody, I pray for them. I'll be praying for you, Lindsey."

She gave me a final squeeze. "I appreciate that."

Then Stuart and I got into the car, and he backed around so we could drive forward down the driveway. I turned in my seat and saw all three of them standing in the grass in front of the porch, watching as we pulled away. When Stuart turned onto the road, he tapped the horn twice in a final farewell.

"That was so not what I expected Mr. Markham to be like," he said as we navigated down the curvy dark road.

"You expected horns?"

"You know what I mean. Alex never said much about his parents, but I always had the impression his father was a real tyrant."

"I think he used to be but apparently not anymore."

Stuart snorted. "Yeah, now that the black sheep is dead and all he has left is a fluffy little white princess sheep, it's easier to be a nice guy."

"Maybe," I said slowly. "But I think he knows his little white sheep has a few black spots herself. I think his attitude really has changed."

"What makes you think so?"

"Something he told Lindsey on the phone. He said he was praying for her." I turned in my seat to I could look at Stuart. "Mama says that a crisis brings people closer to the Lord. I'll bet Mr. Markham turned this crisis over to God, and he changed."

I didn't tell Stuart that I was certain Mr. Markham had begun to trust in the Lord because I had felt a sense of peace exuding from the man. I had looked into Mr. Markham's eyes and seen that he knew he had a rough time in front of him. But he had placed his trust in the One who had all the answers. In my brief meeting of Mr. Markham, I had recognized Jesus peeking out of his eyes. Stuart would think I was a nut case if I told him that.

"You talk about God like He's someone you can walk up to on the street." He shook his head. "That's not the God I learned about in Sunday school."

"Tell me about that God."

Stuart turned the car through a sharp curve before answering. "Oh, you know. All-seeing, all-knowing, sits up in heaven watching everything we do and taking notes."

"Ah, I get it. And one day He'll pull out the book and tally up the good and the bad."

He shrugged. "Something like that. And according to the people in the church where I grew up, there aren't enough good deeds in the world to make up for the big black mark of being gay."

"If that's the way it's going to go, I'm glad I'll have Jesus standing there beside me with a heavy-duty eraser for all the black marks on my page."

Stuart didn't respond. He took a couple of curves in silence. The darkness on this deserted mountain road gave me a feeling of isolation, like we were cocooned alone inside the car, away from the rest of the world.

"Sometimes I get tired of being known as a gay man." He faced forward, never looking away from the road as he continued. "Straight men don't call themselves *straight*. Why are gay people immediately labeled as *gay?*" He sighed. "Sometimes I'd like someone to think of me as a man, period."

I felt a response rising up inside of me and spoke without giving a thought to what I would say, trusting that the Lord would put the right words in my mouth.

"That's how Jesus thinks of you. When He looks at you, He sees a lonely man who needs a friend. And He wants to be that friend, Stuart. Gay or straight doesn't enter into the criteria."

He shifted in his seat. "Are you telling me Jesus doesn't care if I'm gay? Because that is not what Lou told Michael, so his Jesus must be different than your Jesus."

"You just finished saying you didn't want to be thought of as gay or straight. Forget that for a minute. Before I became a Christian, I was just as lonely as you are. Having tons of people around me, even boyfriends, didn't matter. I was like a little kid lost in a big shopping mall, running around all panicky searching for my mother but trying to look brave so nobody would know how terrified I was. You know that feeling I'm talking about?" He nodded, silent. "When I became a Christian, that panicky feeling went away. On the outside, everything was exactly the same, but inside, the panic was gone. Instead, I felt peaceful."

I shut my mouth, feeling like I had said enough. We had reached a main road, and though this one still wound through the mountains, the lanes were wider and the curves gentle. The hum of the tires droned loudly in the silence.

"I know that panic you're talking about." He spoke his admission quietly but with a sense of relief. "Sometimes it's in the background, like when you're hungry but you're too involved in what you're doing to stop and eat so you just ignore it. But sometimes you can't ignore it. Like the night Michael left."

I remembered. I had heard agony in Stuart's voice on the phone that night. The time had come to be bold. *Lord, please don't let me mess this up!* "You don't have to feel that way."

His lips twisted. "And now we come back to the gay issue. I can't just stop being gay." He shook his head. "And I don't think I want to."

I straightened in my seat and hid a sigh. I guess the time wasn't right for Stuart after all. "Last summer I got to the point where letting Jesus fill up the empty places in my soul was more important than *anything* else. I don't think you're there yet."

Depressed, I stared out the windshield, watching the headlights cut a path in the darkness fifteen feet ahead of the car. Just like the Lord does for me, I thought. Sometimes I can't see what's ahead and I feel as though I'm racing blindly forward into who-knows-what. But He always makes sure I have enough light to stay on the right road.

In the middle of my musings, I was thrown forward into my seatbelt strap, and I realized suddenly that the car was *not* staying on the road. Stuart had slammed on the brakes and jerked the steering wheel to the right. The tires skidded onto a gravel shoulder. Had an animal run into the road in front of the car? I hadn't seen anything. The determined set to Stuart's jaw as he maneuvered the car told me we had not just had a close call. He had done this on purpose.

"What are you doing, you idiot?" I shouted, my heart pounding in my throat.

He shoved the shifter into Park before the car had completely stopped rolling. I jerked forward again and opened my mouth to deliver a blistering tirade when I caught sight of his face. His eyes blazed as he turned in his seat to face me.

"I can't stand it anymore. You guys are leaving me out."

"Oh, for cryin' out loud! Out of what?"

"Out of this church thing you've all joined. I want in."

Take a breath, I told myself. *Relax. Don't bite his head off. He doesn't know any better.* "Stuart, Christianity isn't a club you can join like you'd join the YMCA. Christianity is a relationship with a real Person."

"I know that," he snapped. "I'm ready. Let's do it."

I couldn't help it. I put my head against the back of the seat and laughed. "Do what? You think I'm going to zap you with a magic wand or something? Get real!"

I thought he was going to flare up. He took a deep breath like he was getting ready to cut loose on me. But then he exhaled slowly, his shoulders drooping as he did so. "You're right. I'd probably make a lousy Christian anyway."

This was the Stuart I had talked to on the phone, the one who had come all the way to Florida to find someone who could tell him why his life was falling apart. "You would not make a lousy Christian, not if you really wanted to let Jesus be in control of your life."

He caught his lower lip between his teeth. "I think I'm ready to do that."

An expectant stillness tingled in the air around us, as though the world outside had paused to see what would happen in the next moment. I was afraid to move and held myself motionless as Stuart struggled to find words to express what he felt.

"I don't want to turn into a Bible-thumper like Lou. But I do want . . . no, I need what Lou has. What you and Sylvia and Michael have. And if it means I have to quit partying and listening to good music and cheating on my taxes and stay single for the rest of my life, I'll do it." He took a shuddering breath, and I heard pain in his voice. "Because I can't stand my life the way it is anymore."

I reached over and took his hand in mine. "Stuart, you're about to meet the best Friend you'll ever have."

Right there in the front seat of his red Grand Am on the side of

US-460, surrounded by the Appalachian Mountains, Stuart Horten-bury prayed the prayer that would change his life forever. And when he opened his tear-filled eyes, I saw Jesus peeking out of them.

Chapter 17

I crept soundlessly into my apartment at two o'clock in the morning, mindful that Sylvia had probably only been in bed for an hour or so after working the late shift at The Max. I would have gotten home long before, except Stuart was so excited about his newfound life in Christ that he stopped at a Waffle House and questioned me for hours on the finer points of Christianity while I consumed about a gallon of Diet Coke.

Closing the door to my bedroom, I flipped on the light with a happy sigh. Traveling was fun, but coming home was even better.

But where was Harvey? A quick inspection of my room told me he wasn't there. Suspicion niggled in my mind. Sylvia wouldn't have gotten rid of him without telling me, would she? When I spoke with her on Friday, she'd said she had gotten used to having him around. Had the little monster committed an unforgivable task that sent her over the edge, like chewing holes in the couch or peeing on her bed?

Sighing, I put the thought out of my mind. I'd find out in the morning. Right now, my bed was shouting my name like a mother calling her kid inside for the night. I had been awake almost twenty-one hours, and I felt like I could sleep for days.

I awoke to the sound of a door slamming somewhere in the apartment. Hearing Sylvia's voice, I glanced at the clock. She must be coming home from church. I had slept for more than ten hours.

Rolling out of bed, I stretched and then winced as my skin reminded me of my sunburn. My shoulders had started to peel, but a quick glance in the mirror confirmed that my nose was still fire-engine red. Digging the bottle of aloe gel out of my suitcase, I applied a gob before going into the living room to greet my roommate.

"Mayla!" Sylvia turned with surprise as I emerged, yawning, from my bedroom. "I didn't expect you until later today." Her expression turned to one of repulsion as she caught sight of my face. "What is that all over your nose?"

I whimpered in a blatant attempt at sympathy. "Aloe gel. I have a terrible sunburn."

"Sorry about the sunburn, but that stuff looks gross. Like you have a bad cold and wiped your nose the wrong way."

Trying to get sympathy from Sylvia was like getting water from a cactus—you can do it, but sometimes you get stung in the process.

"Who were you talking to, anyway?" I looked around the empty room.

"Harvey. I was just telling him about the sermon." She pointed toward the corner beyond the couch.

I looked and did a double take. There, tucked neatly into the corner between the couch and the wall, sat a rabbit cage. Drawing close to get a better look, I saw that the wire cage sat up on short, wooden stilts. Stored neatly beneath it were plastic containers full of what looked like fresh cedar shavings and rabbit food. The cage door was open, and a ramp led from the entrance to the carpet. Inside the cage, a contented Harvey munched on a wedge of cabbage.

I swung back to Sylvia. "Holy cow!"

She grinned. "I bought the cage at Wal-Mart, and Lou built the legs and the ramp. And you know what? Rabbits are pretty smart, like cats. It only took him a few days to get used to the litter box."

I looked closer and noticed a shallow plastic box filled with kitty litter in the back corner of his cage. "Holy cow," I repeated, shaking my head.

"And watch this." Sylvia reached behind the cage and pulled out a yellow ball about the size of a soccer ball, the kind little kids play with. When Harvey saw the ball, he came hopping down the ramp to the carpet. Sylvia knelt down on the floor and rolled the ball to him. My jaw nearly hit my chest when that rabbit stood up on his hind legs, caught the ball, and rolled it back to her.

"He plays catch!"

Sylvia, grinning ear-to-ear, nodded. "Lou taught him."

"Let me do it." I knelt beside Sylvia and rolled the ball. Harvey caught it and rolled it right back to me. "Amazing!"

Sylvia made a pot of coffee while I played with the rabbit, and then we sat on the couch, sipping coffee and talking. She wanted to hear all about my trip.

As I was describing Lindsey's ultrasound, someone knocked on the door. Without waiting for an answer, Stuart opened the door and came bounding into the room.

"Good morning, fellow Christians!" His face practically glowed with the joy of a new child of God, and he threw his arms open wide as though to embrace the world. "Today is the first day of the rest of my life!"

I rolled my eyes. "I feel like I'm in a commercial. Close the door; you're letting the cold in."

Sylvia's forehead creased as she looked from Stuart to me with wide eyes. "Fellow Christians?"

"That's right," Stuart said, beaming. "Didn't Mayla tell you?"

"I hadn't gotten to that part yet."

Sylvia catapulted across the room and threw herself into Stuart's arms. "I'm so happy for you, Stuart!"

While I refilled my coffee mug, Stuart told Sylvia about his decision and started in on a recap of our midnight discussion in the Waffle House. I sat sipping the fragrant liquid and listening with a deep sense of joy. So what if I didn't have a job or a college degree and had embarrassed myself in front of my pastor to the point that I wasn't sure I could ever go back to church again? I had friends, and they were saved, and life was good.

A knock sounded at the door.

"Probably Lou," said Sylvia.

I stood and crossed to the door, thinking I should call Mama before too long or she'd be worried. I threw the door open wide to let Lou inside, and then froze, stunned. The person standing outside my door was not Lou.

It was Paul.

He stood in my doorway, flakes of snow scattered on the shoulders of his winter coat and in his dark hair. His coat was unbuttoned at the top, and below his square chin, I caught sight of a neatly knotted tie. He had come here directly from church in Salliesburg. When I looked up into those dark eyes, my breath caught in my throat. How had I ever thought Reverend Thomas was better looking than Paul? This man standing in front of me had the ability to make my heart crash to a halt and then flutter like a hummingbird's wings, all within the time it took to draw a shuddering breath.

I saw his gaze rise to my unbrushed hair, drop to take in my wrinkled flannel nightshirt and baggy pants, and finally come to rest on my gunk-covered nose. Horrified, I took a backward step in preparation for fleeing to the safety of the bathroom, which he took as an invitation to come inside. When he stepped through the doorway, I saw what he clutched in his right hand. All thoughts of running away evaporated.

He carried a bouquet of roses.

Numb and with my mouth hanging open like an idiot, I watched as though from a distance as he thrust the flowers toward me. My hand rose like a robot's and took the bouquet from him. Plucking at his collar and clearing his throat, he took a deep breath before speaking the words I had dreamed of but never imagined I would actually hear him say.

"I've come to declare my intentions."

Well, not exactly the words I had dreamed of hearing, but close enough.

"You what?" I asked, displaying my deep intelligence and ability to respond quickly under pressure.

"Declare my intentions," he repeated. "I've already asked permission from your mother. I want to court you."

"Court me?"

"Date you," he explained, as though to someone with an IQ of twelve.

While my whirling mind tried to grasp what was happening to me, Sylvia and Stuart came to my rescue. They swarmed past me and pulled Paul inside, shutting the door behind him and guiding him into the living room. They pointed him toward a chair, which he did not sit in, and then slipped quietly from the room. I knew they were huddled in the kitchen listening to every word, but at least they were trying to give us a semblance of privacy.

I followed Paul into the living room, dazed. "I don't understand. When we talked at Mama's house, you said I was just a friend."

His gaze dropped for a moment. "I know. That's what I thought at the time. But when I heard you were interested in another man . . ." He looked up, his eyelids narrowed. "And that was a terrible trick to pull on me, by the way."

Now it was my turn to look away. "I know. I'm sorry about that."

His hand reached toward my face, and I felt a warm, delicious shock when his fingers touched me. He turned my chin gently until I faced him again. "When I thought you might fall in love with someone else, I knew I couldn't let that happen. And that's when I realized I wanted you to fall in love with me instead. Because sometime during the past nine months, I think I might have fallen in love with you."

There. He had said the words I wanted to hear, had prayed to hear. My breath actually stopped as I fell into the depths of those incredibly passionate eyes. *Lord, I think I'm going to cry. Please don't let me cry, because my nose is red enough already.*

An awful thought sneaked to the front of the tornado in my brain. "You asked my mother for permission to date me?" He nodded. "You realize, don't you, that we're an item all over the church by now."

He nodded again. "Don't worry. Before I asked her, I talked to the board of deacons. They gave their permission first."

Casting my eyes heavenward, I shook my head. Being the preacher's girlfriend in a small country church would certainly mean some adjustments to my independent ways. Asking permission from a bunch of stuffy church people would take some getting used to.

"Well?" he demanded. "What do you say? Will you go out with me?"

I buried my face in the bouquet, mostly to look away from the intensity in his eyes and to take a few seconds to calm the frantic whirlwind of my thoughts. Inhaling the sweet scent of roses helped to clear my poor dazed brain. How should a girl respond to a request from a man of God while wearing red checkered pajamas with gunk smeared all over her nose?

Looking into his face, I stuck my hand out to seal the deal officially. "You bet I will!"

Chapter 18

Flintstones, meet the Flintstones, they're the modern Stone Age fam-i-ly . . .

I flipped my cell phone open with a smile when I saw Grandmother's number on the display. It was Sunday, a week after my return to the biting cold of Kentucky from the warmth of Florida.

"Hello?"

"Happy Sunday," sang Aunt Louise. "I hope I didn't wake you."

"No, I'm getting dressed for church."

"I had to call and tell you my news." The excitement I heard bubbling in her voice could mean only one thing.

"You're getting married!" I shouted.

"I am! And Mother's being wonderful about the whole thing."

"Oh, Aunt Louise, I'm so happy for you! When is the wedding?"

"Not until May, so you have plenty of time to make your plans. We aren't doing anything formal, just a small ceremony in the courtyard of the church. Will you stand up with me as my maid of honor?"

Grinning ear to ear, I said, "I'd love to."

"Thank you! Oh, here, Mother wants to talk to you."

"Hello, Mayla." Grandmother sounded happy. "Did you say you can come for the wedding?"

"I wouldn't miss it," I assured her. "Are you okay with everything?

Aunt Louise getting married will mean some pretty big changes around there."

"I'll be fine. I'm looking forward to the peace and quiet. And they're going to buy a house just down the street, so they won't be far."

An image of the little white house flashed into my mind. "That's wonderful. And let me tell you my news. I got a job."

"Congratulations! Where will you be working?"

"Midstate Insurance and Investments. I'll be doing graphic design and layout of employee communications."

"Isn't that the job that required a college education?"

"That's the one." I opened the top dresser drawer and pulled out a brand new pair of pantyhose, something I had worn less than a dozen times in my entire life. "But they said they were more impressed by my skills than those of anyone else who applied. And not only that, but the salary is almost double what I made at the construction company, so I'll be able to quit my server job and take night classes at Lexington Community College."

"Good. Someone as smart as you should go to college. Have you heard from Lindsey?"

Taking the outfit I planned to wear from my closet, I propped the phone on my shoulder so I could remove the plastic bag it hung in.

"She called a couple of days ago. She has decided to give the baby up for adoption. Apparently, a friend of her father's from church put her in touch with a couple in Ohio who wants to adopt."

"I hope she's doing it legally," Grandmother said. "I've heard about people who buy babies on the black market."

I wadded the plastic bag and tossed it into a corner. "I'm sure she is. She mentioned having an interview with an adoption attorney someone at her church knows."

I had been thrilled when Lindsey told me of the many ways the people in her church were being supportive of her and her family. The Lord had that baby firmly in His hand. Both of them.

My bedroom door opened, and Sylvia stuck her head in. "Stuart will be here in fifteen minutes. Are you ready? Oh!" She stopped when she saw I was on the phone. "Sorry."

I waved a hand, indicating I'd be ready in a minute, and she left. "I need to go, Grandmother. Stuart is being baptized today, and it's almost time to leave."

"Tell him I'm happy for him."

"I will. Tell Aunt Louise I'm so excited for her I can hardly stand it. I love you, Grandmother."

"I love you too. Good-bye."

I tossed the phone onto the bed and sat on the edge, working the pantyhose up my legs with care. The last thing I needed to do was poke a hole in the blasted things. Then I stood and stepped into the skirt. Next came a creamy white sweater, and finally the matching jacket. Standing in front of the mirror, I studied my reflection.

Not bad. My nose was peeling, of course, but that couldn't be helped. At least the color had receded to an unremarkable pink while the rest of my face had deepened into a healthy tan that looked great against the white sweater. I twisted to the right and left, casting a critical eye over the first suit I had ever owned. I had bought it, along with several other outfits suitable for my new job, with the severance check I'd received from Clark and Hasna. The rest would go toward tuition.

Of course, all the new clothes were appropriate attire for a pastor's girlfriend, as well.

"Well, Lord," I said as I studied my reflection, "I hope I look conservative enough to satisfy the deacons."

As I turned my head to see the four earrings in my left ear, the light glinted off the stud in my nostril. For a moment I considered removing it, but I decided not to. I was willing to go only so far in trying to fit the acceptable mold of the preacher's girlfriend. God made me who I am. If they wanted more, we'd have a fight on our hands.

Salliesburg Independent Christian Church would just have to get over it.

Mayla's Bold Beginning

Mayla Strong never liked other people's idea of "normal." So it was no surprise that when she walked into Salliesburg Independent Christian Church, intent on giving her life to Christ, she turned a few heads.

Sporting purple hair, multiple piercings, and a fiery spirit, Mayla displays her personality for everyone to see, and she tries to live for God in the same way. Mayla's new faith brings unexpected friendships into her life and leads to some awkward, amusing, and even painful situations. As she struggles to become more Christlike, Mayla discovers that God loves her—and can use her—just the way she is.

Kregel Publications